GEMINI'S

CROSS

Donna —
May the Lord
richly bless you!

GEMINI'S
CROSS

E.R. WEBB

Tate Publishing & Enterprises

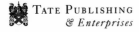

TATE PUBLISHING
& Enterprises

Book design copyright © 2006 by Tate Publishing, LLC. All rights reserved.
Cover design by Lindsay Behrens
Interior design by Chris Webb
Author photo by Stacy Black Photography

Published in the United States of America

ISBN: 1–5988682–3–3
06.11.15

To my God-given partner in life, my wife Vicki—my encourager, friend, critic and love of my life, without whom this simply would not have happened.

Acknowledgements

My warmest thanks to Stuart Brogden, brother in Christ and great friend, for his attention to detail and his honest evaluation of this book. My sincere thanks to Cindy Hosch and to Gwen Craig for their encouragement. Grateful thanks to Pastor Paul Ehmer for his kind input. Thanks to my son, Dr. David Webb for his help in the medical areas and historical events. To my son-in-law Special Agent Scott Anderson thanks for his comments and suggestions regarding police work and the law. To my daughter Lisa Anderson for taking the time to read and to provide honest feedback I owe my sincerest appreciation.

"And he did that which was evil in the sight of the Lord, as his fathers had done . . ."
2 Kings 15:9, KJV

"I do what I do in order to remove any opportunity from certain men who would deceive you in order to elevate themselves. My goal is to reveal them for who they are - just men. For in truth they are false apostles, scam artists, who make themselves out to be in Christ's camp.

"It should not be surprising to us, though. Not one bit–because even Satan himself can present himself as an Angel of Light. It is not a major thing then if one of his ministers also presents himself as a priest of God and His true light. Such ministers shall meet an end in keeping with their works."

—The apostle Paul in a letter to the Church in Corinth, Greece, around AD 57. Author's transliteration.

He wasn't good or evil or cruel or extreme in any way but one, which was that he had elevated greyness to the status of a fine art and cultivated a mind that was as bleak and pitiless and logical as the slopes of Hell.

-from *The Light Fantastic* by Terry Pratchett

PROLOGUE
The Present

His cooling off period between recipients was becoming shorter, and still he had not accomplished his mission—to bring the Light into the world. Perhaps—he was not sure—his last object for introduction to the Light had received a glimpse of it, but nothing more than a tiny glimpse. That was just two months ago, and he was ready to minister again. He was not quite ready for his supreme ministry, however. There still remained the necessity for another interim challenge. He was *almost* there, just not quite. Needing some fine-tuning, he knew just the right subject to provide it. She was so close to the ultimate object that it was exhilarating just to think about her.

There had been a time when he had wondered if he was crazy. It was only a brief span of uncertainty; then he had put it aside. His mission was too crisp, his strategy too clear, his means too perfect for him to be crazy. Also, it had occurred to him that genius was often mocked, considered peculiar and even crazy. Certainly he was not crazy, but it would be an honor to be considered so by others.

Would a crazy person be given the privilege, the tribute, of seeing the Light?

Certainly not.

He had seen the Light—twice. That first time, of course, was when he was six and had died. The other time was in 1980—he was just thirteen. The second seemed more special than the first for a number of reasons. First, it had occurred, not as a result of any physical trauma, but simply, apparently, as a tribute to him, as an accolade of admiration directed toward him. Secondly, it had been accompanied with a message, a message that had given him a purpose and a destiny, which, as a result had provided healing to his psyche. This healing was his third reason for remembering the second sighting. After that he no longer cared how people looked at him, nor what was whispered about him behind their shameful hands, nor who were openly repulsed by him. He was, now, who he was.

Unique.

Special.

Chosen, even.

He remembered lying in his bed, his body damp with sweat. Something had awakened him, a noise, and a movement. The green numbers on his bedside clock face said 3:00.

Then, suddenly, there came the soft refrains of music. But, not really music—more like an orchestra tuning up, except softer and more melodic. Then came the gentle breeze, cool and quiet.

At once there had appeared a dim, steady light at the foot of his bed. He sat bolt upright, fully awake now, his skin prickling. Growing brighter, the light emitted a greenish glow. Beginning slowly, it drifted upwards until it was about even with his feet, where it remained, about the size of a softball, slightly bobbing up and down.

The voice was in a low whisper.

I am truth and light.

Straining to hear, his trembling wouldn't stop.

I have chosen you; you have not chosen me. You are special to me, and you shall be my special envoy. Do not be afraid to do what I say. I will be with you. You will bring my light into the world to whomever I will.

The light brightened as the music rose to a screeching crescendo. He did not care that everyone in the house might be awakened. The light became so brilliant, the breeze warm then hot, and the shrieking dissonance so loud that he had to cover his ears and close his eyes. Strangely, no one came into his bedroom to rescue him or investigate the ruckus.

Then it stopped. The room was cast in darkness and became utterly quiet. The only sound was his rapid breathing. He fell backwards onto his pillow, heart pounding, perspiring profusely.

It was true.

It was confirmed.

He *was* chosen

Then, improbably, he fell asleep.

ONE

Two Months Ago

These were not the first photographs that John Parella had seen of a dead person, nor would they be the last. Nevertheless, Parella, homicide detective in the Spring Precinct Four Constable's Department, was struggling to maintain his composure. Staring at the horrific photos of the child's mutilated body, he could not, nor would he ever be able to, comprehend how someone could do this to another human, especially to a completely innocent fifteen-year-old girl. She was victim number five. He was certain there were no more than five, since all of the victims had been placed where they would be easily discovered. This victim had been found at Raveneaux Country Club, less than five miles from Parella's office.

Playing Raveneaux's old course, hitting twenty-nine and lying two on the 361 yard par four hole six, it was not a great day for Jim Stoddard. He was not happy with either his approach shots or his putting. He would likely not break a hundred on this outing. His partner, Harrison Clooney, was in the fairway about thirty yards ahead. Stoddard had shanked his second shot to the right into the woods.

As he had entered the woods to look for his ball he thought, "They need to put up a Watch-for-Snakes sign." He began to thrash around in the leaves with his seven iron. It had taken several long, mind-wrenching seconds for Jim to register what he was seeing.

The realization had been a process. First he had seen torn cloth mingled with leaves, then a shoe, then matted blond hair.

"What the...? Clooney!" he had screamed for his partner, who was further over in the woods looking for the errant ball. "Get over here! Now!"

"What is it?" Clooney had asked, running over to where Stoddard stood, trembling, having no earthly idea what to expect.

Jim didn't say a word, but just stood, dazed, his club lying in the leaves, pointing, his eyes wide with astonishment.

Just like the four previous victims, victim number five had worn the killer's motif—his identifying mark. They had each had a white silk ribbon tied around the left ankle. The sick psychopath had wanted to make certain that everyone knew that this was his handiwork, as if it could not be plainly seen from the horror that he had inflicted upon his victims. They each had the left side of their face pulverized, beaten to a bloody pulp. The left eyeball was missing, nowhere to be found, apparently plucked from the socket. The police, of course, had not revealed these details to the media for fear of copycat murders.

Such dreadful things had always brought Parella low. He would battle his melancholy with a fierce doggedness, determined that his wife, daughter, and colleagues would not see it. He was just not able to objectify himself—to disconnect—the way most of the other officers seemed to do. The fact that he had a beautiful fifteen-year-old daughter, Genevieve, amplified his compassion—and his pain. He would not allow it to affect his work, however. He used the pain, pushing it away from him, like Sisyphus rolling his boulder uphill. It allowed him to keep his focus, to aim his anger toward the right target, toward the warped madman who was doing this. As Al Pacino had explained to his wife in one of Parella's favorite movies *Heat*, "I have to hold on to my angst. It keeps me sharp—where I need to be."

At five feet eleven inches and 180 pounds, Parella had worked hard at staying trim. He had determined when first becoming a cop that he would not succumb to the "doughnut syndrome." He ran three miles three times a week and worked out regularly in his home gym. At thirty-four he was in excellent condition. He wore his sandy hair closely cropped for no reason other than it was simpler. His eyes were clear hazel and direct, hinting at the pain of having seen too much, too soon. His mouth wore a disarming half-grin most of the time and was quick to break into a full smile, one of his defenses against the recurring depression. All combined, his appearance was a strong asset for interrogating suspects—his open sincerity and friendliness quite often served to break through their defenses.

He studied an aerial map taped to the wall. Five different colored stickpins were stuck in five different nearby neighborhoods. Next to the map were multiple dreadful photos of the preceding four victims. He had been introduced to the little town of Spring, Texas, northwest of Houston in the humid swelter of August 2003. He had been brought on board as team lead investigator at a time when there were only three victims. He had been placed over a team of twelve. It was almost two years now, and still nothing had broken—no real leads, no witnesses, and no snitches. Nothing but two more victims.

Unlike most newcomers to the Houston area, the humidity didn't bother him. He, his wife Annie Louise and daughter Genevieve "Jenny" Marie were coming from the Big Easy—N'awlins—Crescent City. It was always humid in New Orleans.

The New Orleans Police Department had been basically good to him—up until that last month when the only words District Commander Joseph Michienzi had ever spoken to him eyeball to eyeball were something along the line of "I recommend, son, that you find yourself a spot elsewhere. Somewhere other than Louisiana."

Parella sat, letting the words sink in. The use of the word *son,* had offended him—it was crass and condescending. At the moment he was wondering what could have ever prompted him to leave Atlanta for New Orleans. For the life of him he couldn't remember the motivation; only how excited he and Annie Louise had been at the prospect of moving to New Orleans—a new exciting city, new friends, new beginnings.

Finally, Parella stood.

"Yes, sir," John said, laying his Glock 19 and his badge on the Commander's desk. "Since you explain it that way . . ." He saluted crisply, turned and walked out of the oversized office. *No problemo,* he thought.

It had been a political thing, and Parella hated politics.

It had all come down in June of 2003—on a day that was stressing every air conditioner in the city of New Orleans—a searing day that burned your lungs to breathe. Parella was in his car in the middle of the afternoon on Canal Street when a 62R, residential burglary, came in.

The call-in was for the Faubourg Marigny neighborhood, on Clairborne Avenue. He was close so he acknowledged the dispatcher, stuck his light on the car's roof and hit the siren. He was there in six minutes.

As he slid to a stop at the address, he saw an elderly woman on the front porch next door, wringing her hands. A bag of groceries was on the porch next to her feet. She hurried down the steps and approached him as fast as she could.

"Thank God, you're here," she said. She was clearly a woman of means who had likely lived in this neighborhood for more than fifty years. "I think someone is in my house," she said, her lip quivering, a shaky finger pointing in the general direction.

"Yes, ma'am," Parella said. "Why do you think someone is in your home?"

"I came home from the grocery store and the front door was partially open." She placed a frail hand on his arm and whispered, "I'm sure I heard noises from inside."

"I see," he said. "I'll check it out for you. It would be best if you went back to your neighbor's porch." As he spoke, a patrol car pulled up. He motioned to the officer to go around back.

"Please be careful," the lady said.

Approaching the house, his hand on his Glock 19 at his waist, Parella had a feeling this would be something. Some calls were nothing—some were something. This was something. He placed his back against the side of the open front door. He could see signs of forced entry.

"Police," he shouted. "New Orleans Police Department. Come forward with your hands visible." There was no response—no sound. He unholstered his weapon and snaked around the doorframe. The lighting in the house was subdued.

He checked the parlor on the left. Nothing.

Standing to one side of the hall closet door, he flipped it open. Nothing.

The living room was on his right. He scanned the room quickly. A wingback, maroon sofa was in front of a fireplace. On each side were cushioned Sackback Windsor chairs. A large Boston fern was behind the sofa. Nothing here.

The formal dining room was next. As he entered the room he heard a noise behind him, from the living room.

Crud! He thought. *Missed it. Missed it. The breaker had been behind the sofa.*

He quickly backed into the dining room in case the perp was armed. He heard scraping and scrambling from the room next door.

"Police," he said again. "Give it up."

The perp bolted, heavy footsteps on the wooden floor. Parella whipped around the door, leading with his weapon, two-hand hold. He was just in time to see the intruder disappear out the front door. He was dark, probably African-American, green jacket, jeans, and 5'6" at 130 pounds.

He charged after the burglar. Parella was in good shape. He had good wind.

The instant he exited the front door he saw the perp at the corner of the front yard. He was pointing a weapon in Parella's direction.

I am not believing this, Parella thought. *He's going to shoot!* He heard the angry snap of the bullet past his ear, the thud of splintering wood, then the *crack* of the weapon almost simultaneously.

Parella fired three quick rounds, the shell casings arcing over his right shoulder.

The man slumped to his knees, and then pitched forward on his face.

Parella approached cautiously, his weapon ready. In his peripheral Parella could see the other officer to his right, his weapon aimed at the man on the ground.

The man's weapon had fallen from his hand and lay in front of him. Parella kicked it away. He knelt and felt the carotid for a pulse. Nothing.

Parella holstered his weapon and turned the man over.

Parella's heart lurched. *Oh Jesus,* he thought. *It's just a kid.*

The boy's eyes were open and glazed. A thin trickle of blood edged from his nose. He couldn't be more than sixteen. There was a four-inch pattern of three dark holes in the center of his chest.

"Call this in, please," John Parella said to the officer, and stood slowly.

"It was justified," the policeman said. "A legitimate shoot, detective."

"Yeah," Parella sighed. "And some Momma's got a dead baby

boy. Jeez," he exclaimed, rubbing the back of his head. He looked up into the sky. "Just call it in."

It hadn't taken long for the circus to come to town. Every black group within a thousand miles had arrived to decry "the senseless murder of another promising young black."

Promising of what—more efficient burglary? Parella thought. But, still, the kid was dead, and that was a tragedy.

He was placed on suspension with pay. An inquiry would be held within a week.

The cry went up that a child murderer should not receive pay while awaiting justice. Some critics said that he should have apprehended the boy, Tyree Simpson, behind the sofa, and this tragedy could have been avoided.

Perhaps he could have gotten the boy behind the sofa. Perhaps he could have gotten a bullet between the eyes. One never knows.

All of which served to prove that Monday morning armchair quarterbacking was not worth a bucket of warm spit at half price.

So, John Parella was sacrificed. Didn't matter that the perp had fired first, that John was simply protecting his own hide. Nothing else mattered. The weather was hot, tempers were hot, and the town fathers did not want a Watts riot. He was told to walk, so he walked.

He would not miss New Orleans. Well, he might miss grillades and grits with smothered greens for breakfast at the Café Dumonde. Or maybe Beignets and Café au Lait. But he could and would turn his back on the city that had abandoned him.

Au revoir, N'awlins.

TWO

The Present

David Corwin Baxter sat staring out his Spring, Texas, office window at the traffic on Louetta Road in Northwest Houston. He noted that the majority of vehicles were SUVs and pickups. He himself owned a 2004 Chevy Tahoe. He loved the car, especially the fact that the large vehicle could have such a tight turn radius. His only regret was that he had selected a black one, which, during sweltering Texas summers made it more difficult to cool the interior.

At thirty-eight, David's six foot two inch frame was that of a professional athlete. No one would guess that he was a desk bound attorney. His hair, dark and naturally curled, had been the object of covetous women since he was a tot. His light blue eyes conveyed a sense of honest sincerity, and would fix upon whomever he was conversing with resolute interest. The eyes seemed to carry a sense of some intriguing private humor.

It was the eyes that had first attracted Lillian Jean Hansen to David. They were in the fourth grade at Westlawn Elementary in LaMarque, Texas, where Lillian had confessed to her girlfriends that David was "So-o-o cool." As have such matters for countless years, the word got back to David. Completely flummoxed by the revelation, he did at the time the only thing with the information that he knew to do—he ignored it.

Both David and Lillian were raised in La Marque, Texas. Although a separate community from nearby Texas City, the two towns shared their heritage, businesses and living areas; and were lovingly called the Twin Cities. Incongruously, La Marque was originally known as Highland. It was all of twelve feet above sea level. The name was changed to La Marque in 1882 when the Post Office came to town.

Located south of Houston and north of Galveston Island, the Twin Cities lay claim to multiple industries, including a tin smelter, oil refineries, metal fabrication, chemical plants and shipping. The bustling port distributes grain, cotton, sulfur, petroleum and chemical products. Swimmers and sunbathers on Galveston beaches continually see tankers and freighters coming and going to and from port and plying their way across the distant horizon. It was in this environment of industry and commerce, amongst a skyline of metal smoke stacks pouring out steam and smoke mixed with the briny air blowing in from the Texas Gulf, that Lillian Jean realized at the ripe age of nine, that she would one day change her name to Mrs. David Baxter. She, at the same time knowing that David Baxter had other things on *his* mind at the moment, determined, with a wisdom that God seems to bestow upon females of all ages, and not males of *any* age, that she must wait patiently.

And that she did.

David had gone through his phases—his preoccupation with Royal Ambassadors at church, his greater interest in boys than girls (girls were just no *fun*), but mainly his obsession with sports (*especially* football and baseball), until gradually he had begun to notice her more and more. Oh, he had known she was around, even in the fourth grade, but Lillian had known that she had occupied only a minuscule pinch of his time, and even less of his thoughts.

Then, in the ninth grade, as the football season had drawn on, David had begun to become quite the talk in the local barbershops and pool halls as perhaps having the potential to be the best little wide receiver La Marque had ever seen. There was a subtle change occurring within David Corwin Baxter. Girls had gradually become something more than a strange segment of the human species to be ridiculed and occasionally tolerated. Now they were *interesting*. And *mysterious*. And of all things *pretty*. And, while Lillian used to look sort of like a boy, only skinnier, she now looked, well, *different*. Certainly no longer like a boy.

It was 1983 when all of this amazing change was occurring. Lillian had made cheerleader that year and the year before, so she attended all of the games. It afforded her more opportunity to be seen by David, although it was something he never overtly seemed to do. Then one Thursday, when there were only two games left in the season, Lillian bolstered up her courage and managed to bump into David in the hallway between first and second period.

"Hi, David," she said, smiling up at him.

"Ah, hi, Lillian," he said. His voice changed pitch in the middle of her name, and his face turned immediately crimson.

She ignored his embarrassment and forged ahead. "You think we'll beat Friendswood tonight?" He rubbed the back of his neck, shifting his weight from one foot to another. "Oh yeah," he said, "We'll cream 'em."

"Alright," she smiled. There were only a few moments before the second period bell would ring. "Listen, could I . . . would you let me walk you off the field . . . after we cream 'em?"

He paused before answering. Lillian knew that Maybelle Schuster, another cheerleader, had walked him off the field after a few of the games. She prayed that Maybelle had not already asked him.

"Sure," he said, finally. Her heart leaped with joy.

"Okay, then," she said, touching him on the arm. "Have a good game." She turned, her fair, golden hair twirling, and walked with a spring down the hall.

He stood, transfixed, watching her walk away.

They had beaten Friendswood handily, 27–7. David had caught seven passes for 185 yards and two touchdowns. Lillian had greeted him on the field after the team had knelt in prayer.

"You creamed 'em," she squealed.

"Well, yeah—*we* creamed 'em" he grinned broadly.

"Here, let me take that," she offered, reaching for his blue, gold and white helmet. She hooked the face guard in the fingers of her right hand, and placed her left hand in his right. She had noted that he had a soft touch when catching the football. Scouts from various colleges had already noted it as well.

Swinging hands and laughing, they strode from the field of victory. David was happily flushed both with the feeling of winning and the feel of her hand in his.

He had no inkling then that his life had just been immutably changed.

David now considered himself to be truly blessed of God. He could ask for nothing more in his life. His loving wife Lillian and daughter Meredith doted over him, he had a flourishing family law practice, he was considered to be a pillar in his church—God had beyond doubt smiled upon him. And Lillian was the crown jewel of his life. He could not ask for a better partner. They had faced some hardships together, but nothing like the burden they would soon be required to bear.

# THREE

Two Months Ago

Summer Blevins Chase hated her life. She hated her middle name, she hated her hair, she hated her body, and she hated her Mom.

But most of all, she especially hated her dad.

The one person she had never hated was her best friend of twelve years, Loosey Goosey Suzie Muncie. They were fifteen and had been through it all together, fun times and absolutely lower than low times, and they had stuck together like super glue.

They had sustained one another through their parents' ugly divorces. Suzie's had been first, then eighteen months later Summer's folks Fred and Mary Chase had dissolved their union. The girls had cried on one another's shoulders through all the mish-mash feelings of guilt, anger, helplessness and hopelessness. Their worlds would never be as they once were. Now they would somehow have to figure out how to divide their love between their mom and dad, being careful not to infer that one was loved above the other.

The girls were similar in size and just beginning to develop. When together, they were both in awe of what was happening to their bodies. Suzie could not wait for the process to be complete.

"I hate it," Summer said.

"Why?" puzzled Suzie. "You're gorgeous, Sum!"

Summer would simply let the flatteries drop.

They shared similar tastes and traded clothes on a regular basis. Summer was ash blond, with straight hair to her shoulders. Suzie's dark hair was cropped at the nape of her neck. They had dark, even tans, spending most of their inseparable, waking hours during the summer outdoors. They were instrumental in helping their swim team, the mighty Swordfish, make it to and take first place in the regional finals. They had done the same for their soccer team.

Where one was, the other was nearby. They seldom slept apart—except when Summer began visiting her dad.

As for boys, they had made a pact when they were eleven never to have anything of any significance to do with boys. Boys were anathema to the girls. The girls pinky swore to have only the most minimal of transactions with the rude and crude creatures.

Now that they were fifteen Suzie was developing a chink in her armor of resolve towards boys. His name was Eddy Tindale. He was sixteen and a little on the wild side, which for some reason, not clear to Suzie, mysteriously appealed to her. But, above all things, Eddy had a car. Eddy and Suzie had skipped school together on three occasions. They had gone to Cypress Park where Eddy had taken a little traveled trail road, which was nothing more than two tire tracks, into the woods. On each occasion he had produced a six-pack of beer. Each time Suzie had had two cans. It tasted nasty, but it had given her a buzz. And Eddy had kissed her, three different times.

None of this had been hinted at to Summer. If Summer knew, Suzie was convinced, it would be the end of their relationship forever.

As for Summer, there were three boys who had mustered the courage to approach her, only to be devastatingly rebuffed with something like, "Oh, sure, like I want to relate to a Neanderthal." As far as Summer was concerned, Suzie was the only friend she needed—ever.

Now, seven years since her parents' divorce, Summer was totally convinced that if it were not for Suzie she would be crazy. Stark, raving looney-toons.

Or dead.

She had eventually decided to tell Suzie what was going on when she visited her dad. After that, things had pretty much snowballed out of her control. Suzie insisted that Summer should tell someone—some adult. Then came Child Protective Services, the District Attorney, and *her* attorney, Mr. Baxter. He, at least, was one adult that seemed to be real—and really cared. She certainly didn't hate him.

Nevertheless, her world had gone into a tailspin.

The inside of her head had continually felt like a bowl of cold spaghetti. Her mom had said often, "I love you, Summer." But it was only words. Her mom had never *done* anything to show it. She could at least have protected her somehow these last years. Even though her folks had divorced seven years ago, her mom could have done *something*. Anybody with a thimble full of brains could've seen that something was majorly wrong—that she was messed up big time.

But her mom had cried and said over and over, "But I didn't know, sweetheart. I didn't know," her small frame racked with helpless sobs.

Her dad, too, before she had ratted him out, had said, "I love you, baby." Many times. Of course he did. Especially when he was...

It had started six years ago; one year after her parent's divorce. For the longest time Summer had thought that both the divorce and what her dad was doing were her fault. Or at least her responsibility.

Her dad started when she was eight years old, and she had cried from the pain, physical and emotional—and the confusion.

This can't be right. Can it? But he's my dad; and I love him. And he loves me.

She remembered back when she was four. She had had elaborate plans for a regal wedding. She would marry her father. She had not given any thought to what would happen to her mother. Just that she would still be her mother. There would be flowers, and bubbles, candles and cake. Strawberry cake. With peach tea.

By the time she was nine she dreaded visiting her dad. She would lie in bed and wish with all her heart that he would die. Then guilt would consume her and she would cry slow hot tears. Then she wished *she* would die, then cry some more. Then, as time went by and it was clear he would not stop, she developed ways to push it out of her mind. Soon she was in complete denial. It simply didn't exist.

Except that it did exist.

Once, she had seen an evangelist on her television, talking about family and how God had designed the family. He had said that without God in a family it could not be the kind of family that God had planned. She had asked God then to make her family a good family. The preacher had gone on to say that fathers were not to exasperate their children. She was not sure what the word meant, but she was sure that must be what her father was doing.

One day, two months ago, finally, Summer had had enough. Her decision to tell Suzie was triggered, not by her father visiting her bedroom once again, but by the fact that he said he would not buy her a car. She would be sixteen soon, and she wanted a car. But she did not threaten her father, or attempt to bribe him for it. She had known somehow for some time that something awful bonded her and her dad, and that somehow she held the power in it. He was bigger and stronger, and could do whatever he wanted with her, but in some way she *knew* she had the power.

So she used her anger at being denied a car to open the years of anger that had filled the reservoir behind her dam of denial toward her father and the anguish he had caused her. She told Suzie.

She had made subtle hints before. Had Suzie picked up on them

Summer would have told her the whole thing. But Suzie had not. So, finally, Summer told her plainly. And Suzie had freaked.

"Oh. Crimey, Sum!" Suzie had exclaimed. "Are you serious? This is not right!"

Suzie began pacing her bedroom floor, back and forth, kicking clothes out of the way as she paced.

"What're you going to do?" Suzie asked, stopping in the middle of the room, then began pacing again. "We have to tell *somebody*."

So Summer had told her mother.

"Summer," her mother had responded, "Why are you doing this?" She removed her glasses, rubbed her eyes, and with pained expression continued, "You know that your father loves you. Why would you try to get him in trouble like this?"

Summer could not believe her ears. Why would her mother take up for her father like this? Why could her mother not *hear* her?

"*Mom!*" she exclaimed. "It's not right! What he's doing is not right!" Tears of exasperation flowed.

"Well, I just . . ." her mother continued as if Summer had not said a thing. "I just don't understand why you would do such a thing."

The next day, numbed by her mother's response, Summer told Mrs. Amato, one of the counselors at Klein High school. She had obtained her permission slip, walked over to the office in the Pavilion building after second period and had given the pass to Beth Cummings, the counseling secretary. Beth had seen the same look that was on Summer's face many times on many young girls. She told Summer that Mrs. Amato was waiting for her and to knock on Mrs. Amato's office door.

"Come in, please," Mrs. Amato had said.

With approximately 3500 students enrolled at Klein High, divided amongst ten counselors, Mrs. Sharon Amato, as was the case with all the counselors, found little time to breathe. She had allotted ten minutes for Summer. Mrs. Amato had the Bum-Di (or as she called it "the bumpity") section of the alphabet, which made Summer Chase one of hers. Feedback on Summer had been that she was quiet, moody, few friends, good attendance and a fairly bright student when she tried. Hopefully this would be a quick session.

Mrs. Amato shook Summer's hand and motioned to one of two armless chairs in front of the miniature desk. Mrs. Amato took the other chair. Their knees almost touched as they faced each other. The office was small and neat. A thin stack of papers was squared up in the middle of a desk calendar pad. The pad was full of notes, appointments and doodles. Sharon Amato doodled when she talked on the phone—mostly small hearts of all shapes. A notebook computer was on the left side of the pad. To the right was an In/Out basket with an empty In, and a few forms in the Out basket. The overall effect was that this was the office of someone who was neat, tidy and meant business.

A pot of red begonias sat in the middle of the windowsill. The clear glass window looked out westward toward the red-bricked Main Building. Half a dozen pine trees, branches gently maneuvering in the almost constant breeze that funneled between the structures, intervened between the two buildings.

Summer briefly told her story while mostly looking down at her hands in her lap.

This is not going to be ten minutes, Sharon thought, and notified Beth to block out an hour. Beth was not surprised at the request.

Mrs. Amato responded nothing like Summer's mother. She was compassionate and caring, and gave Summer a comforting hug.

"Summer, I am required to notify CPS—Child Protective Services—they are an organization that helps children who don't have the family support they need. Do you understand?"

"What for?" Summer asked. "What are they going to do?"

"Well, they will ask you some questions, and they will find you a temporary place to stay while they get things sorted out. Okay?"

"I guess," Summer said. She seemed to have no other options. She looked out the window at the pines, the limbs swaying more briskly now. The sky had grayed over and a fine mist had begun to fall. Somewhere distant thunder rolled.

David Baxter had received the call from Bill Hogerty at CPS, who explained the situation at Klein High, and asked if David could meet him there.

"When?" David had asked.

"Fifteen minutes."

David felt that Bill was not the sharpest knife in the drawer over at CPS, and the two of them had had a couple of run-ins over what David had considered to be minor issues. But Hogerty was one of those types that considered everything to be an emergency and would not let matters lie.

"If your pants are on fire, or all the blood in your body is running out on the ground–that's an emergency," David had once said.

The characterization notwithstanding, Bill had pestered David to do some things that David had considered to be unnecessary and a waste of time. David had some family time scheduled for the weekend and finally had told Hogerty to do the reports himself if he wanted reports on his desk Monday morning.

The topic was never revisited.

So David considered pushing back on the "Fifteen minute" thing, but it sounded as if a young girl could use his help.

"Sure," he had said. "See you there in fifteen minutes."

Mrs. Amato arranged for a meeting room, with soft drinks and bottled water. The room was sparse with a rectangular laminated table surrounded by ten brown plastic chairs. The levered panel windows provided a southern view of the campus. It was raining harder now, with frequent flashes of lightning.

Summer was not thirsty. She sat against the wall with her arms folded.

"Hi, Summer," Bill Hogerty extended his hand, and Summer took it limply. "I'm Bill Hogerty, case worker with Child Protective Services. And this is your attorney David Baxter." Hogerty was fat, balding and red faced. His white shirt was too small and gapped between buttons, revealing a white cotton undershirt. His blue polyester trousers hiked up above his brown shoes, showing white socks.

"Hi, Summer," David waved his hand and smiled broadly. "Circumstances aside, it's good to meet you." David was trim and athletic, dressed in khakis, a dark blue pullover, with Top Siders casual boating shoes. He conveyed a sense of strength and confidence.

"Hi," Summer said, looking at David and ignoring Hogerty. In the brief moments of their meeting, Summer had taken an immediate liking to David, and just as immediate disliking to Bill Hogerty. The reasons were subtle and mostly subconscious to her. David was direct and forthright with his eyes, and non-pushy, with a genuine smile. Bill Hogerty, on the other hand, was shifty, self-absorbed, pushy and not to be trusted.

"Well, why don't we get started?" Hogerty said, leaning back in his chair. "First of all, Summer, I need to get . . ."

"Just a second, Bill." David raised a hand slightly. "Let me have a few moments with my client."

"But I need to get a statement so that . . ."

"Soon enough, Bill." David smiled. "I need to explain a few things to Summer first."

"I . . ."

"In private, please."

Bill stood, his face fallen, and left the room.

Summer sighed audibly, reaching for a bottle of Dr. Pepper and opened it.

David said, "I expect that things are spinning pretty fast for you right now."

"I don't like Hoggy," she said simply.

"You mean Mr. Hogerty?" David asked. He had to suppress a smile.

"Yeah, I don't like him. He's nasty."

"Well . . . okay," David acknowledged. "Does that mean . . . ?"

"I don't want to talk to him," she finished the sentence.

The next day Summer had been assigned to Mrs. Esparanza Chavez, a young, pretty Hispanic woman who wore her long black hair in a tight bun. She had been with CPS for only eight months.

"My name—Esperanza—means 'hope' in Spanish." She placed her hand on Summer's shoulder. "With God there is always hope." Then she had asked Summer if she could pray for her, and Summer had said okay. Esperanza had taken her to the Sonic drive-in on Louetta Road to get a malted.

"I will pray for you as a friend," she had said. "Not as a CPS caseworker."

Suddenly it struck Summer, and her heart began to race. Just two nights ago she had recognized the same evangelist that she had seen on her TV when she was nine. She remembered having prayed back then that God would make her family better. She prayed again the other night, asking God to show Himself to her if He was indeed real. She asked Him specifically to send someone to help her.

Esperanza continued, "But before I pray I need to make sure that you understand something."

"What is it?" Summer asked, sipping her strawberry malt.

"You need to understand that what has happened between you and your father was not your fault. Not by any stretch is it your fault. It is entirely your father's fault; he alone is responsible for the horrible things that he has done to you. The Bible tells us though, that we are all sinners, Summer. Including you. But this thing with your father is not one of your sins." Esperanza looked intently at Summer. "Do you understand what I am saying, Summer?"

"Yes . . . I think so," Summer replied, wiping her mouth with a paper napkin.

"You have need for a Savior, Summer, as we all do. Because of your sin. But make sure that you know that it has nothing to do with your father. Let me pray for you, then we will talk some more."

Esperanza had prayed an eloquent but simple prayer, asking God to touch Summer, to fill her with his grace and healing, and to intervene in Summer's circumstances. She then explained again that we are all separated from God by our sin, and that every one of us is a sinner. She explained that only the sinless blood of Christ is adequate payment for sin, and when we repent of our sin, believe individually in Christ's atoning death, and confess Him as Savior we receive eternal life. She then asked Summer if she had ever trusted in Jesus as her personal savior, and Summer had shaken her head no, but she said that she would like to. Esperanza led her in a prayer of repentance, thanking God for forgiving her sin, and thanking Jesus for dying on the cross for her.

"Dear Lord," Summer had prayed, "I believe that you died on the cross for me, and that you rose from the dead in three days. Please come into my life, save me, make me whole, make me the person that you want me to be."

Such a peace came over Summer—she felt as though she were floating. She couldn't wait to share the exciting good news with Suzie. As soon as the two of them could get together, Summer shared the thrilling event of the day. Summer shared the things that Esparanza had told her, and led Suzie in the same prayer of repentance and salvation that she had just prayed that day.

That night Summer had slept with a tranquility that she had not known for years.

The following day Esparanza had taken Summer to Dr. Oscar Villarreal's office in Tomball. It was raining heavily, with bright flashes of lightning and immediate deafening peals of thunder. They said little to each other on the way over.

The experience could not have been more horrible for Summer. It was demeaning and humiliating. The examination room was small and cold, and she had had to remove her clothes and put on a stupid wraparound gown that opened in the back.

The doctor had been totally insensitive and impersonal, the instruments had been cold, and the doctor never looked at her. No one, including the gruff nurse, seemed to have any feelings. It was as if she were not even there. Summer gritted her teeth, swallowed her tears and said nothing. It was at least as bad as being with her dad.

She had come away from the experience vowing that no man would ever touch her again.

The only man she came even close to trusting now was her attorney, Mr. Baxter. He listened, and he cared.

FOUR

The Present

Some people in life made a difference in the world. Most didn't. Darrell Phelps knew that he was one who made a difference—a big difference. He had clearly made a difference, several times over now. He would continue to make such an impact. And the real measure of his nobility and graciousness was that he exercised his magnanimity in secrecy.

The true measure of greatness in a person, he thought, *is that he does not need plaudits, he does not need applause—he does not need payment. He does not need others. One such as this needs no reward.*

"*I* need no reward," Darrell spoke aloud as he drove his black Chevy Tahoe toward the law office on Louetta Road. "*I am*, is my reward," he smiled. "I am that I am. I need no one. I need no thing."

He had felt the call to ministry when he was eleven. He had begun first ministering to small animals, developing the cunning and prowess to minister to people when he was sixteen. It had been a clear calling, crisp and lucid. Circumstances in his life had decreed it. When his mother left him, he knew that he was on his own. When everyone else abandoned him there was no question regarding his destiny.

And, of course, most of all, he had seen and been instructed by the Light.

But there was one paradox, he knew. Although he could function behind the scenes, without notoriety, in order for the Light to be revealed in glory he must see that those for whom the Light was intended would be able to find the way. They would not be able to do it on their own. He must reveal *some* of himself. Accordingly he had begun to leave a bare minimum of clues that would eventually be discovered—a pointer here and there. There was especially the white ribbon, symbolizing the purity of the Light that he was disclosing. Ultimately, he would soon have a special delivery just for David.

He parked in front of a Radio Shack store, two doors down from the law office that had a painted sign on the door reading:

ATTORNEY AT LAW
DAVID BAXTER
MON—FRI
9 A.M. TO 5 P.M.
SAT—SUN CLOSED

It was Saturday, but David's office was open. The routine had been established over the last two months. He had named the girl *Lucerna* because he had not yet discovered her real name. The new name fit because it meant light in Latin, and she would be most instrumental in helping usher in the light. She was perfect for the next step because she was close to David, and it fit so well into his overall plan. It was clearly something the others couldn't do.

The others were just minor apostles: Daumer, Berkowitz, Gacy, the BTK guy—*what was his name? See—just his point*; his name was not indelible. Those others brought a spark into the world—a tiny spark. He, on the other hand, would introduce the everlasting Light. The Healing Light. He knew there would be opposition. There were those—groups, entire factions—who did not want healing to come into the world. The Hippocratic hypocrites in the medical industry did not really want healing. They would be virtually ruined if he were allowed to bring the healing Light into the world. So, most certainly, he would be opposed.

Lucerna was in the law office right now. It had become somewhat of a pattern. He had been in the Wimbledon Estates subdivision earlier that morning, watching the house when the woman and Lucerna got into the gray Honda Civic and backed out of the driveway.

Darrell drove straight to the law office, getting there ahead of them, to see the woman pull up behind parked cars to let Lucerna out. He thought that the woman was not Lucerna's mother. There was zero intimacy between them. He hadn't figured it out yet. Perhaps the woman was an aunt or a friend of the family. She probably went shopping while Lucerna was with David. The session typically lasted an hour. Darrell could not imagine what they were talking about every Saturday.

FIVE

The Present

David considered that the transformation he had seen in Summer over the last several weeks was nothing short of a miracle. She had *blossomed.* She had begun to radiate a glow and joy that was infectious. She smiled all of the time and talked about almost nothing but what Jesus had done in her life.

Her father had pleaded guilty, and the judge had set the sentencing for a week from this Tuesday. David had counseled her regarding what to expect and what her options were. Summer had opted to have the courtroom emptied of all unnecessary people. She just did not want everyone in the world to hear her have to describe all the sordid details.

Summer had told David at their second meeting that the CPS lady, Mrs. Chavez had introduced her to Christ. He had congratulated her and revealed that he too was a Christian.

"I was baptized in a little Baptist church in La Marque just after my eighth birthday," he shared. "My father baptized me. He was a deacon in the church. It was quite a thrill."

"No chance my father will baptize *me*," she shrugged. "I don't even see how I can get baptized since my fosters don't even believe in God. They won't let me go to church. They say it's waste-of-time-nonsense."

David had already had Summer moved once. CPS had first placed her with the Hendricks, who were an empty nest, their three children having moved out, married and produced eight grandchildren. Summer was uncomfortable with the way that Mr. Hendricks looked at her, and, besides, he was overly affectionate in Summer's opinion. Way too touchy.

So David had talked with CPS and they had re-placed Summer with George and Marsha Greer. George was an electrical engineer at Hewlett Packard, and Marsha was a stay-at-home mom, raising their five-year-old, Georgie junior. They had moved to Wimbledon Estates in 2002, the year that HP had bought out Compaq, the local computer company.

They were nice enough, Summer felt. The only thing was they were agnostic, and would not provide a ride to church. No one else that Summer knew was interested in going, except Suzie—but she didn't have a ride either.

David had approached CPS, and they had refused his request to change fosters to a specifically Christian home. They had been more than flexible, they said, having changed counselors and fosters already. Besides, religiosity was not a requirement for being a foster home they said.

So David had said to Summer, "Let me make a suggestion; why don't we have church right here in my office? We can meet on Saturdays. I don't think it would be such a great idea at this point for me to take you to my church."

The Greers had agreed to bring Summer to the office each Saturday since David was also providing legal counsel during these meetings as well. Suzie's parents, on the other hand, would not let her come. Her dad did not want "some attorney filling my daughter's head with some mumbo-jumbo garbage." So Summer had begun to mentor Suzie, passing along the things she was learning from Mr. Baxter.

David and Summer met, for the sake of propriety, in Sharon Maybree's, the secretary's, office in front and in open view of the large window. They sat in front of her desk.

Summer had her brand new maroon leather bound Bible that David had given to her, open on her lap. He had told her that it was okay to take notes in it.

"Write in it," he said. "Take lots of notes. Use your highlighter. It's a study tool. It's God's personal letter to you—meant to be read, meant to be understood."

He had suggested she read the Gospel of John on her own at home. Already it was filled with her meticulous tiny notes, and several verses were highlighted.

"Okay," David began. "So, before we start, let's pray. It's always good to ask God to open our hearts and minds to what *He* wants to teach us. Really, we want to be on His agenda, not our own. You want to pray?"

"Sure," she said, and bowed her head. "Dear God, thank You for loving us, and saving us. Thank You for Mr. Baxter and what he's doing for me. Thank You for my best friend Suzie. Help us both to grow—and help her parents to understand what she needs. Help Mr. Baxter and me understand what You want to teach us today. In Jesus' name, Amen."

"Thanks, Summer," David smiled. "You remember what we said last time about *paradox*—about what it means?"

"Yep," Summer waggled her head back and forth, and punctuated the air with her index finger. "It means, like, a sort of contradiction and stuff."

"That's right, and we said that God is a God of paradox. What does that mean?

"Well, it means that . . . um—God wants us to, like, do the opposite of stuff."

"Good, close—real close. Can you give me an example maybe?"

Summer toyed with a snow globe on the secretary's desk. "One is: *if you want to be first you must be last.*"

"Absolutely," David grinned. "Good one. Can you think of another?"

"Oh, yeah," she brightened even more. "If you want to live, you have to first die—to yourself, that is."

"Great. That's good. Thing about it is, God is that way about *everything*. To receive you must . . . ?"

"Give," she finished with a flourish.

"To be great we must be . . . ?"

"Teensy."

"To lead we must . . ."

"Get a leash," she giggled.

"Well, alright then. So today let's talk about something that tends to be pretty difficult for most of us—at least, I know that it's *real* difficult for me. What is it that you usually want to do when somebody does something that's mean, or bad to you, like your father did? What do you want to do?"

"Get even," she became still for the first time that morning.

"Yes, me too. What else; anything else?"

"Yeah, sure. Hurt him and stuff." Her eyes watered and she looked out the window. "Sometimes I want him to die."

"Well if we get back to God and His paradoxical ways, guess what He says?"

"To . . . not hurt 'em?" she looked back at David.

"Close, but, really, even more than that. Look at Romans 12:19. Read it to me, please."

She flipped through her New King James Bible and found Romans. She read the verse out loud, "Beloved, do not avenge your-selves, but rather give place to wrath; for it is written, 'Vengeance is Mine, I will repay,' says the Lord."

"What does that mean in your own words?" he asked.

"It means that we should not get even—should not even *try* to get even. That it's God's job to do it—He will take care of it Himself." She hesitated a moment, then asked, "So—we're supposed to just not do nothing—just forget about it, like it didn't happen?"

"Good point, Summer. Now comes the really hard part. Take a look at Mark chapter eleven verse twenty-five."

"And whenever you stand praying, if you have anything against anyone, forgive him, that your Father in heaven may also forgive you your trespasses."

Summer read it then said, "So, the paradox is, when somebody does something really bad to you, and you feel like you want something really bad to happen to them or you would like to do something to hurt them back, what you're really supposed to do is forgive them. Right?"

"Right. Think about it," David said. "Who is most affected when someone holds a grudge against another person and is bitter in his heart toward them?"

"What do you mean?" Summer asked, puzzled.

"Okay, say I'm really bitter towards you. Who is affected most by my bitterness?"

"It would really hurt my feelings if you were mad at me," Summer said, quietly.

"Me, too," David said. "But the thing is, the person most hurt is the person holding the bitterness in their heart. It can even make a person physically sick. So, a good rule of thumb when it comes to doing what God wants us to do is: Do the opposite of what you *feel* like doing."

She laughed and said, "'I see' said the blind man."

"What part did you not get?"

"I got it," she said. "If you feel like choking somebody, hug 'em instead."

"Good analogy," David said, closing his Bible. "Do you have any questions about what is going to happen in court a week from this Tuesday? Any questions?"

"Well, I think I can remember most of the stuff you told me already." She blew out a puff of breath. "I think I'm just mostly scared."

"Well, you know I'll be praying for you. I think you'll be fine." He stood. "One other thing not related to forgiveness."

"Sure, what is it?"

"The Bible says that whatever Satan means for evil, God intends it for good. Remember that. God can turn any horrible thing to work for His good purpose. Okay?"

"Okay." She looked out the window and saw Mrs. Greer's car in a slot across the lot. She gave David a quick hug around the waist.

"Thanks, Mr. Baxter. See ya."

"See ya," he said. "Next Saturday if not before."

SIX

The Present

John Parella was staring at the map with its small cluster of five pushpins on the wall, the gruesome photographs pinned next to it. Something had to materialize soon. Something had to break. Unannounced Detective Sergeant Vincent Cramer burst in. His voice was raised half an octave with excitement.

"John, you're not going to believe this," Cramer panted.

Vince's physical appearance would place him more at a thief's convention than in the police department. He was short, 5' 7," portly, and dark. He sported a constant five o'clock shadow. His black slicked back hair added to the picture. The only thing missing was the dark, pinstriped suit, with black silk shirt and white tie. Instead, Vince wore navy blue trousers, standard white button down shirt with no tie, and a gray sports jacket.

"We got prints, man!" Vince pumped his fist and laughed. "Hoowa."

Parella was nonplussed. "What are you talking about, Vince? Haven't we gone over everything three or four times?"

"Yeah, right—but not on the inside," Vince said mysteriously and waited. He was childishly enjoying this—relishing knowing for a brief moment something that his boss didn't already know.

"Well?" Parella encouraged him.

"Mitch at the lab was just fooling around, and on a whim or something, he looks inside number three's little pink purse. And there it is—big as day. A fingerprint. Right in the middle of the inside of the purse. Good one, too. Only slightly rough around the edges."

Parella's mind was racing. *The attacker had used gloves. There were no prints, no hair, no DNA. Why a print on the* inside *of her purse? Hidden, but there to find for the persistent. A hidden, intentional clue? It didn't compute.*

"You said 'prints'—plural," Parella said.

"Yeah, right. Victim number four also. On the *inside* of her right shoe. Same print." Vincent sat, out of breath with excitement. "Slightly smudged. But good."

"Don't we as a rule look for prints in shoes?" Parella asked.

"Not down inside the toe," Vincent smiled.

How crazy does it get? This morning they had zip. Now they had two prints from a killer who had not left another single clue—not one. It made no sense. Why would a sicko this smart risk being caught by providing two good findable prints?

The books said that criminals subconsciously want to get caught, so they unintentionally leave lots of clues. But that theory, Parella surmised, assumed that they had some feelings of guilt. And wanted to be caught and punished. The problem was these clues were not unintentional. The book didn't apply here—it didn't apply to sick, psychotic, sociopaths like this character, who had about as much feelings of guilt as a mud turtle.

"We're running an ID through AFIS right now," Vincent said, heading off Parella's next question. "Should know something real soon."

SEVEN
The Present

Darrell had planned as best he could. He had gotten the layout of the house from city records. The only thing was, he didn't know which room the girl slept in—or the boy. There were no security lights on so he went through the back wooden gate and quickly picked the lock to the utility room door. Three bedrooms up, one down. She was sure to be up. There were two bedrooms on the north side of the house, a bathroom in the hallway, then a bedroom on the south side. The boy would most likely be in that one since it was the largest bedroom and he had lived there before Lucerna.

He went to the northwest bedroom first and slowly opened the door. There was enough light through the blinds to see that the bed was unoccupied. He tried the northeast room across the hallway.

Locked.

It must be the girl's room. The boy was too young to want his door locked.

Then his senses leaped. A slight noise behind him. He turned slowly to see the small, dark form of the boy in the dimness of the hallway. Darrell froze, holding his breath. The boy shuffled toward him, then turned into the bathroom. After several moments there was the sound of the toilet flushing. The boy reappeared through the door, turned away from Darrell and headed for his bedroom.

Darrell waited until he was absolutely certain that the boy had settled back down.

He had the door unlocked quickly and was inside. Her bed was against the far wall. She was deep asleep, breathing slowly and evenly. Lucerna was lying on her stomach, her pillow covering the top of her head. She was facing the wall.

Quickly he simultaneously put his knee in her back, placed his left hand over her nose and mouth and with his right, jabbed the hypodermic needle into her left common carotid artery. The Diprivan would work quickly. He waited patiently with his hand over her mouth, allowing her to breathe through her nose. After several seconds he slowly removed his hand. She was out.

Relishing the moment, he pressed the button on his penlight and scanned the room. It was modestly furnished, a small, white dresser against the north wall next to a two-door closet. A mirror hung on the wall above the dresser. A white, four-drawer chest of drawers was against the opposite wall. On top was a framed photograph of another girl, a snow globe from Disney World, a jewelry box, and a rock, upon which was inscribed:

THE
LORD IS
MY **ROCK,**
MY **FORTRESS**
AND MY **DELIVERER**
PSALM 18:12

On the wall next to the dresser were two posters. One had an abstract background in blues upon which was inscribed:

WHATEVER
is true, whatever is noble, whatever is right,
whatever is pure, whatever is lovely,
whatever is admirable—

if anything is excellent or praiseworthy—
Think about such things.
Philippians 4:7–9 NIV

The other poster depicted a bright light out of which was a hand, palm upward. It said:

SEE!
I will not
Forget you . . .
I have carved your name
On the palm of My hand!
Isaiah 49:15, 16 NIV

Hmmm…It appears that we have a zealot here, Darrell thought.

He swung the penlight around to the bedside table. Next to the lamp was a maroon Bible. Holding the penlight in his teeth he picked up the Bible and flipped the pages. Some pages were full of handwritten notes in blue ink—small, neat printing. Text on several of the other pages was highlighted in yellow. He turned to the cover pages. On one page a short note was written:

Nov. 20, 2004
Dear Summer,
I thank God for you and for what you have meant in my life. It has been a real encouragement to me to see Him work in you. I have faith in you, but more importantly God has faith in you.
I pray for your continued blessings and that you will clearly know His plan and purpose for your life.
Jude 2
David Baxter

"Perfect," he whispered to himself. "Perfect, perfect, perfect."

EIGHT

The Present

The Greers finally took Summer to church.

Her shiny, bronze casket had to remain closed due to the grievous nature of her wounds. The coffin was heaped with mounds of flowers of every color and kind—red and white chrysanthemums, red, pink and white roses, white lilies, wreaths, sprays, and pots of live greenery, bows of all colors—the arrangements filled the altar area and much of the choir section behind it as a tribute of friendship in death from many to a girl who, in life, had so few friends.

Strains of "Amazing Grace" drifted softly from the ceiling speakers. It had been quickly determined that David's church in Spring, where he was a Pastor-Elder, would not accommodate the potential crowd. The sanctuary area there would seat only 200.

David's office and the Greer's home had been inundated with phone calls, cards and emails honoring Summer and asking for details of the funeral. Today, clearly, White Fields Baptist Church would not be large enough to accommodate all of the mourners either. All sanctuary seats were taken, and the foyer was beginning to rapidly fill where 150 folding chairs had been set up. It was 8:50 a.m.; ten minutes before the slated start time.

Fred Chase had filed a petition to attend his daughter's funeral service. His request had been denied, and he had wept in bitter remorse. He considered her death as his punishment for what he had done. He had been housed with other pedophiles, with his first response being *I am not like **them**.* After four weeks of counseling he had begun to develop some sense of the terrible nature of his actions. He had been actively considering suicide.

Mary Chase sat on the front row of the church's family section, mostly hidden from the main congregation. She stared straight ahead, not moving, blinking only occasionally. Her face was pasty, purple bags hanging beneath reddened eyes. Her mouth was a tight red line. There was not a hint of a tear. She had spent hours alone in her empty bedroom, howling like an animal ensnared by the steel teeth of a trap. What had she done, what terrible act of commission or omission had she perpetrated to bring this awful thing upon her daughter? She was drained dry, numb, with not a glimmer of hope or an idea of how she could go on. She sat next to the Greers with considerable space between them.

Marsha Greer wept openly behind her dark glasses, occasionally blowing her nose into George's handkerchief. He had several in his jacket pocket. Occasionally he would bring a finger to his eye to wipe a tear from behind his glasses.

Suzie and her parents sat next to the Greers. Suzie sobbed uncontrollably, wringing her hands, her grief unbelievably consuming at the thought of the horror that had happened to her friend, and that she would never, ever see her again. Suzie's father sat, stiff and stoic, looking straight ahead. Suzie's mother dabbed at her reddened eyes with a tiny kerchief.

Included in the family section was Esperanza Chavez, Summer's CPS caseworker. She sat, quietly praying, her black-gloved hands folded in her lap. She wore a black netted and ribboned, small-rimmed hat, a newly purchased loose-fitting black dress, and black, medium-heeled shoes. Her black clutch purse was at her side. And although, she knew that Summer was at this moment in heaven with God, Esperanza's heart and mind were anesthetized by pain of the horrid nature of Summer's untimely death.

The congregation was full of Klein High Schoolers and their parents. Audible sobs regularly issued from the assembly. It was not necessary for them to have known Summer, they were united by the stunning suddenness of her horrific death, and the knowledge that their lives were equally as tenuous. There was a morbid unity in their anguish, and the questions that derived from it. *Why did this happen . . . Summer was young . . . How could God allow such a terrible thing . . . She was a good girl . . . What did she do to deserve such a horrible death?*

John Parella stood at the rear of the church at the right hand side. Vincent Cramer was opposite him on the left. Penny White-side was positioned behind the choir seats at the entryway to the right-hand steps leading into the baptistery where she could see out but not be seen. Luke Beeman was opposite her on the left side of the baptistery. Sitting in the middle of the congregation near the front was Joyce Kilmer. Near the back was Tom Nash.

A remote controlled camera had been installed in the ceiling above the choir. Jim Knight and Percy Black controlled and moni-tored the camera from a classroom in the rear of the church. Before the service would be over, everyone in the sanctuary would be cap-tured on tape for about seven seconds. The team estimated that there were about 500 people in the congregation.

There was no such setup for the foyer. Kevin Lacy and Patri-cia Greene on either side of the foyer were taking digital photos of everyone as surreptitiously as possible. Many of their shots were of necessity profiles. There were about 150 attendees in the folding chairs. In the process Kevin and Patricia received several reproving looks.

In the parking lot four officers were taking stills of each license plate on about 200 vehicles. Two others were scanning the area and the perimeter for any strange or unusual behavior.

The team communicated via radio transceivers in their ears. They were monitoring the audience carefully for any peculiar behavior. It was not unusual for serial killers to attend the funerals of their victims. In this instance, however, Parella did not have much confidence. This guy was smarter than most.

However, there had been another print. On the dedication page of Summer's maroon Bible. A slightly smudged print was right there—right in the center of the page signed by David Baxter. It matched the other two prints.

David Baxter was not at all confident that he could deliver Summer's funeral message. The Greers had asked him right away if he would do it, and without hesitating he had said yes. But this reminded him of another funeral. A funeral in 1974. He had said goodbye to his best friend Birdy who had died clutching David's wrist. He would never shed himself of the heavy grief. Now this was being added to the scale.

He removed Birdy's photo from his wallet and read the inscription on the back: Job 19:25–26, KJV.

"I know that my Redeemer liveth... and though after my skin worms destroy this body, yet in my flesh shall I see God."

As he sat on the podium, his palms sweating, he listened to his wife Lillian, singing Rich Mullins' "Our God Is an Awesome God."

Our God is an awesome God,
He reigns from heaven above,
With wisdom, power and love,
Our God is an awesome God . . .

David prayed, *Dear Lord, give me strength.*

He loved his wife. Her voice was absolutely beautiful, and she was doing so well. But she was finished with her song and was sitting down. Taking a deep breath, David stood.

You can do this, he thought. He flipped the switch on the lapel mike clipped to his belt.

Clasping each side of the podium to steady himself, David began. "Summer Blevins Chase was born September 5th, 1989. She went to be in the presence of her Lord and Savior, Jesus Christ on February 3rd, 2005. She is survived by her parents, Fred and Mary Chase, and a number of aunts, uncles and cousins.

"It saddens us when a young, promising life is cut needlessly short. It is proper and healthy for us to mourn—even to be angry at the cruel nature of Summer's death."

We were just talking about forgiveness, weren't we, Summer? I don't know if I can forgive whoever did this to you. I certainly can't ask you to. That's something you'll have to discuss with the Lord. Maybe you already have.

"But we are here this morning to celebrate. We are here to celebrate Summer's life, and especially the impact that it has had on the lives of many just recently; and to celebrate the eternal life that God has available for each of us. Scripture is clear about this. John 10 in the New King James Version says,

> My sheep hear My voice, and I know them, and they follow Me. And I give them eternal life, and they shall never perish; neither shall anyone snatch them out of My hand. My Father, who has given *them* to Me, is greater than all; and no one is able to snatch *them* out of My Father's hand. I and My Father are one.

"I know without a shadow of doubt that Summer has begun the glory of her eternal residence in Heaven. She is rejoicing at this moment before God our Father, who just three days ago said to her, as He welcomed her into His presence, saying, 'Well done, My good and faithful servant.'

"In the book of Job we read, in Chapter 19, verses 25 and 26 in the King James Version, 'I know that my Redeemer liveth... and though after my skin worms destroy this body, yet in my flesh shall I see God.'

"We conclude from this that if we have been redeemed through faith in Christ, we will one day see God. And if the redeemed shall see God then we will certainly see one another. I have no doubt that I will see Summer again.

"I am fortunate to have been associated with Summer these past two months, to see the power of God at work in her life; to see her bloom from someone who was hopeless, depressed and desolate, to someone who was full of life, full of hope and full of joy. I know that this transformation did not go unnoticed by many of you, and I will give you the opportunity to share some of your thoughts regarding Summer with us this morning."

David went on to more detail regarding God's miraculous work in Summer and his recent weeks studying the Bible with her.

"God wants to do the same for you," he said. "Put your faith in Jesus Christ and in what He has accomplished for you on the cross."

As David was in the midst of his appeal, Vincent received a call in his earpiece. His face drained of color.

"What?" he whispered. "Say again?"

Vincent stood, dumbstruck. He could not make his voice work.

"John," he said. "John."

"Go ahead."

"John, we got the FBI results on the prints."

The mile long funeral procession wound its way to Louetta Road where it turned east. The motorcycle policemen skillfully worked the long line of cars and the intersections to keep the motorcade moving smoothly.

One particular policeman had little patience with drivers not in the procession who would try to pass the entire line. He would roar up to the front of the trespasser's automobile, his palm toward the driver.

"Where *you* going in such an all-fired hurry?"

"Sorry, officer."

"Sorry, my foot," he said, turning his motorcycle around. "You stay right there. Don't let me see you move." And he roared off toward the front of the line. The motorcade turned south on IH45 three miles to Beckman Cemetery. The fresh site could be seen from the gate as the hearse entered. There was the green canopy, the flowers covering the new mound of earth, and a few folding chairs for the family.

David kept the graveside service brief. He opened with a prayer, and provided one more opportunity for those there to accept Jesus Christ as their personal savior.

"It is not about religion," he said. "Religion is man's attempt to please God, to be good enough to make it into Heaven. It's impossible," he said. "You can no more be good enough to make it into Heaven than the best broad jumper in the world can jump the Grand Canyon. The Bible clearly says that man's righteousness is as filthy rags to God. The only acceptable payment for our sin, yours and mine, is the blood of Jesus Christ, which was poured out on the cross for you. God has done His part. Your part is simply to accept by faith what he has done for you individually. It is about a relationship—your relationship with God your Father to whom you now have access through Christ. Once you have received Christ, nothing can change that. Scripture says to us in the book of Romans: "For I am persuaded that neither death nor life, nor angels, nor principalities, nor powers, nor things present nor things to come, nor height nor depth, nor any other created thing, shall be able to separate us from the love of God which is in Christ Jesus our Lord.

"Let's pray," David said. "Father, we thank You for the great privilege of prayer that we have. That we, as Your children can approach the throne of the King of the universe, the Creator of all things, with boldness is an amazing thing. We can do just that because of the blood of Your Son. So we come now, thanking You for Your grace, thanking You for Your patience with us, and thanking You for Your peace that passes all understanding. I pray especially now for Your peace—Your supernatural peace for those here, and others, who mourn the passing of Your dear child and our Sister-in-Christ, Summer Chase. We know that she is rejoicing with You at this moment. Keep us mindful of who You are, and who we are without You. We praise You and we bless Your holy name. We pray this in the name of Jesus Christ our Lord. Amen."

David stood at the head of the casket, greeting mourners for several minutes. As they filed away in ones and twos, John Parella and Vincent Cramer approached.

David extended his right hand toward Parella. "It was good of you gentlemen to come," he said warmly.

Parella deftly clasped a handcuff on David's wrist.

"David Corwin Baxter, I am arresting you for the murder of Summer Chase. Please place your hands behind your back."

NINE
Present Day

Darrell sat on the sofa, beer in hand, with potato chips at his side, his feet up on the hassock, watching the evening news. He giggled regularly. It could not be more delicious.

David Baxter, Spring attorney was arrested today for the murder of fifteen-year-old Summer Chase who was found four days ago, brutally murdered, stuffed in a trash can in a Spring soccer park.

The anchorwoman looked directly into the camera.

Ironically, Baxter had just completed delivering the funeral service for the murdered teenager when the Spring police arrested and handcuffed him. It is not currently known upon what grounds Baxter was arrested. Police are not saying at this time if this arrest has any connection with five previous murders of teenage females in nearby neighborhoods.

The TV showed Baxter being assisted into a patrol car, stunned disbelief on his face.

In other news, an apartment fire in southeast Houston claimed the life of an elderly . . .

Darrell clicked off the TV, taking a sip of beer.

"Good, good, good, good, good," he chirped.

Lucerna had been special. He sighed, recollecting the moments. He was entirely convinced that she had seen the Light. There had been a brief span when she had been uncommonly lucid. Somehow the drug had momentarily lost its potency—just briefly. She had said something to him, barely a whisper.

Leaning over, his right ear near her mouth, he had asked, "What, my precious?"

"I forgive you."

"What?" He jolted upright.

Then there was that look in her eyes, the look of calm peace. There was not that look of raw terror that had claimed the others. There was only one way to explain it.

Surely, surely, surely—this one had seen the Light.

 **TEN**

February 14, 1967

Jolene Waters' heart simply stopped beating during the process of giving birth.

Dr. Ethan Chesnee had not expected that the babies would choose to arrive a week early. There had been no indications. He had planned to move the mother on the very next day from the Halbert Substance Abuse Felony Punishment Facility in Burnet, Texas, to the better-equipped hospital Galveston CID Medical Facility 270 miles southeast. But the babies elected not to wait.

Chesnee worked for twenty minutes to get Jolene restarted, but it was useless. Perspiration glistened on his brow beneath an abundance of pristine white hair. The doctor knew of no good reason for heart failure in this young girl. She had no known history of alcohol or drug abuse, or anything that would compromise her heart. It was never clear why Jolene ended up at Halbert. She was one of few there, including the staff, who did not use drugs. The fact that she was there, however, clearly proved to be Providential.

The doctor pronounced her at 11:27 p.m., February 14, 1967. With Dr. Chesnee's signature, Jolene Waters, TDCJ #337275, was officially deceased.

Outside, a cold, steady drizzle fell. Highway 281 South was empty of traffic. Husbands and boyfriends had completed their purchases of candy, flowers and cards, and by now had dutifully delivered their valentines to wives or girlfriends.

Darlene Phelps, RN, made no attempt to hide her tears as she cleaned the babies. Such a sad story—another sad story. There were 601 sad stories in this women's prison. 602 sad stories counting Darlene's. Today was just another holiday to remind her that she was alone and lonely, with no prospects for change.

The woman lying there, who had just given birth, and whose body was still warm, added to Nurse Darlene's sense of misery. And though the nurse was quite familiar with death, she would never be able to accept it gracefully.

"What're you going to name them?" Dr. Chesnee asked. His eyes, filled with heavy weariness, fixed upon his nurse of nine years. He had watched her decline emotionally over the last two or three years. All of the telltale signs of depression were there. The flat affect, her dull, straight hair, the lethargy. The two of them had made a good team, and they had become close friends. Dr. Chesnee and his wife Ilene had invited Darlene to their home on a regular basis. Lately they both had felt inept and frustrated in their attempts to somehow cheer her up—to help her.

"What?"

"Someone needs to complete the certificates and give them a name. Might as well be you." He removed his gloves and deposited them in the receptacle. At sixty-two he was thin and lanky. His health was excellent. Cholesterol, heart, lungs, kidneys and prostate were all good. His only known ailment was a touch of arthritis in his wrists and elbows. It wasn't enough to prevent him from playing tennis though—which he did at least twice a week.

"Right. Okay." She placed the bundled infants in empty desk drawers that she had padded with blankets. They had no basinets in the prison. "I . . . um . . . I'll have to give it some thought."

"Sure. All right, then. I'll call Delmar's to come get the body." He started to leave, then stopped and turned to face Darlene. Sadness clouded his face. He reached out and touched the corner of the gurney. "Her family disowned her, you know."

Jolene would be buried in the small prison plot, which held those inmates who had no one to care for them.

"I know," Darlene said. "Sad."

"Yes, it is. I should notify them anyway." The doctor pursed his lips, running his hand through his hair. "I reckon I'll head on home then. You going to be okay?"

"Yes, sir." She managed a smile. "Sandi relieves me in a couple of hours. See you tomorrow."

"Good night, then."

But it was not a good night. Darlene heard Doctor Chesnee's footsteps fade down the empty clinic hallway, and her shoulders shook with quiet sobs.

ELEVEN
The Present

Sitting in the holding cell at the Precinct Four Station in Spring, David could make no sense of the events of the last couple of hours. He knew nothing other than he was being held for arraignment for murder before a judge in the morning. He had no idea what evidence they thought they had. They had questioned him briefly, but only briefly, and surprisingly to him they had not been very forceful. They had taken a DNA sample, which to David meant exoneration since he had done nothing. Lillian and Meredith were clearly bewildered by the occurrences.

Although Lillian trusted her husband implicitly there was still that niggling question mark.

*Do you ever really **know** someone?* She hated herself for thinking it.

Meredith on the other hand was stoically fixed in her faith in her dad. He could never—would never do anything like this. She believed in him utterly.

A brief, chaperoned meeting had been allowed between David and Lillian in a small room across a table; no touching.

Lillian had sucked in her breath audibly when David had entered the room in his bright orange jumpsuit, chains rattling, ankles and wrists shackled.

"Lillian," he said, his voice almost a whisper. "I did not do this. I couldn't. They have made some colossal mistake."

"I know, sweetheart." A tear formed in her eye. She had determined, no matter what, that she would not cry. But she had not been prepared for the troubled look on his face, nor the jumpsuit and shackles. This was beyond anything she could ever have imagined—her husband, her kind and gentle husband shackled and chained like a common criminal.

"How are you? Are you okay?" he asked.

"We'll be okay. We're okay," she said, shaking her head. "It's just that—it's just so—*unexpected.*"

"I know," David said, looking her in the eye. "It's not like you *prepare* for something like this."

"What are we going to do, David?"

"Get everybody praying. Call everybody." He tried to manage a smile. "Then give Palmer a call and get him down here tonight. He needs to be here for the arraignment in the morning. Okay?"

Palmer Hutchins, a friend of eight years whom David had met at Baylor University, was a criminal attorney in Plano, Texas. David knew that Palmer would drop everything to come to his aid.

"Lord, watch over my wife and daughter. Keep them in Your hedge of protection," David prayed aloud. "You know all things—You know what is going on here. We put this all in Your capable hands. Keep Palmer safe as he flies down here. In Jesus' name, amen."

"I love you, Hon," Lillian said.

"I love you, too," David said. "Pray—don't worry."

She waved as David rose to be escorted out of the room.

"Go ahead and remain seated," the policeman said. "You have another visitor."

Evan James had been David's pastor for the last four years. He came into the visiting room wearing jeans, a gray sweatshirt and loafers with no socks, sporting his consistent broad grin.

"David," he said.

Evan's dark hairline was receding, cropped short. Although his hair was raven black, his mustache and goatee were gray.

David extended his right hand, but Evan ignored it and grabbed him, encircling him with both arms, patting his back heartily.

"Gentlemen," the guard said. "No contact, please."

The men sat, David's chains rattling.

"What's going on, David?" Evan began.

Even though Evan was David's pastor, or mentor, he was not *the* pastor of the church. There were nine Pastor/Elders at Community Fellowship, a fundamental, non-denominational church. Evan had founded the church six years ago, and David, Lillian and Meredith had started going two years later.

David had become one of the Pastor/Elders after attending for six months. Each of the Pastor/Elders mentored one of the other Pastor/Elders. They considered accountability to be of utmost importance, fostering an atmosphere of healthy openness among one another. Each Pastor/Elder also shepherded a "flock" of fifteen to twenty families, known in the congregation as "the little churches." Each little church would meet at someone's home at least every other week, and all the little churches would gather together on Sunday morning for corporate praise and worship, teaching of the Word and usually fellowship around a potluck meal.

"I don't have a clue, Ev." David shook his head. "I don't know why I'm here—or why they would charge me with Summer's death."

"Do you have an attorney?"

"He's on his way as we speak. Name's Palmer Hutchins, a long time friend from law school. He presently resides in Plano—an excellent criminal attorney. I expect him to be here soon."

"Well sir," Evan smiled. "I guess my job then is to encourage you in the meantime."

"I can certainly use it. I'm pretty bumfuzzled right now," David acknowledged, pinching the bridge of his nose with thumb and index finger.

Evan laid his small Bible on the table. "Well, mostly what I've got to say, you already know."

"I don't know about that, Ev, but in any case it is always good to hear it again."

"Yes, it is. Let's pray." Evan bowed his head and began. "Father, we praise You tonight for who You are; and we thank You for loving us and caring for us the way You do. We know that You have a purpose in all of this; because we know and trust that You work all things according to the counsel of your own will.

"I pray right now for my brother David. Give him supernatural peace in the midst of this difficult time for him and his family. Encircle Lillian and Meredith in Your loving arms. Let them know the presence of Your Spirit with them.

"Father we know that You know the end from the beginning. You already know the outcome. We simply pray that Your name would be honored and glorified in it, and that Your justice would be truly served. We pray in the name of Your precious Son, and our Savior Jesus Christ."

"Thanks, Evan," David said, his lips firmly pressed together.

"The other thing to bear in mind," Evan said, "Is Ephesians 6:12, where Paul wrote to his church at Ephesus," Evan did not open his Bible but quoted from memory: "For we wrestle not against flesh and blood, but against powers, against the rulers of the darkness of this world, against spiritual wickedness in high places."

"As you know, my brother, Paul clearly says that we're not actually fighting people that we can see; we are not fighting against each other in this battle. Instead, our warfare is with spiritual wickedness in high places. We battle against Satan and his well-organized forces in this world; a ruthless, conniving, murderous, maliciously evil army that has been operating contrary to God and

His purpose on the earth since Lucifer was evicted from Heaven. But the thing in which we exalt is that, even though this is a battle between good and evil, it is not a battle between equals. There is no comparison between God and His all-encompassing powers and Satan with his measly bag of tricks. God's power is unlimited; Satan's on the other hand is finite, and, in fact decreed by God. Satan, as you well know, my friend, is on a short leash held in the firm grip of God Almighty."

"Amen," David said. He was sitting more upright and was, in fact, encouraged by Evan's words.

"And we know that Satan is a liar, characterized by Christ as the Father of lies. He gains his limited power through lies, through deceit and through half-truths. He advances through the darkness of believed lies and has done so throughout history. He is defeated only by the truth and the power of God. We humans cannot war against him physically; we must do it as Christ did in the wilderness when He resisted Satan's tempting with the truth of scripture. And as He did when He confronted various demons during His ministry, by the power of God through the Spirit of God who dwelled within Jesus."

"Have you ever encountered a demon?" David asked. Although Evan had mentored David for three years they had not delved into this subject in detail.

"Only once. Although I have no doubt that demons are at work amongst us, and that Satan's unwavering goal is to replace God, and during the process to kill, steal, and destroy as Jesus said in John 10:10, I don't believe that there is a demon under every rock."

"Tell me about the one occasion that you encountered a demon," David said.

Evan shrugged, "Well, it was on a Saturday morning. John Casey and I were ministering on the geriatric floor at Cy-Fair hospital—just praying with some of the elderly, you know. John had gotten saved just about a month earlier, so this was all new to him. We rounded the corner of the hall and went into this one lady's room. She was probably in her mid to late seventies I would guess. Anyway, there she was, lying on her right side, facing the door as we came in. I could see that her feet were bound, and tied to the foot of her bed, and that her hands were tied in front of her to the side railing. John was right behind me as I entered the room, and the instant my foot crossed the threshold her eyes flashed right into mine, and she said in this deep, raspy, loud whisper,' What are *you* doing here?'

"I mean the hair on the back of my neck went up, and a chill went through me that I won't forget," Evan chuckled. "This was not a little old lady talking to me. This was a voice, I immediately knew, that had centuries of existence behind it."

"What did you do?" David asked.

"Well, my first instinct was to turn and run as fast as I could, but instead, I turned to John, upon whom it appeared, none of this had really registered. I said, 'John, this is a demon that we are confronted with.' His reply was an expletive from his former life, so I said, 'Just pray—silently.' I approached the bed slowly, with John on my heels. I cannot describe the malevolence in those eyes. It was just pure, unadulterated hatred. Her lips were drawn back over clinched teeth, and she was hissing like a snake.

"I said, 'In the name of Jesus, be quiet and let me speak to the woman.' Just like that her eyes changed from hatred to pleading. I asked her, 'Do you want to be released of your tormentor?'

"She nodded and mumbled something like, 'Num ma mumma num.' She couldn't speak, so I asked her, 'Do you believe that Jesus Christ is the only Son of God, and that he died on the cross for your sin, was buried and rose again on the third day, ascended into Heaven where He now reigns at the right hand of the Father, and will, one day, return to receive you into His kingdom where you will reside for all eternity?'

"She nodded her ascent, so I commanded the demon to leave her, which, it was obvious, it did. Finally, gradually, she got to the point where she could say, as plainly as you and I, 'Jesus is Lord.'

"All the while I was thinking of Jesus' explanation in Luke 11:21 that it is not good to cast an unclean spirit out without replacing it with the Spirit of God, otherwise the demon will return with seven others more evil than himself, and the latter state of that person will be worse than before.

"Before we left her room, David, she was speaking plainly, asking us to pray for her brothers."

"Wow," David said. "Quite an experience."

"Yes, it was," Evan said somberly. "Haven't had an encounter since."

"I did have an opportunity to speak at length with a *curandero*, a Mexican witchdoctor," David said. "He got saved as a result of God healing his little girl through an American evangelist. I forget the man's name, but he said that whenever he encountered a Christian, he knew that their power was stronger than his. He remarked that it was too bad that the Christians didn't know this."

"Ain't that the truth," Evan responded.

"Something else the man said that was interesting," David continued. "He said that he received his knowledge and power for practicing his art through *Moses*. He said an individual who called himself Moses would appear to him and would reveal things to him—how to heal certain diseases, how to counsel someone in financial or family trouble. He knows now that this was a demon. And he could never heal his own daughter."

"Yeah, that's Satan for you," Evan said. "Give a little, take a lot."

"Gentlemen," the guard approached the table. "You need to wrap it up." It was 7:00 p.m. according to the large numbered clock encased in a cage above the only door to the room.

"Okay, thanks," Evan said. "Let me just pray real quick with my friend."

They bowed together, Evan saying a brief prayer for peace, strength and wisdom.

They stood, and Evan embraced David again in a powerful bear hug.

"Gentlemen," the guard said. "No contact, please."

"Do you have your Bible?" Evan asked.

"No," David said. "Lill is going to bring it tomorrow."

"Here, take mine," Evan handed the small Bible over towards David.

The guard extended his hand. "May I see that, please? And he took the Bible and ruffled through it. "Okay, here you go," he said, handing the Bible to David.

"Well, hang in there, buddy," Evan said. "We'll get everybody to praying. Let me know if you need anything at all."

"Alright," David said. "Thanks for coming. I appreciate it."

Evan was let out of the door, and David followed immediately after, escorted to his cell where he could read his Bible.

✵ ✦ ✵ ✦ ✵

Palmer arrived a little after 8:45 p.m. He and David met in the same room where David had talked with Lillian and Evan.

"Hey, buddy," Palmer stood, calling out as David was escorted into the room. "How're you holding up?"

"Thanks for coming, Palmer," David said, shuffling across the room. "Please sit down. I'm doing okay, I guess. Evan James, my pastor, was just here. We had a good time together—very encouraging. I had been just completely blown away by all this. I haven't a clue about what's going on—or why they're charging me with Summer's murder."

Palmer sat for a long moment, looking into David's eyes, seeing nothing but puzzlement.

"What?" David asked.

"It's not good, pal," Palmer said, shaking his head.

"What do you mean?" David asked incredulously.

"I talked to the DA. They believe they have you cold."

"What? *Cold*—what do you mean *cold*?"

"They are considering charging you with other murders as well—maybe as many as five others. But at least two others."

David's heart pounded, and his face drained of color.

"They have fingerprints, David—yours. And DNA. They have a hair. It's yours as well."

David could only sit and stare. His mind would not work. Nothing made any sense.

"Now that I am here," Palmer said, "The police will want to question you some more. They will probably want to offer you a deal if you will confess."

"A deal? Confess? I didn't do anything, Palmer!"

"They will probably offer life without possibility of parole instead of death by injection," Palmer went on as if David had said nothing.

"I didn't do this, Palmer."

"David, they have all that they need to convict."

"I don't care, Palmer. What they have is wrong."

"What they have, David is hard, irrefutable evidence. If you can't explain it, then you have no defense."

Am I crazy? Did I go out and do horrible things without knowing it? Am I a Jeckle and Hyde—a multiple personality? David's mind whirled.

There was nothing about this that he could explain.

The Present

Darrell paced the floor excitedly. His plan was working just as he had foreseen. He giggled and sang one of his many little ditties, "The purveyor of light is here, the proof is frighteningly clear; he will fly quietly near, whisper into your ear, and you'll beg, 'Please take me, please take me, from here.'"

He danced and twirled across the floor with fluid motion.

He would play this present scenario with David to the hilt and then change at the proper moment. The plan was that David would have to dangle on the hook for a time. Then would come the ultimate move, which would, regrettably let David off the hook. Were there a way, Darrell would keep the heretic dangling forever. Alas, it could only happen one way. But through it all, he would accomplish two things: he would usher in the Light, and he would gain sweet, sweet revenge against David who had brought so many years of unbearable pain into Darrell's life.

It would mean an exchange of pain in David's life. As long as exchanges were properly made everything would be copasetic. In truth the second pain would be much worse than the first for David—worse than the pain he was presently experiencing. He would likely wish that he could die rather than bear this pain. And with that would come the Light.

His excitement was mounting. He felt the need to go outside. With David in the cell probably Meredith would not be out and about, but then again maybe she would.

He would go and see—perhaps just to take a quick peek.

THIRTEEN

The Present

Palmer had been exactly correct. Denise Nichols, the Assistant DA, and John Parella, Lead Homicide Detective had met with David and Palmer, and had presented their evidence against David. Denise had done most of the talking.

The ADA was formal and proper, with rimless glasses, short auburn hair just below the earlobes, curved inward at the ends, sienna lipstick, tight gray suit with a large black bowtie with ends hanging loose for several inches. She wore black, frilless pumps.

John Parella was the antithesis to the ADA. He wore loose fitting khakis and a blue pullover, with black and white Converse basketball shoes. His sandy hair was cut in a military style flat top. He never took his eyes off of David, studying him intently.

"You are clear, Baxter, that we have your prints, and we have your DNA? You understand this?" Denise had asked, standing, hands on hips.

"Asked and answered. My client has already stated that he does *not* understand this. In making his declaration of innocence he does not understand how it is possible for you to have such so-called *evidence*," Palmer stated firmly.

Denise did not look at Palmer. Placing both hands on the table she leaned toward David.

"Baxter, you're a smart man. You're an attorney for Pete's sake. You know what is happening here. When we walk out that door, if by then you have not accepted our offer then the offer will no longer be on the table."

"I never claimed to be smart," David said, meeting her eyes. "All that I know is that I have never murdered anyone. I am innocent of the charges that you have made against me. I know what it looks like to you, with your evidence and all. I have nothing I can say about that, except that I did not do what you say."

"He's innocent," Parella said to Denise as they walked to their respective cars.

"Bull," the ADA said, her pumps clicking on the sidewalk. "We have him cold. What are you talking about?"

"I can't say specifically," Parella said, shaking his head. "He doesn't have the demeanor—he doesn't have the moves of a serial killer. No matter how I look at him, I can't see it. He is wholly confused and bewildered. Serials maintain their haughtiness, no matter what. This guy is—I don't know—he's in turmoil. He's not playing the serialist's game with us."

"So, what are you saying, John?" She stopped and looked up at him. "We got the wrong guy? How can that possibly be? Is he a multiple personality?"

Parella pursed his lips. "All I am saying, Denise, is that this does not feel right. You know? You're a woman, dadgummit. I'm talking about intuition here. Multiple personality? I'm not even sure I even believe such a thing exists. In Baxter's case I sense no guilt at all—they say that even in multiples there is some residual guilt."

"So, what are you suggesting that I do, John?"

"What else can you do?" Parella shrugged. "You have him cold."

✵ ✦ ✵ ✦ ✵

Judge D. Howard Allen had disallowed all forms of cameras from his courtroom. All seats and three walls were packed with reporters and the curious, which overflowed to the outside hallway.

"Let me make myself perfectly clear," the judge had begun after the bailiff had announced the case. "I expect you folks in here to be as serious as I am about the importance of this case. I expect that you will be, since you are here. If there are any outbursts in this courtroom during these proceedings, or any undue interruption, I will place the perpetrator in confinement for not less than one day for contempt, and I will fine him or her 200 bucks."

He looked over at the ADA. "Prosecutor?"

"We are ready, Your Honor."

"Defense?"

Palmer rose. "Ready, Your Honor."

"Approach the bench, please," the judge said.

The attorneys walked together to the judge. He looked at Palmer.

"What in thunderation is going on here, young man?"

"Pardon me?"

"The DA here," he flicked his gavel in Denise's direction, "has made you a perfectly good offer."

"It's no longer on the table, Your Honor," Denise said.

"Just let me finish," Judge Allen held up the hand with the gavel in it. "Why didn't you take it?"

"Because my client's innocent, judge."

"Oh, for . . ." the judge looked heavenward, then back at Palmer. "This is not going to be a 'by reason of insanity' thing is it? I'll just tell you right now, that won't fly in my court."

"No, sir, Your Honor." Palmer looked squarely at the judge. "This is a simple *not guilty*."

"Your man knows the evidence against him?"

"Yes, sir, he does."

"And he is pleading not guilty?"

"Yes, sir."

"You've advised him of the consequences of his plea—life and death—all that?"

"Yes, sir, I have. We maintain that he is innocent."

"Well, I for one want to see this," the judge said. "You better give those folks their money's worth." He flicked the gavel toward the crowd of reporters and onlookers.

"Yes, sir," Palmer said, and turned to leave.

"One other thing," the judge said.

Palmer quickly turned back toward the bench.

"Don't waste this court's time."

"I don't intend to, Your Honor." Palmer said, and turned again to leave.

"One other thing," the judge said.

Palmer once again quickly turned toward the bench. "Yes, Your Honor?"

"Don't leave till I tell you to leave."

"Sorry, Your Honor."

"You may leave." The judge flicked his gavel.

David Baxter guessed that it was after 11:00 p.m. They had taken his watch, wedding ring and shoes, and had replaced his street clothes with the orange coveralls. They had processed him—fingerprints, mug shots, identifying marks, and all pertinent information. In the short time that he had been there he could no longer remember what it felt like to feel normal. At arraignment the judge had set the trial date for two weeks from today, significantly quicker than the usual process due to the enormity of the case, and the fear that had permeated the community of Spring. Grasping David by each elbow two constables shuffled him off to his cell. He had tried unsuccessfully to sleep. This was the nightmare to end all nightmares. He tried to pray, and it seemed as if God had secluded Himself behind a massive locked door and was not answering. He tried to think, and nothing happened. How did he get here? Suddenly, he was jolted by memories of another night when his world had been flipped upside down.

It was early February 1983. Dinner had been uncommonly quiet. David Baxter, sixteen, the only child to Herbert and Lila Baxter, had known that something was in the air. Something major. Normally there would be general, cheerful banter around the table. They would be discussing the Redskins win over Miami in Superbowl XVII, or whether Ronald Reagan was a good president. Or they would discuss his school day—anything but this bizarre, heavy silence.

Even Major Dundee, his yellow lab, lying at David's feet, seemed to sense something was amiss. He wrinkled his brow and wagged the tip of his tail nervously.

David's dad seemed to have difficulty looking up from his plate. He was a thick-necked, red-faced man, whose broad frame gave him an air of fearlessness. He had worked for twenty-seven years at the Kiefer-Marigold Refinery in Texas City. Retirement was just around the corner, which he viewed with mixed feelings. The one fear that he revealed to no one was the dread he carried concerning what he would do when he no longer went to the refinery. What would he do with his battered tin lunch pail? His hard hat? His steel-toed safety shoes? What would he do with his life? He dreaded his retirement; it was a signal, a signpost, that his life was coming to an end.

David's mom, on the other hand, had never had a paying job,

but she was one of the hardest working people David knew. She was constantly doing something around the house, or puttering in the vegetable garden. David could not recall ever seeing his mother sit quietly and read a book.

At the age of forty-four she maintained the same size seven she wore when she had married her high school sweetheart. She was Herbert's "beautiful blond with the girlish figure." Tonight she smiled apprehensively and looked away whenever her son caught her eye. She pushed her food around in her plate nervously.

At last the grueling meal was over. David had never seen his parents so agitated.

He could not imagine what this was about. Did one of them have a fatal disease?

Were they getting a divorce? Impossible.

Finally, Mr. Baxter cleared his throat. The blood had drained from Mrs. Baxter's face, making her lipstick remarkably crimson.

"David," Mr. Baxter began, clearing his throat again. "David, there is something your mother and I need to tell you. Something very difficult for us to bring up."

What could this be about? David's mind buzzed.

"First, we love you very much, we want you to know that."

"I've never doubted it, Dad.

"I know, but we want you to keep that in mind, as we talk-as we discuss what we need to discuss."

"Okay," David said, twisting in his seat.

"David," Mr. Baxter began again, "I don't know any other way to do this, but just to say it." He paused and took a deep breath. "We feel that you need to know that . . . that it's time that we told you that you are not our natural child." Mrs. Baxter was crying openly now. "David, you are adopted. We adopted you when you were just three weeks old."

David's mind was really spinning now. Was this some kind of

crazy joke? Adopted? These were his folks-the only parents he knew. His heart pounded. This was his dad and his mom.

A million questions flooded his mind.

He tried to say something, but it stuck in his throat, and he began to cry. He kicked his chair back, and it fell over with a crash. He fled to his room.

He could hear his mother sobbing aloud. "David," she cried. "David-don't."

He slammed his door, locking it, throwing himself onto his bed.

Adopted? It was incomprehensible. His mind had whirled like a dust devil. *Adopted?* Who am I?

Here he was at sixteen, and his world, which had been in perfect order just that morning had been turned completely upside down. Feelings of betrayal and anger overwhelmed him. Clenching his teeth, tears flowing, he pounded his pillow. How could his parents-or whatever they were-do this to him? For the briefest moment he wished that they were both dead. Immediately overwhelmed with guilt he asked God to forgive him of such horrible thoughts.

Now twenty-two years later, lying in his cell, on his hard bunk, staring up at the dappled pattern of light on his ceiling, his world was in greater turmoil than he could have ever imagined. He couldn't make sense of any of it.

FOURTEEN
February 14, 1967

The boys were a Godsend—a miracle—in Darlene's lonely life. They had arrived at just the right moment.

It had occurred to her like an epiphany after Doctor Chesnee had left—God was giving her a baby. And the doctor had asked her to name them. She knew that she could not raise them both. It would not be fair to either one. But which one should she keep? She would take them both home tonight and somehow decide. It was so exciting. She had not felt this lighthearted in years.

She had stopped at Meyer's Supermarket, bundled the babies in a shopping cart and bought everything she could think of that the boys might need: formula for later since they would initially be drinking boiled sugar water, baby bottles and nipples, diapers, wipes, pacifiers, rattles, Butter Cream receiving blankets, tee shirts, gowns, overalls and socks. To celebrate her great, unexpected fortune, Darlene bought herself a six-pack of cola, a large bag of potato chips and a bag of chocolate covered raisins. She went over to the book aisle, and sure enough there was a book entitled *What to Name Your Baby*. It was only $4.67. She put it in the basket.

Putting the stuff in the trunk of the old 1959 Ford Fairlane, she placed the babies in the back seat. She couldn't wait to get home. The boys had started to fuss a little.

"Shhh, shhh, shhh little chickies," she cooed. "We'll be home in just a minute."

When she had arrived home she carried the boys into the house, arranging them on the divan. They were becoming a little more restless. She hauled the stuff into the house and set it on the dining table. In short order she had warmed two bottles of sugar water. She propped the boys on the couch at a low angle to feed them, a bottle in each of her hands. They both sucked greedily, finishing at about the same time. She burped one; gently patting and rubbing his back until a loud, undignified belch erupted, and then did the same with the other.

Clearing a spot on the dining table she laid them on it to change their diapers, and to inspect them. She placed them side-by-side on a blanket, naked. Immediately she noticed how almost synchronized their movements were; except on opposite sides. One would stiffen his right arm; the other, his left. Almost every movement was a mirror of the other.

She turned them over, mystified by what she saw. One of the boys had a reddish-purple birthmark on his left hip; the other one had the exact same mark, only mirrored, on his right hip. The marks looked like small butterflies, with one wing slightly, but noticeably, larger than the other. On the baby with the mark on the left side, the right wing was larger. On the infant with the mark on the right side, the left wing was larger. She examined the marks closely, and in every way they were identical—except mirrored.

She had heard of mirrored identical twins in nursing school. It was very rare. She also knew that these boys were extremely fortunate that they had arrived separately, and not connected. Siamese twins were fairly common among mirrored twins.

She bundled the boys up and laid them on the bed next to her pillow. Getting into her pajamas, she poured a coke over ice and opened the bag of chips and the chocolate covered raisins. Flipping on the bedside lamp she crawled into bed with the baby-naming book. She thought about the fact that they were the same, but different. What would work?

Scanning the names she noticed that there was an added bonus. The book not only provided name suggestions, it gave the meaning of each name. Give the boys names that were different, but meant the same thing? Possible.

Retrieving a pencil and pad of paper out of the nightstand drawer, she began to scribble. She wrote *Valentine, love, heart, gift, friendship, friend*. She scanned through the book. There was nothing at all for *Valentine*. Nothing sounded good that meant *love*. She found several names for *friend*. She especially liked Baldwin and Corwin. After further searching and scribbling she settled on two names for *Beloved*. They were Darrel and David. Except that she didn't like Darrel with only one "l" so she changed it to Darrell.

Beloved Friend. They both would be Beloved Friend. "Works for me," she said. "How about you guys?"

So that gave her David, Darrell, Baldwin and Corwin. She wrote *David Baldwin, Darrell Corwin, David Corwin*, and *Darrell Baldwin*.

She took a swig of coke and popped some chips into her mouth—then decided.

"Lefty" the one with the mark on his left hip would henceforth be known as

Darrell Baldwin Phelps

"Righty" would be dubbed David Corwin Phelps.

Now, which one would she keep? That was the biggy. She would sleep on it.

She didn't sleep on it of course. At 12:50 a.m., the boys began to wail

in unison. The level of sound from those tiny throats was unbelievable. Groggily, she slid her feet over the side of the bed. When it occurred to her what she was doing, her heart was thrilled anew.

She had Darrell and David fed, burped and changed in no time. They were thoroughly satisfied. Equally at peace, Darlene was once again asleep moments later.

The event recurred at 4:30 a.m. Happily, in short order, she had the boys comfortable again, and returned to her dreams—pleasant for the first time in months.

Her "alarm clocks" aroused her again at 8:05. She looked at them, exercising their lungs to the utmost, their little hands balled into demanding fists, and smiled. What could be more blissful than this?

What's more she had decided which of the boys she would keep. It would be Darrell. If anyone were to ever ask her why, she would not be able to provide a cognitive answer. It was just that he was the one who tugged at her heart.

Darrell Baldwin Phelps would be her son. She would add him immediately to her medical insurance. She was a firm believer in insurance. She would be responsible, unlike her father, who had died without insurance, leaving her mother penniless.

She would pour her heart into her son. He was the "left butterfly" one. She vowed that she would make him happier than any one boy ever had the right to be.

FIFTEEN
The Present

Sitting next to David on his cell bunk it was clear that Palmer had had no sleep either. His eyes were rimmed with red, his brown hair disheveled; his jaw line sported a two-day growth. He spoke without a trace of animation. In the years that David had known him he had never seen Palmer this low.

"We have nothing, David. There is no defense. Houdini himself could not get out of this. I'm sorry."

David clasped Palmer's shoulder. "Palmer," he said, "You have absolutely nothing to be sorry about, believe me."

"The point is that now they may no longer accept a plea bargain."

"Palmer," David said, fixing his eyes upon his friend, "You are not hearing me. I am innocent. I did not do this. I will *not* plea bargain for something that I did not do."

"I do hear you, David—loud and clear. You need to hear this— that they may strap you to a gurney, stick an IV into your arm, and pump you full of lethal chemicals until you are dead. It doesn't get more serious than that."

"I am not confessing to something that I didn't do. God is in this equation, Palmer, and He is just. I have put myself in His hands."

Palmer inhaled a long breath through his nostrils, held it a long time then finally exhaled. "Here's what we're left with, then. Our only defense is to put you on the stand and let the jury hear you say that you didn't do it."

"Then we pray," David smiled weakly, "that the jury can hear God."

John Parella walked in the grass among the pine trees on a knoll next to the Precinct Four parking lot, a cup of steaming Starbucks in his hand. His head pounded, and his joints ached. He had realized perhaps two hours total sleep. Annie, as she had demonstrated so many times in the past, had been supremely patient with him, listening to his rehash of his thoughts from as many possible approaches as he could develop.

Now he walked among the pine needles to be alone with his thoughts. His team had gathered reams of data on David Baxter and had interviewed every conceivable connection to him and his family. One of the FBI's best profilers interviewed David for more than six hours.

Marcus James, twenty-two years with the FBI, nine as a profiler, had a stellar reputation. A short, balding man with a full, graying beard and the uncanny ability to get into criminal minds had come away from his time with David Baxter with one conviction.

"This man is no serial killer. He's not a killer at all. Unsullied and as untouched by evil as any person that I've ever met. It is uncommon to find a virtuous man. Baxter is one."

Denise Nichols would certainly not bring James' findings into evidence. Unfortunately, through the process of discovery, which required the prosecution to reveal case evidence to the defense, Palmer could now certainly bring James to the stand.

Parella had not been surprised by James' report. He had shared with Annie all of his own doubts and issues regarding David through the long night.

"The guy is pure, Annie," he had said, their bedroom TV on low volume in the background. "Everyone who has talked to him at any length is convinced of his innocence. Voice analysis and body studies indicate that he is not lying. No one can fake it like that, Annie. Lots of folks—not just me—think he is innocent."

"Except Denise," Annie added.

"Yes, except Denise," John sighed. "And I guess that I can understand her position. The only evidence that exists is damning, and it points to Baxter—and Baxter only. That's what gets me. We have three prints and one hair. Enough to convict in any court." He took a sip of Diet Dr. Pepper from a can on his nightstand.

"But . . . ?" Annie urged.

"But . . ." John continued, "We have combed his car, combed his house and combed his computers, personal and work, with not a smidge. Zip. It just simply does not fit. I cannot think of a time— never, ever—when we did not find some corroborative evidence. There's always something else. These guys that do these kinds of things need stimulation between their crimes. They take trophies— pictures, videos, clothing, body parts—they keep newspaper and magazine clippings, they have hard drives full of porn . . ."

Annie winced as Parella spoke.

"Nothing like this came up with Baxter. It's just . . ." John shook his head, " . . . not right."

Annie rubbed the back of her husband's neck. "So, is Mr. Baxter being framed?"

John looked at her. "I've asked myself that." He shrugged, "It's a very long shot, I guess. The hair would be extremely easy to explain—it's nothing really—the prints not so easy. I can't see how someone could transport someone else's print—such a pristine print—to a crime scene. It may be possible to lift and move a smudged print—but nothing at all like these prints. They've got to be originals. Not second generation."

"Which follows that the only source for the prints is Baxter?" Annie asked, but it was more of a statement than question.

"Seems so," John said, offering her the Dr. Pepper can, from which she took a swig.

"So, what are you going to do?" Annie brought the conversation to a head.

"I don't know, A." John gave her a wan smile. "Catch the real perp, I guess."

SIXTEEN
The Present

As he guided his black Tahoe through the Kleinwood neighborhood, Darrell was hoping for a glimpse of Meredith—just a glimpse. He needed it for momentum, for energy. Things were about to go into high gear, and he needed to see her. It was all that he was allowing himself right now. Just a look. Anything else would be counter-productive to his overall purpose. It was not yet her time, and she was not on her usual routine. Understandable, probably—in view of her father's recent incarceration. Meredith was probably with her mother. He had driven by the house on Kleingreen once already. He knew that he could not continue to make passes. Someone was always looking. The neighborhood would be somewhat less edgy though, now that David was put away for the time being.

Okay, then. He would make one more pass by their house.

It gave him nothing but disappointment. No one was in sight at the Baxter homestead. The black Tahoe was in the driveway, but no one was in sight.

As he drove away he sang a little song under his breath that he had decided to publish soon.

Roses are red, my love
Bruises are blue-oo-oo,
Roses are red my love,

Soon I will be with you.

He left the neighborhood on the south side, turning right onto Cypresswood Drive. He would stop by Kroger's supermarket and pick up a few things.

Tomorrow promised to be a big day.

SEVENTEEN

February 10, 1974

Darrell Baldwin Phelps was upset. He sat on the ground in the backyard and threw pebbles at the China Berry tree, trying to ricochet them off the trunk into the empty cement birdbath. He was probably the only kid he knew who still slept with his mother at the age of seven. Well, he wasn't exactly seven—but he *would* be seven on Thursday, and today was Sunday. They would start celebrating his birthday today. His plan was to tell his mother that he wanted his own bed in his own room. She had her "sewing room" which was really a junk room. He had never once seen her sew. She could change that room into his bedroom. It would be easy. She wouldn't like it, he knew. But then again, there were things she did that he didn't like—so this would make them even. He wanted to grow up, and she didn't want him to. It was clear.

It should be just as clear that there were lots of things that he could do by himself now. Lots. She really hadn't wanted him to do anything on his own. He had to just keep telling her, that's all— *Mom, I can do it myself!*

He could . . . put on his clothes . . . tie his shoes . . . bathe himself. He could even cut his own chicken-fried steak. He had really had to fight for all these things. He was growing up, and no one better try and stop him.

His mom was in the house getting ready. It took her *forever.* She was taking him to Marble Falls for a hamburger at the Bluebonnet Café, and some peanut butter pie, and then a movie at the Driftwood Theater. She had wanted to do some shopping, too, but Darrell vetoed that. He hated shopping—unless it was in the toy section. He didn't even have to throw a fit. He just simply crossed his arms tight, stuck out his bottom lip real far and said, "It's *my* birthday." And that was it.

"Darrellsweet." It was one word.

Yech, bleh. Why couldn't she just call him by his *name?* He hated it

"You ready to party hardy?" She was at the back door.

"Yeah, mom. Sure" He flung one more rock at the tree and missed it altogether. Didn't matter. The crowd still went wild.

"C'mere." Darlene Phelps smiled broadly. "Let me fix you."

"Aw, mom," he turned his face and scrunched it into a frown. "It's okay."

"No, no. No, no," she chirped. "You can't go out like *that.* Your hair's sticking up in back." She wet her fingers with her tongue and pressed the spike of hair down. Then she wiped his cheek.

Good grief. Darrell pulled away. "Let's just go," he said.

"Okay, sweetie pie."

Once in the white '69 VW Beetle, Darlene switched on the radio. John Denver was singing "Sunshine on My Shoulders."

If I had a day that I could give you

I'd give to you a day just like today

If I had a song that I could sing for you

I'd sing a song to make you feel this way

Sunshine on my shoulders makes me happy

Sunshine in my eyes can make me cry . . .

She loved that song.

"Buckle up, sugar," she said, patting her son on the knee.

What a beautiful day.

EIGHTEEN
February 13, 1974

6:50 Wednesday night, and it was time for church. Each Wednesday evening David Baxter's parents would drop him off near the portable building at the west side of Brightview Baptist Church in La Marque, Texas. Then they would go into the main sanctuary. This had become a regular routine since he had turned six a year ago—old enough to join the Royal Ambassadors. He would go to his RA meeting, and they would go to their prayer meeting. He looked forward to each Wednesday night with eager anticipation.

Some people called the RA's the Baptist Boy Scouts. They did everything—crafts, campouts, sports, and projects. David's RA chapter was named the Charles and Becky Haupman Chapter, after a Southern Baptist Missionary couple.

All of David's friends belonged to the chapter. His best friend, "Birdy" Tindale, had already arrived at the meeting. His real name was Bridy, but in the first grade, when everybody was learning to read, they all automatically read Bridy's name as Birdy. His mother hadn't liked it, but that made no matter. His name, by consensus and collective dyslexia, had been changed forever to Birdy.

"Hi, David." Birdy smiled and waved as David approached.

"Hi, Birdy," David said. "Whatcha doing?"

"Nothing," Birdy shrugged. "Just waiting. You're the first one besides me. I brought a cake."

"You did? What kind?"

"Strawberry. My mom made it."

"Hey—my favorite. Strawberry."

"Yeah, well—my mom probably asked your mom."

"Yeah—I'll bet."

Some of the other boys began to trickle in.

"Let's talk later," Birdy said.

"Sure, okay."

Last month in mid-January the RA's had gone tent camping in the Big Thicket at Indian Mound Camp and RV Park. Twelve boys, ready for whatever nature had to offer, along with their three leaders, had packed into the thick tangled woods that held nine kinds of trees. They had found the perfect spot next to Tepee Creek, a cypress black water slough that purportedly held some monster large mouth bass. The trees were so thick that the sun splashed the ground in only a few spots.

It had been a tremendous adventure for David, heightened by the fact that his dad was one of the overseers. He appreciated the fact that his dad cared enough to be involved.

David's father was a deacon in the church. So was Birdy's father. The only difference was that Birdy's father was too preachy. Even Birdy said so. David was glad that Birdy's dad didn't get involved. He would have preached them to death during the two-day campout.

Doug Fairchild, the main leader of the RA's, was also an object of David's admiration. It seemed to David that Mr. Fairchild, although younger than David's father, knew almost all there was to know about camping and outdoors stuff.

He had shown the boys how to attach six tents in tandem, forming one long rooftop, two ends, a back and an open front. In front of the open tent they had made, based on Mr. Fairchild's instructions, a reflecting fireplace of stones stacked about six feet wide and four feet tall. The boys had collected enough wood, piling it nearby, to keep the fire going for two weeks. And it had worked perfectly, the stones reflecting the heat, keeping the inside of the open makeshift tent marvelously warm.

They had sat in their tent before the fire that first night, watching the orange sparks swirl upwards, disappearing into the dark night. They roasted marshmallows and they munched on S'mores, while listening to the men tell scary ghost stories.

"Oooooh," they would say in unison at the appropriate parts of the stories. And marvel of marvels, out in the thick, dark woods, filled with strange night sounds, far from home—the boys were not the least bit afraid.

They had awakened the next morning with frost on the ground, but they had been snug and toasty through the cold night, thanks to Mr. Fairchild's neat tent and fireplace idea.

Tonight, though, at the RA meeting, one of the activities would be David's surprise birthday party. It wasn't really a surprise, though, because Mr. Fairchild did it for everybody when it was their birthday. So tonight they would have strawberry cake and sing "Happy Birthday" to David, before resuming their regular meeting.

He would be seven years old tomorrow. He had decided to tell his folks and Mr. Fairchild that he wanted to be baptized next Sunday.

It was something he should do, after all, since he was growing up.

NINTEEN

February 10, 1974

"Did you like the movie, sweetie?" Darlene asked her son. They had seen *The Little Prince*.

"Nah, I guess," he said. "It was okay."

"My thoughts exactly," she said. "Matter of fact I thought it was a little dull. Besides, *you're* my little prince."

The sun was high in the west in a cloudless Texas sky. The temperature was a comfortable sixty-eight degrees. The Bug was pointed north toward Burnet.

"Are you happy, sugar?"

She was always asking that dumb question. "I s'pose." Darrell twiddled his fingers and swung his feet back and forth.

"What does that mean, 'I s'pose?'"

"Mom, c'mon."

"No, really. I work hard to make you happy. You should know if you're happy. Right?"

She looked over with a giant smile. "You're either happy or you're not. I want you to be happy."

"I want my own room and my own bed," he said in a low voice.

"You what, sweetie?"

"I want to sleep in my bed, in my room," he said louder.

"You want—what? For your birthday?" Unexpectedly there was a lead ball of panic in her chest. "You're too young."

"No, mom," Darrell looked at her, his eyes determined. "I'm not."

She noticed an eighteen-wheeler approaching in the rear view mirror.

"I want to sleep by myself in my bed, in my room. I'm getting bigger."

This was beginning to feel like the old brush-off she had experienced from so many other men before. *I need space* or *this is just not working out* or *I like you a lot, but* . . .

"Yes, you are, sweetheart," her voice cracked, and her eyes began to fill with tears. "But you're not *that* big, you know." That bed of hers could be so lonely. Darrell couldn't know. He was supposed to be an end to all that. Now . . . now . . . what? What was he doing? The tears were flowing now.

"You're only six," she blubbered.

"I'm seven, Ma. Don't cry. I don't want you to cry."

Tears clouded her vision, the road blurred, and she didn't make out the curve in the road ahead. Besides she was looking at her beloved son.

The truck driver behind the white VW later explained to the police what had happened.

"The road curved to the left," he said, "and the Beetle didn't."

It had become airborne over a twenty-foot culvert, the nose slamming into the other side, flipping it end over end three times, crashing on its top into the rock. The vehicle was flattened to less than half its normal height.

Darlene's skull was crushed, her neck and spine broken in three places. There were multiple other fractures and internal injuries, none of which she felt. She was dead instantly.

Darrell Baldwin Phelps was less fortunate, managing to survive in a small pocket of the tangled metal and jagged glass. It took the rescue team thirty-five minutes to extricate the boy from the mess. His injuries were massive. Everyone on the team would have wagered that Darrell would not make it through the night.

TWENTY

The Present

David Baxter had been allowed to exchange his orange jump suit for street clothes. He wore a light gray suit, with white shirt and light blue large patterned tie, with black Italian style loafers. His dark hair was freshly trimmed and combed back. The turmoil in his stomach was not visible on the outside. David appeared to be calm and rested. He and Palmer were seated at the defendant's table on the left. Behind them sat Lillian and Meredith on the front row.

The courtroom was jam-packed with the professional and the curious, and had been abuzz with speculative chatter until David and Palmer had entered. The room had become suddenly, eerily quiet, all eyes on David, trying to get a "read." At least three sketch artists had their pencils furiously flying.

Denise and her team of two other attorneys were at the right side. Their deportment was that of quiet confidence. Denise was a spider in her web, with the prey already entrapped. All that remained was for her to wrap her catch in a silk cocoon and store him away for a future meal.

Announcing the judge the bailiff said, "All rise."

Momentarily, Judge D. Howard Allen entered, entreated the

courtroom to sit, and flicked his gavel at the bailiff, who asked the clerk to call the day's calendar.

David's ears were roaring so loudly that he heard little of it.

"Harris County versus David Corwin Baxter . . ."

David swallowed hard, trying to clear his ears.

" . . . for the murder of Summer Blevins Chase."

David felt the perspiration pop out on his forehead. He was sure that he appeared as guilty as sin. There was a jury pool of sixty prospects. David could feel every one of the sixty pairs of eyes on the back of his neck.

Palmer had petitioned the court for a change of venue, stating that the flood of material and information that had been released upon a voracious community had saturated the environment. "Chances are nil to none that we can raise an impartial jury in this town. This well has been thoroughly poisoned by the press." Palmer's argument was to no avail

Judge Allen was making his explanations to the jury prospects. "This phase of our proceedings, ladies and gentlemen, is called the voir dire. Fancy talk for how we select a jury. It means literally "to speak the truth." All of you have filled out forms, which have provided some information about you, which the attorneys and I have reviewed. Based upon your answers some of you may perhaps be excused—for example, if you know the defendant or one of the attorneys, or if you don't like district attorneys. Also, the attorneys will summarize their cases within certain limits, so that you have some idea of what is going on. They will then ask some of ya'll a few questions based upon your questionnaire, or upon the trial summaries that they have made to you. They each, of course, are trying to determine how you as a prospective juror might vote when you're locked in that room with eleven others. Might you be inclined to acquit? Would you be able to convict? These lawyers here wish they were mind readers. Fortunately they are not. If one had a better crystal ball than the other then the system wouldn't work." The judge leaned back in his chair. "Any questions so far?" There was silence from the prospective jurors.

"Okay, then," he said. "You lawyers go to work."

Denise was first. She rose and faced the prospective jurors. She held a ballpoint pen in her right hand. Walking around her chair to approach the potential juror box, she began in a calm even voice.

"Good morning, ladies and gentlemen. My name is Denise Nichols. I am the prosecuting attorney for this case. These are my associates Georgia Wainwright and Thomas Jones. I want to thank you, ladies and gentlemen, for your willingness to fulfill your responsibility as a citizen. Let me thank you for the state of Texas, for Harris County and for the city of Spring. Judge Allen was just speaking to you about the system working—the simple truth is that it would not work without you. So, thank you."

Denise walked to the front of her table.

"If you are selected as a member of this jury I regret to have to tell you that you will be subjected to some extremely horrendous sights—some horrendous photos and descriptions of the victim. This is a murder trial. We will ask for the maximum sentence, which, I'm sure you know, in Texas is death by lethal injection. We have asked each of you if you can deliver a sentence of death in this case. We trust that you each have searched his or her conscience before answering this question. Do not take it lightly. You may very well find yourself in the jury room with the defendant's life in your hands. So, that said, I want to ask once again if any of you who said on your form that you can support the death penalty would like to now change your mind. It will not be held against you." Denise paused, giving the prospects time to consider.

After several seconds prospect number nine, a young woman in her early twenties slowly raised her hand.

"Thank you," Denise said. "We appreciate your honesty," she looked at her prospects sheet, "Mrs. Turnage." Denise turned to the judge and said, "Number nine, Your Honor, Mrs. Joanne Turnage." When she turned back to the box there were two more hands in the air.

"Hmm," she said. Studying her sheet "And you are Mr. Cramer?" The older gentleman in coveralls with his right hand partially raised nodded his head yes. The prospect sheet said. *Frank Cramer, Occupation—dairy farmer.* Frank needed to get back to his cows. "And you would not be able to vote for imposing the death penalty, Mr. Cramer?"

"Vote for? No, Ma'am."

"Alright, then." She turned her attention to an elderly lady on the back row of the box. "Mrs. White?"

"Yes."

"You would not be able to impose the death penalty"

"No, after thinking about it like you said, I just couldn't do that."

"Your Honor," Denise said, turning back to the bench, "that's number nine, Joanne Turnage; number seventeen, Frank Cramer; and number twenty three, Mae White."

"Okay, Counselor. Mrs. Turnage, Mr. Cramer and Mrs. White. You folks are excused. Thank you for your time. You may go as soon as we take our next break."

Denise continued. "As I said, this is a murder trial. Sitting over there," she pointed her pen like a weapon, "is the accused. The facts of this case will show that he is not who he seems to be. In one life he is a pillar of the church and an attorney who practices family law. In his other life, his secret, diabolical life, we will show that he is a killer of children, that he . . ."

Palmer was instantly on his feet. "We object, Your Honor. There is only one charge against my client."

"What exactly are you objecting to?" the judge asked.

"To the DA's use of the plural, Your Honor. To *children*."

"It was a general statement, Your Honor," Denise said.

"I'll sustain it." He pointed his gavel toward Denise. "There is only one victim in this case, Counselor. Keep it singular."

"Ladies and gentlemen," Denise resumed. "We will show conclusively that the defendant is a murderer, that he killed in cold blood and without remorse the victim in this trial. We will show that he is a killer of the worst kind, that he preys upon innocent, defenseless children . . ."

"Your Honor, please," Palmer shouted.

"Sorry, Your Honor," Denise said. " . . . that he has preyed upon an innocent, defenseless child. One who had a future and an entire life in front of her." She pointed the pen once again at David. "He took that from her, and he took her from her family and replaced her with a burden of grief that they must somehow bear alone. We will insist upon the death penalty in this case. That will provide justice in this instance, but it will not take away the unbearable pain, nor bring the children . . . child, back to us."

Denise sat and stared straight ahead.

Palmer rose, placed his left hand upon David's shoulder and faced the prospective jurors. "Good morning, ladies and gentlemen. My name is Palmer Hutchins. I too want to thank you for your service. We know that it is a sacrifice for you to be here today, but it is one of the things that make our nation great. Although our system is not perfect, it is the best there is. Our system says that the accused in a trial is *innocent* . . ." David paused at length to let the word sink in. " . . . until proven guilty. By the way, my client's name is David Baxter. He *is* a leader in his community, an elder in his church, and a prominent family attorney. He is married and has a fifteen-year-old daughter." Palmer paused again. "So please let these words sink in. David Baxter is innocent." He patted David's shoulder. "This man is innocent. It is up to the DA's office to provide compelling proof that he is not innocent. They must show you without a shadow of a reasonable doubt that he is guilty. Say that to yourselves—*reasonable doubt*. Reasonable." Palmer paused once again. The word *reasonable* emanated from the box in a collective whisper.

"My job is simple, really," Palmer smiled at the prospects, and several women on the panel wished that they would be selected for the jury. "Picture the prosecution's case as a giant red balloon. All that I am required to do is poke it with a tiny needle, and—*pow!*— the state's case goes away. My job is to introduce one tiny needle-doubt, and *pow!*"

Darrell Phelps' skin was hot and itchy behind the full-face disguise. It had taken him almost an hour to apply the latex and the makeup around his eyes and mouth properly. Then the light brown wig had to be just right. He was not concerned. It had all worked at the funeral. He had seen the police at the service, scanning the audience. There was no inkling of suspicion toward him. Things had gone without a hitch. The only thing that he could not hide was his left arm and hand. He was confident that he could pull this off, though. He always did.

Not a bad job, Palmer, Darrell thought. *Not bad at all.* But the fact remained that David was on the grill because Darrell had put him there, and Darrell fully intended to let him roast a while longer before he let him off.

Just a wee while longer, David, then I will let you hop out of the frying pan. Right into the old fire. Darrell chuckled to himself.

TWENTY-ONE

February 10, 1974

Darrell Phelps was wheeled into Burnet Hospital ER, his head completely swaddled in blood-soaked gauze. He was covered with a gray blanket, his left arm lying atop the cover, taped to a papoose board to immobilize it.

Dr. Herman Alcott met the paramedics in the hallway and walked alongside the gurney the few steps to the ER. The EMTs had called in to say that it was really bad. Doctor Alcott knew both of the emergency techs; Raymond Trent, thirty-one, balding and overweight; and Lonnie Farberg, twenty-eight, full of energy and never-ending talk, a weekend racecar driver. Raymond and Lonnie had a combined EMT experience of seven years, and neither had ever seen anything like this.

"What've we got? " he asked the EMTs as they rolled into the ER to Bay Two, which was staffed by the four capped and gowned members of the trauma team. The crew was eager to spring into action.

"Auto crash, one dead. This one's stable," Raymond, the driver, responded. "BP's 130 over ninety; respirations are eighty-six. Massive face, jaw and skull trauma. Massive. He lost his left eye, doc; and I mean lost. We couldn't find it anywhere—inside the car or out."

"I looked all over," Lonnie said. "Everywheres. You'd think you could find a dad gummed thing like 'at." Lonnie shook his head in deep resignation. "Don't know what good it woulda done to find it though—know what I mean?"

Raymond continued the rundown, trying to remain professional and objective, but obviously shaken by the damage to this young boy, and the death of the woman, whom they assumed to be his mother. He couldn't understand why this had to happen to anybody, much less a little kid.

"Also, there are multiple fractures of the left arm and hand; probable internal injuries," Raymond finalized.

"The car was just totally smashed," Lonnie offered. "Like a beer can."

Darrell was lifted onto the bed, and quickly hooked to the monitors. Juanita Mendez, head nurse, began unwrapping the bandages.

"Start him on Ringers," Dr. Alcott said in his calm ER voice, assessing immediately that he was in way over his head. He would have to do the critical component ABC's comprised of Airway with cervical spine control, Breathing, and Circulation with bleeding control, however long that took; then transport him, probably to Scott and White Hospital in Temple. The insult to the left side of the boy's face was obscenely horrible. Entire sections of flesh and muscle were missing, as if scooped away by a large spoon, starting from the Frontalis muscle, or brow, across the Obicularis oculi around the eye socket, down to the Masseter muscle of the lower jaw. And there was the dark, empty hole where the eyeball used to be. By contrast, and by some miracle the right side of the face was untouched.

Dr. Alcott dealt with all of the bleeders in the face. After they were stopped Nurse Mendez began cleaning dried blood and debris from the facial wounds, probably unaware that little whimpers of sympathetic pain were coming from her throat. She would occasionally whisper, "Niño pobrecito; Niño pobrecito." Poor little boy.

The victim was a sure candidate for hypovolemic shock, due to crush injury trauma, but strangely, it didn't happen. His blood pressure, pulse and capillary refill were all within normal range.

The EMTs had done a good job of clearing the airway of blood, teeth and other debris. He appeared to be breathing well, with no difficulty. The trauma team would likely not have to intubate or bag him.

Then, without warning, the steady beep of the monitor changed.

"Uh oh," Lonnie said.

"He's throwing PVC's," Carl Parmeter, a male nurse, said, meaning that suddenly there were premature cardiac ventricular contractions. PVC's often preceded cardiac arrest.

"Let's get the defib over here, please," Dr. Alcott said, asking for the electrical heart shock machine. It seemed certain that he would need it.

"Okay, he *is* fibrillating," Parmeter said, a moment later.

"Mm, Mm," Lonnie said. "Need to get on this. C'mon, boy. You hang in there." Lonnie had helped cut David out of the tangled mess. He wanted him to live. Now the boy was fibrillating.

Darrell's heart had begun to beat so chaotically that it could not deliver adequate blood to the brain or the body—especially the brain. If the brain were deprived of oxygenated blood at normal body temperature, for longer than four minutes there would be irreversible brain damage. If the heart continued to fibrillate, the boy would die.

"Start the clock," Dr Alcott said. They would need to keep accurate account of the length of time that the heart was not doing its job. "Hand me the paddles, please."

He placed one paddle on the breastbone, the other between the left nipple and the armpit. The paddles were large for the seven-year-old frame, but they would work.

"Shock, please," the doctor said.

Nurse Mendez depressed the "shock" button on the defibrillator. There was a sharp clicking sound, and the boy's torso jerked slightly.

A high frequency whine followed as the machine recharged.

"Still fibbing," Parmeter said.

"Shock," the doctor said again. Again, the *click* and the quick spasm. Several in the trauma room were beginning to think the same thing, with some measure of guilt.

How badly do we really want to work to save this boy? And for what purpose? What kind of life can he expect with a face like that?

It was being assumed that the Post Traumatic Shock resulting from such horrible, disfiguring injuries would be insurmountable.

The Hippocratic Oath says, "Do no harm."

Which would be more harmful, to save this boy or to let him go?

"Shock," the doctor said.

Nothing happened.

He looked over his mask at Nurse Mendez. "Shock, please, nurse."

There was a pause as there eyes locked. Hers began to brim with tears.

Click.

"Nope," Parmeter said. "No change."

"Time?" Dr Alcott asked.

"A minute fifty," Parmeter replied.

The heart had been beating anomalously for one minute and fifty seconds.

"God, help us," Alcott breathed a prayer, not absolutely certain of what he was asking for.

He was about to shock again when the heart rhythm suddenly changed. It became steadier, but progressively slower.

"Pulse sixty-five," Parmeter announced. "Sixty. He's probably going Bradycardic." Bradycardic was a slowed heart rate to less than fifty beats per minute.

Then there was no beep from the monitor, no jiggling green trace.

"Flat line," Parmeter stated, unemotionally.

"Time?" the doctor asked. "Two ten," Parmeter responded. Two minutes and ten seconds without oxygen to the brain.

The doctor placed the paddles and once again said, "Shock."

Sometimes it proved to be easier to restart a stopped heart than to defibrillate one.

In this instance there was no response.

The trauma room was eerily quiet. Everyone was fixed upon Dr. Alcott. He was in charge—captain of this boat; and they were in rough shoals.

"Ten CC's of epi, please." He was handed a syringe filled with epinephrine, which he administered directly through the sternum into the heart.

"He's cyanotic," Parmeter said. "Two forty-three" At two minutes and forty three seconds the boy's lips were turning blue. What was left of the good side of his face had grown pale and waxen. The dark spectre of death had certainly come into the room. Occasionally he would outfox the team and win one. They hated it.

"Three minutes, doc."

Some brain damage had probably already occurred. No way of knowing.

Dr. Alcott said. "Let's shock him again."

Nurse Mendez depressed the button again. There was no change. The boy's face was the color of cold ashes.

"Almost four minutes."

Dr. Alcott exhaled loudly, overwhelmed by a sense of helplessness. He was about to open his mouth to pronounce Darrell's time of death when there was a sudden harsh clatter against the sidewall of the OR. Inexplicably, a metal cart had crashed into the wall and overturned, spilling trays, sending surgical instruments clattering across the floor. To a person everyone in the room turned their heads in the direction of the startling noise.

As the trauma team recovered from the shock and turned back to the unhappy business at hand there was a collective audible gasp. Some involuntarily stepped back.

On the gurney the shattered young boy was looking around with his one good eye. His face was as pink as a peach. The monitor was still flat lined. Dr. Alcott stared transfixed at the monitor.

"Hello?" Nurse Mendez said. "Can you hear me?"

Darrell looked in her direction. Instantly there was a jiggle on the monitor's trace. Then another.

Then, "He's got steady rhythm. Good BP."

Darrell was breathing steadily.

"Good boy," Lonnie said. "Good boy."

"Well, alright," Dr. Alcott sighed, and smiled slightly. "CBC and full x-rays. We need to know what he looks like inside."

"Will somebody tell me what just happened?" Parmeter asked.

Predictably, there was no answer.

TWENTY-TWO

February 17, 1974

David's father would baptize him today. His heart fluttering with excitement, David finished tying his shoes. He thought that he might be too excited to eat his breakfast, as he scrambled down the stairs to the smell of cooking bacon.

He had announced his desire to be baptized to his folks the previous Wednesday evening. They had beamed at the news, especially when he had asked his father if he would baptize him.

"What a wonderful gift to *us* for your birthday, David," his mother had said, giving him a giant hug. "You could not make me happier."

"I am really proud of you, son, and it would be an honor for me to do it." David's father shook his hand, and then gave him a bear hug.

"You men come sit down," Mrs. Baxter said. "Before it gets cold."

She had made an obvious celebratory breakfast—scrambled eggs with peppers, patty sausage, bacon, pancakes, hash browns, cantaloupe, sliced tomatoes, giant biscuits, flour gravy, orange juice and coffee. With the admixture of aromas and the sight of the table full of food, David's appetite suddenly reappeared with a vengeance.

"Let's pray," David's father said, and they took hands around the table.

"Heavenly Father, we thank you for this day that you have made, and we rejoice in it. Father, I thank you for this family, and the many, many ways that you have blessed us. I ask you to especially bless my son, David, who has chosen to follow you in faith and in baptism. Bless him. Father, I thank you for my wife; bless her. And bless this great meal that you have provided for us this morning, in Jesus' name. Amen."

David wolfed down his breakfast and then had another helping of pancakes smothered with crunchy peanut butter and syrup. Now he was ready to be baptized.

He was growing up, no question about it.

TWENTY-THREE

The Present

Judge Allen announced a recess at 3:30 in the afternoon, to resume at 9 a.m. the following morning. A jury of seven women and five men had been selected.

"What do you think?" David had asked Palmer. "Am I a cooked goose?"

"I think we have a pretty good jury," Palmer said, sitting next to David on his cell bunk. "Women can be pretty tough on people who do bad things to children, but at the same time they are wont to depend on their intuition. In this case I am betting that their intuition will tell them that you are innocent. Plus, I think you have good curb appeal."

"Too bad I'm not selling a house."

"The men, on the other hand will decide early. Some of them have already decided, I expect."

"I thought men were supposed to be more logical," David said.

"They are," Palmer said. "That's my point. Logically, based on news reports, and the fact that a grand jury indicted you because of evidence, you are guilty. Logically. Problem is, their logic is illogical."

The closest that Lillian and Meredith had been allowed to David was four feet behind him in the first spectator row. Had Lillian been closer, she would have reached out and touched him—guards be hanged.

At one point during the proceedings Lillian had said in a stage whisper loud enough for most to hear, "I love you, David." The judge had given her a quick stern look, but he said nothing.

When the judge had announced the recess until the following morning, David had turned as the guards were escorting him out.

"I love you, Lillian."

How sweet, Darrell thought to himself as he slowly drifted with the crowd, edging toward the doorways. *Sweet love blooms. We may have to do some pruning in the garden.*

Darrell made his way to his car, which he had parked two aisles over from Lillian's. He had discretely followed her and the girl to the courthouse and would follow them home. He got into his car and switched on his radio to a local news station while he waited for them to show up.

. . . jury selection this afternoon. The jury will be comprised of seven women and five men, with two female alternates. It is generally believed that the trial will be an uncommonly short one, perhaps no more than three days. Sources indicate that the District Attorney plans to call only two expert witnesses to testify regarding DNA and fingerprint evidence.

Lillian and Meredith appeared, approaching their car, neither of them speaking. They both looked depressed, it seemed to Darrell.

He gave them a moment's head start and then pulled out, allowing two cars between them.

He just wanted to see the girl. For now that would have to suffice.

He checked his mask and makeup in the rearview mirror. It looked okay. Although it was uncomfortable, it did the job. It kept people from staring at him.

TWENTY-FOUR

The Present

Denise Nichols' fingerprint expert was an ex-FBI forensics expert, now a full-time consultant whose sole vocation was testifying at criminal trials. His reputation was such that he could afford to be very selective, limiting his travels to once a month, and still maintained a standard of living to which his wife had become addicted. His name was Royce Brown, forty-five, from Baltimore, not quite six feet tall with dusty brown hair over his shirt collar, which he wore as a mild rebellion against the previous conservative requirements of the bureau. He dressed casually in khakis, tie-less, blue button-down shirt and oxblood loafers. His left eye was crossed, skewed inward toward his nose, which was distracting and stole from his attempt at conveying an air of authority. Consequently, Royce seldom looked anyone straight in the eye. He compensated with his work, which was always thorough and detailed, compensating for the minor flaw of his turned-in eye.

John Parella had convinced Brown to meet with him to discuss the fingerprints that, it seemed to John, had been deliberately placed in the shoe, the purse and the Bible.

"What is the possibility that these prints could have been planted?" Parella had asked.

Brown rubbed his brow and thought. Finally he said, "The

quality is too good. It is possible to transfer a print but you usually get, say on a scale of one to ten, a three or less. These prints were more like eights or nines."

It was Parella's turn to pause and think. "Why just an eight or nine? Why not a ten?"

"In normal conditions a ten is rare. The print has to be made under very controlled circumstances"

"So an eight or nine is common?"

"No. It depends. It depends on the surface quality, the oil content of the finger, the jeopardy to the print after it has been laid down—in other words the environment that the print is in will of course affect its quality. Over time prints will deteriorate. There are a number of variables."

"Don't you find it unusual—the location of these prints, especially?" Parella asked. "I mean—here we are—three victims and not a single clue, then *whammo*, three prints. Three *hidden* prints that, seems to me, are intentionally placed to be found at some point in time. And placed in such a way that they are *protected*, if you will. *Inside* a purse, *inside* a shoe and *inside* a Bible."

Brown rubbed the back of his neck. He did not want to commit to anything that may crop up in court and get him caught in a bind. He was always careful to be as certain of his answers as possible before committing. He tightened his lips as if not wanting the words to escape.

"It *does* seem to me to be somewhat uncharacteristic to have high quality prints on the *inside* of a foundation—I should say, a *single* print on each platform—with no prints, or even partials on any other surface," he finally said.

"Would you say that the prints were intentionally placed?"

Brown shook his head. "I couldn't conjecture on that. No."

"Well," Parella persisted, "In view of the fact that it is *somewhat* uncharacteristic to have one good print on the inside and nothing on the outside, what *can* you say about the probabilities?"

The expression on Brown's face was almost pained. "I have no way to quantify what you are asking for, John. Conjecture has no place here."

"But you do find it uncommon—out of the norm?"

"Yes."

"Have you ever seen anything like it before, in your experience?"

An extremely loaded question, Brown felt. But they were talking about a man's life, and Brown had to admit to himself that the circumstances around these prints were *unusual* to say the least. He breathed a long sigh. "No, I've never seen anything like this before."

"Good," John smiled. "Thank you very much."

Royce Brown got up to leave when John said, "One other thing?"

"Yes?"

"Did you correlate prints from David Baxter's youth—when he was in the RAs—or did you use the prints from his processing?"

The question hit Brown as if the roof had just fallen in. Brown's response was halting. "We used prints from his childhood. That's what was in the database. We didn't have his processing prints yet."

Unbelievable, Parella thought.

"So, what exactly are you saying John?" Nothing of Denise's tone was lost through John's cell phone. She was clearly upset and defensive.

"I am saying, Denise, that we did not do due diligence on this." John was careful to use *we* to avoid adding fuel to the flame. "These prints in the database were done so long ago, shoot, we don't even know if they are Baxter's. They may be corrupted-any number of things. We need to correlate the crime scene prints with Baxter's processing prints. We need to do it immediately. Royce Brown has everything he needs to have it done tonight."

"Have you told Palmer?"

"No–not yet." Parella paused. "Are you suggesting something?"

"Just wait. That's all. I don't want to get Baxter's hopes up."

"Are you telling me that you are concerned about Baxter's feelings?"

"I'm a compassionate female." John could feel her smiling over the phone.

Parella laughed. "I doubt that you would find many of your prosecutees to agree with you."

Denise laughed aloud. She was not worried much about what others thought. Nor was she concerned about the results of Royce Brown's tests. Neither did she mention the obvious–the hair. She already knew that it was tenuous evidence at best, being so easily planted in a crime scene. The hair would simply be the cherry on the sundae.

"If the results are in David's favor," John continued. "I will let them know immediately."

"And me," Denise said.

"And you."

Denise hung up.

Parella watched as Royce Brown did his thing. Brown had a custom forensic laptop computer that he had assembled himself. Everything in the computer, the processor, hard drive, memory and graphics was the fastest and largest capacity that he could accrue a year ago. It greatly facilitated his work. Since then there had been some improvements and advances, which he watched closely, but nothing that warranted retrofitting or upgrading anything just yet.

Brown already had the prints from the crime scene scanned to a file in his laptop. He had run a correlation program comparing the three prints which showed 99.8% probability that they were the same print. Which, interpreted, meant that they were fingerprints from the same person. Matches didn't get much closer than that.

Brown was scanning the prints that were taken at David Baxter's processing into the system. Once he had them stored into a file he selected David Baxter's fingerprints and placed them in the correlation window on the right side of the computer screen. He placed the fingerprint from the Bible in the left correlation window of the screen, placed the cursor over the "start" button on the screen and doubled clicked the left mouse button. Immediately the application began to compare the whorls and swirls in the two prints, marking and filing matches in a histogram and data files. After about five minutes the comparison was complete. A window summarizing the findings appeared in the center of the screen. The first line said: PROBABILITY OF MATCH: 91%.

"I'm guessing that's not all that good," Parella said, looking at Royce Brown's frown.

Brown continued looking at the screen, as if expecting it to change. "It's not as good as the first time with the earlier prints. It's certainly not what I expected."

"What's the difference?" Parella asked. His heart rate begun to increase. He had had a feeling.

"The first fingerprint from Baxter's youth was mainly a center print-it had not been rolled well when taken, consequently the outer ridges were not printed. Quite often the Boy Scouts and such groups let the boys print themselves; the prints are provided to the police, where they can be retrieved by AFIS. It's better than nothing."

Parella nodded his head. "I see."

"Plus," Brown went on, "the prints from the crime scenes were also center prints with smudged and missing outside ridges. There was still a 91% probability of match-good enough to convict."

"So what is the difference now?"

"The limiter before was Baxter's youth print. And the amount of outside ridge that was missing. We now have 30% more print to compare, using the jail print. These particular outside ridges . . ."

Brown pointed at an area on the screen. "are close, but not a certain match to the crime scene prints."

"So you are saying to me," Parella said calmly, keeping his voice free of accusation, "that when you didn't have as much print to work with, you got a better match? Is that crazy or what?"

"The software can only compare what it sees."

"You mean that it doesn't derate its findings based upon how much actual fingerprint there is to compare."

"The software considers that 60% of a print will provide sufficient data to provide a match. If the middle matches, the outside matches as well - usually."

John Parella pointed to the screen. "It doesn't match here."

"True. Highly unusual."

"Do you believe that this is the same man?"

"Most certainly not," Brown shook his head.

Parella's heart ratcheted up a notch. "How then do you explain this?"

"It is almost the same man." Brown looked Parella squarely in the face with his right eye, forgetting about his skewed left eye.

"What in the world are you talking about? How can it almost be somebody?" Parella's frustration was clearly conveyed in his voice.

"It means," the fingerprint expert said deliberately as if on the witness stand, "David Baxter is in all likelihood an identical twin."

TWENTY-FIVE

February 14, 1974

Dr. Herman Alcott at Burnet Hospital had done the important basics as far as Darrell Baldwin Phelps' injuries were concerned. He had performed a splenectomy, repaired a torn liver, set the left leg and put it in a cast, and sutured a number of lacerations. Three pints of blood had been administered in total on the day of Darrell's arrival to Burnet ER.

What Dr. Alcott elected not to even attempt was repair to the destroyed left side of the boy's face and the demolished left arm and hand.

For the head and arm trauma Dr. Alcott had transferred Darrell to Scott and White Hospital in the small central Texas community of Temple.

Darrell had arrived by ambulance two days ago. He had immediately been "adopted" by the nursing staff when they discovered that he had absolutely no family. Then when they had discovered that it was Darrell's birthday they went all out. Margie Townes spearheaded the party.

Twenty-three-year-old Margie, an RN, graduate of Texas Women's University in Denton, Texas, was a tireless package of energy. She was constantly volunteering for extra hours. A typical six-day week for her was sixty plus hours.

The likelihood that Darrell, in his morphine fog, would remember any of his party was small. Margie and the others were doing it anyway, on the chance that it would be embedded in his subconscious, and would affect his overall morale. So, they brought in flowers, stuffed animals and balloons, and hung a "Happy Birthday" sign across the top of his window.

Darrell's head was enveloped in bandages, with a hole for his right eye, a hole for his nostrils for his oxygen, and a hole at the right side of his mouth for a straw by which he could take small sips of cold water.

There would be no candles because of the fire hazard with the oxygen, so the five girls, and Larry Brenham, the one male nurse, gathered around Darrell's bed and sang "Happy Birthday" to him at 6:00 in the morning, just thirty minutes before he would be prepped for his first of fourteen visits to the OR.

Dr. Angus McWhorter had practiced at Scott and White for eighteen years. He had been chief resident surgeon for ten of those years. He would take the Phelps case, assisted by Dr. Lois Dryden, a young but skilled cosmetic surgeon. Angus was happy to have her on the team. She was as nimble-fingered a surgeon as he had ever seen.

Having just scrubbed, Lois entered the OR where Dr. McWhorter was already standing beside the patient. Tchaikovsky's Sixth was playing softly in the background. Angus liked classical music while he was working.

"Good morning, Lois," Dr. McWhorter said, smiling behind his mask. "Good to see you this morning."

"Glad to be here," Lois said. "What do we have?" She walked around the table so that she could get a good look at the left side of Darrell's face.

"Oh, my..." she said. "What happened?"

"A car wreck. His mother was killed," Angus said.

This morning was to be an evaluation/planning session. There would be multiple scans, x-rays, super-8 and stills made of Darrell's head from every possible angle. Every skull and facial bone fracture, hairline and otherwise, would need to be discovered and addressed. Then they would decide what to do about missing facial muscle and tissue.

Lois assessed the injuries. *Poor kid,* she thought, then putting her feelings aside, she began to evaluate objectively. The entire left side of his facial muscle and skin had been ripped away—from the left Frontalis muscle, back across the Temporoparietialis, down the Zygomaticus Minor and Major, including the left ear. The Orbicularis Oculi along with the eyeball and optical nerves had been torn out. Some shred of sinew hung where the Buccinator, Masseter, and Depressor Anguli Otis had been attached to form the left cheek and jaw structure. A large chunk of jawbone and most of the teeth on the left side were missing. Burnet ER had sutured the left side of the tongue back to the root.

"We're going to need at least four films," Lois said. "A Waters view, a Caldwell view, a lateral view, and a submentovertex view. We'll need a CT as well, of course."

She turned toward the other doctor. "There is no way to repair all this, Angus," she sighed.

"I know, Lois." Dr. McWhorter placed his hands on his waist. "All we can do is the best we can do. Do you think we can make him presentable?"

"Perhaps to a leper colony," she said, shaking her head. "Obviously, we can't recreate any muscle structure. My first thought for a foundation is silicone–like in a breast implant. I'll have to figure out how to attach it—shouldn't be too difficult. Then we harvest some skin," she said, shrugging her shoulders. "Not a good story for a

seven year old. How this kid will deal with growing up looking like
an ogre will be between him and God."

TWENTY-SIX

The Present

David Baxter could not believe his ears. John Parella had notified Palmer immediately after discovering the dissimilarity of Baxter's print with the crime scene prints, and Palmer had come right over with the news.

"So what is the DA's office saying?" Baxter asked his friend. "Are they dropping charges?"

"They're thinking about it, David. Denise Nichols is tenacious. She's a bulldog. Something about DAs—once they've crossed the line they don't want to go back."

"Commonly known as pride," David said.

"Yeah, I guess," Palmer said. "But whatever—she may want to forge ahead. The pro of it is that now the fingerprint guy is as much ours as he is hers. I think the detective—Parella—is our witness now. Plus, throw the profiler on our pile as well. Seems God is answering some prayers."

"He does that, you know," David smiled, feeling suddenly much lighter.

Providing coffee and doughnuts, Denise had called an emergency meeting. It was 8:45 in the evening. Gathered in the cheaply paneled conference room of the DA's offices, seated around the long table were Georgia Wainwright, administrative assistant; Thomas Jones, research assistant; Peter Darby, another ADA; Charles Parker, DNA expert; Marcus James, the profiler; and Royce Brown, the fingerprints expert.

Denise stood in the corner in front of the artificial plants. She cleared her throat and began. "We have an issue. It seems that the match probability on our fingerprint is not as good as we had first thought it to be. Further evaluation has determined that there is a 91% probability of match between the print on the Bible at the crime scene and Baxter's processing prints. Did I say that right Royce?"

"Couldn't've said it better," Royce said.

"So what I want to know before we leave tonight is, number one; *should we go on?* And number two; *what are our chances?* Okay? Any questions?"

"What are the alternatives to going on with the trial?" Marcus James asked.

"In my mind, there are none," Denise responded.

"You're saying that there's no possible plea bargain—reduced sentence, anything?"

"You might wanna think about it, Denise," Peter Darby said.

"I don't think so, Peter." Denise's arms were folded across her chest, and she shook her head emphatically. "What are you going to testify, Royce?"

"What you just reiterated, Denise. That there is only a 91% probability of a match between the two prints."

"Do you have to say *only*, Royce? Can you phrase it a little more positively?

"Sure, I can say that there is a 91% probability of a match. Then I get cross examined."

"Yes, you will—but let me ask you something, Royce. Have you ever seen a 91% probability of a match before? Ever?" Attorney rule number one said *Never ask a question that you don't know the answer to.* But this was not in a courtroom, and she needed to know the answer. She might ask the question tomorrow.

"No," Royce said.

"Never?"

"Never."

"What do you typically see if fingerprints match?"

"In the high 90% range," Royce said.

"Come on Royce. Give it to me. 96%? 98%?"

"98% and above is more likely."

"So when you don't have a match, what do you usually see, 91%?"

"No," Brown said, shaking his head. "Nowhere near. More like 50% or less."

Denise was smiling now. "So 50% or less probability of a match means...?"

"It's not the same person," Brown finished.

"And 91% probability of a match means . . . ?"

Royce Brown sat silent. He felt somewhat trapped. Finally, he said, "Inconclusive."

"That's not what you told Parella is it?" Denise had lowered her voice. "Parella said that *you* said that it is not the same man."

"That's what I said, yes." Brown remained calm. He had been in this position in the courtroom many times.

"Just now you said *inconclusive?*" Denise was not attacking. This was her witness after all. Were she attacking, she would be more in his face.

"It is not a high enough probability match that one can say that it is the same person that made these prints," Brown said evenly.

"But neither can one say that it is not the same person, right?"

"Not with absolute certainty."

"So it is possible that the prints may belong to the same person?"

"There is a very small probability that it might be the same person."

"Okay, back up," Denise said. "That's a yes or no question, Royce. If we go with this tomorrow, just answer yes or no. Don't embellish. Okay?"

Royce sighed heavily. The scientist in him was feeling restricted.

"So, rewind. Here we go. Mr. Brown, it is possible that the prints may belong to the same person?"

"Yes."

"Okay, then. Great." Denise walked to the other end of the table so that she could face Charles Parker, the DNA expert.

"So, Charles, let's make this quick, okay?"

"My pleasure," said Parker, a balding, pinch-faced man with rimless glasses on a large hooked nose.

"You have a sample of DNA—a hair—from the crime scene?"

"Yes."

"And a DNA sample from the accused?"

"Yes, that's correct."

"What can you say regarding the two samples?"

"That they came from the same person."

"And that person is . . . ?"

"The accused, David Baxter." Charles Parker almost pointed.

"Will you tell the jury the probability that these DNA samples are from the same person?"

"Yes," Charles said. "99.9%"

"Absolute certainty?"

"Yes," Parker smiled.

"Thank you, Mr. Parker." Denise walked around to the other side of the table so that she could see Marcus James the profiler.

"So, Mr. James, you have met at length with the accused?"

"Yes, Ma'am, I have."

"And what are your findings?"

"Well, I found that David Baxter's personality and demeanor is not consistent with that of a serial killer, Ms. Nichols."

"We're not accusing him of being a serial killer, Mr. James."

James was nonplussed. He felt himself wedged between the desire to be a good witness for the prosecution and the desire to avoid placing himself in a vulnerable position on the witness chair.

"Would you say that the accused has the personality or demeanor of someone who, perhaps, has killed *one* person?"

"No, I couldn't say."

"Why not?"

"One, victim perpetrators are not—do not have a quantifiable matrix by which to profile them."

"English, please."

"Um—there is not enough information regarding a single victim killer by which to make a judgment."

"So you can't rule out, from your meetings with the accused, the possibility that he may be a murderer?"

"No, ma'am, of course not."

"Okay," Denise clasped her hands together. "That's our case folks. What do ya'll think?"

No one said anything for several long seconds, then Peter Darby, the ADA spoke up.

"I think, perhaps, that I was wrong," he smiled. "You may just pull this off, Denise."

"What do ya'll think our chances are?" she asked.

"Fifty-fifty?" Georgia Wainwright, her assistant, said. It was more of a question.

"I think fifty-fifty works," Darby said.

Denise looked around the room. When no one else said anything she said,

"Fifty-fifty sounds good to me. Georgia, call Palmer on his cell and tell him that we will see him in court."

TWENTY-SEVEN

April 15, 1974

In early March, after three operations on his face, Darrell began speaking his first words since the accident. His words were thick and garbled. Margie Townes was one of few who could understand him.

"Verse mah mahn?" he would ask, over and over, unable to control his lips or tongue.

"Where's my mom?" Margie interpreted to the others. "He's asking for his mom. I've been telling him that she is not here; she is somewhere else. But he keeps asking."

Finally, Dr. Henry Perkins, Chief of Psychiatry said. "We need to tell him. He strongly suspects anyway."

It was decided that Margie should tell him, and if necessary they would sedate him. Margie got little sleep the night before, sorely dreading what lay before her the next day.

That morning she pulled up a rolling stool next to Darrell's right side. Bandages covered the left side of his face. His face on the right was incredulously smooth and unblemished. His eye was open staring at the ceiling when she sat down.

"Hi, Darrell," she said, her voice soft and gentle. Taking his right hand in both of hers she continued, "How're you feeling this morning? Okay?"

"Mmmm," he said. "Ochre." He turned his head slowly toward her. The right side of his mouth curved up slightly in an attempt to smile.

"Darrell, I have something to tell you. It's something . . . not good."

"Mmmm?" he said. His eye widened a little.

"It's about your mother."

He fixed his eye upon her face. It was filled with foreboding.

"Darrell . . ." she took a deep breath, wondering why she had ever wanted to be a nurse. "You were in a bad car wreck with your mother. Your mother did not survive Darrell. She was killed. I'm so sorry."

His grip tightened on her hand, but he uttered not a sound. He turned his face toward the ceiling and closed his eye.

Darrell had remained silent for a little more than a month until today. At almost precisely 3:00 in the morning a long horrifying shriek issued from his room. It was so woefully heartrending that it froze the two nurses on duty in their tracks. It manifested horror with no indication of letting up.

One nurse was behind the nurse's station; the other was at the opposite end of the hall. Immediately call-lights up and down the hall lit up. Both nurses broke into a run toward Darrell's room. They found him sitting up in bed, ripping at the bandages on his face with his right hand. The wail of a soul trapped in Hell surged from his mouth.

Nurse Steward immediately stuck a syringe of morphine into his IV, while Nurse Washington pulled his arm away from his face. Gradually the cry mellowed to a whimper, then silence.

"My heavens," Nurse Washington said. "Have you ever heard such a thing?"

"Never," replied Nurse Steward as they left the room to calm the other patients.

TWENTY-EIGHT

The Present

Denise had decided to put her DNA expert, Charles Parker on the stand first. It was basically going the same as the evening before, except that this performance was before a packed house, and an intently attentive jury of seven women and five men.

"So, in your expert opinion, there is a correlation between the DNA at the crime scene and the DNA of the accused," Denise pointed her pen at David Baxter.

"Yes, absolutely."

"To what degree is the correlation—or match—between the crime scene DNA and the accused?"

"99.9%"

"Which means . . . ?"

"It means that without a doubt, the source of the DNA is the same person."

"That person being the accused?"

"That is correct."

"David Baxter?"

"Yes, correct."

"Thank you, Mr. Parker. No further questions for this witness Your Honor." Denise turned and walked to her seat without looking in David's direction.

"Counselor?" Judge Allen pointed the handle of his gavel in Palmer's general direction.

Palmer stood at his chair and did not approach the witness.

"Good morning, Mr. Parker," he began.

"Morning," Parker replied.

"No doubt in your mind that my client is the source of the DNA in question?" Palmer asked, his voice even and safe.

"No, none at all."

"Have you ever been wrong?"

"You mean about . . . ?"

"I mean have you ever been wrong about a DNA match—for example you thought it was a match when it wasn't?" *The basic rule,* Palmer thought. *Know the answer before asking the question. Didn't matter here.* He had a plan. "Or you thought it was not a match when it was?"

"No, I have never been wrong."

"Never, ever been wrong?"

"Not with regard to DNA matching, no."

"A commendable record, Mr. Parker. How many DNA tests have you performed?"

Parker had a ready answer. "About 1500."

"You have performed one thousand five hundred tests without being wrong?"

"Yes, correct."

"Do you perform these tests yourself?"

"No, not always. Sometimes I'm involved—it depends upon my schedule." Parker shifted in his seat. Denise perked up. *Where was this headed?* She had expected the simple "The hair was left in the Bible by Baxter as a result of Baxter's innocent contact with the Bible and the victim" defense.

"So—help me understand, please—you are *involved* in *some* of the tests?"

"That's correct."

"What does *involved* mean, Mr. Parker?"

"It means that I am overseeing the testing."

"Overseeing. So, you are telling operators, or testers—whatever you call them—you are telling them what to do? Telling them how to conduct the test?"

"Not *telling* them exactly. No."

"May I approach the witness, Your Honor?"

The judge nodded his assent.

"Mr. Parker, please bear with me. You are a scientist, and I don't have a scientific bone in my body," Palmer smiled, approaching the witness stand. "So, I think that I am hearing that the operators pretty much know how to run the tests, right?"

"Yes, that's fair."

"So you don't actually run the test?"

"No, not actually."

"And you are not always at the test lab while tests are being conducted, correct?"

"That is correct."

"Okay. So you—what?—You interpret the test?" Palmer was now within three feet of Parker and gradually drawing closer. He could see a thin bead of sweat on Parker's forehead.

"I am . . ." Parker hesitated, looking for words. "I participate in interpreting the test."

"Is that the same as being *involved*, Mr. Parker?"

Denise had to do something, so she stood. "Badgering the witness, Your Honor."

Judge Allen shook his head. "I don't think so, Counselor. I'll allow it."

There was a brief silence, and then Palmer said, "Please instruct the witness to answer, Your Honor."

"What was the question?" Parker was showing some signs of agitation.

The clerk read, "Is that the same as being involved, Mr. Parker?"

Parker readjusted himself on the chair. "You might say that," he responded, wishing that Palmer would go away.

"Okay, well forget all that. The point, I think, Mr. Parker is that someone else does the testing, right?"

"Yes."

"And someone else does the interpretation, is that also right?"

"Yes."

"Do you always use the same lab?"

"No."

"You use different labs?"

"Yes."

"So your job, then, is . . . ?"

"I present the findings."

Palmer was now within one foot of the witness. "You present the findings?"

"Yes."

"To whom?"

"To interested parties."

"Ah, to interested parties. Is this jury an *interested party*?"

"Yes."

"Do you present your findings to anyone other than juries, attorneys, judges and onlookers at trials?"

"No."

"What is your occupation, Mr. Parker?"

"I am a DNA expert."

"That's how you make a living?"

"Yes."

"I see. Did you make more than $200,000 last year?"

"Objection," Denise was on her feet.

"Sustained," the judge said, tapping the gavel handle on his bench.

"Okay. So, let's wrap this up Mr. Parker, Okay?" Palmer asked.

"It's your call," Parker said, struggling to maintain his composure.

"Have you ever heard of Zylac Laboratories right here in Houston?"

"Yes."

"Have you ever been involved with them, Mr. Parker?"

"Yes."

"Was Zylac used for this trial?"

"No."

"Why not?"

Parker instinctively looked at Denise, a movement noticed by most everyone in the courtroom. Denise kept her poker face, remaining rigid in her chair, her insides in turmoil.

"It was decided to use Kadco Labs in Ft. Worth." Parker wanted to remove his handkerchief from his back pocket and wipe his brow, but he couldn't decide which would be worse, the rapidly accumulating sweat which would be rolling off his forehead any moment, or wiping his brow with a handkerchief. His wife had always said, "Don't let 'em see you sweat." *I'm glad she's not here to see this,* he thought. He opted not to remove his handkerchief.

"Would you please instruct Mr. Parker to answer the question, Your Honor?"

Before the judge could say anything Parker said, "There was a problem with Zylac." His motive now was to get this over with, get his check, and get out of town.

"Oh?" Palmer said, mock surprise in his voice. "A problem?"

"Yes, they had an issue with their processes. With process control."

"What processes, Mr. Parker?" Everyone knew what the answer would be.

"With DNA processes."

"DNA testing and matching?"

"Yes."

"Can you apprise us of the scope—the magnitude—of this problem?"

"It is still under evaluation."

"I see. Are you familiar with the results thus far?" Palmer turned to face the jury box.

"Over 250 cases, so far, have been affected."

Palmer pivoted on his toes to face Parker so quickly that Parker recoiled in his chair. Someone in the audience sniggered.

"What!" Palmer almost shouted. "250 cases? Affected? What in heaven's name does *affected* mean Mr. Parker?"

"It means that some and maybe all of these cases may be overthrown."

Palmer placed both hands on his head. "I can't..." He began to walk in circles. "250 *criminals* may be let loose on the streets to do whatever evil they're prone to do? Unbelievable!"

"Your Honor," Denise said calmly. "We can do without the histrionics."

"I agree. Ratchet it down a notch, Counselor."

"This is *serious* Your Honor."

"I agree. It just doesn't have a whit to do with *these* proceedings. Kindly wrap it up."

"Yes, sir." Palmer walked back over to the witness. "I want to thank you for your time, Mr. Parker. I know that you are a busy man and have places to go." Palmer placed himself so that his back was to the judge, Parker was to his left, and he was facing the jury.

"Let's do this, I will summarize what I think your testimony has been. If I am wrong in any way, please, interrupt. Okay?"

"Sure," Parker said, relieved that this was almost over.

"Here we go. First, Mr. Parker, you don't actually do any testing or interpretation of testing. Your function is to travel to various trial locations and present data that someone provides to you." Palmer paused and looked at the witness.

"Correct."

"And to say that you have never been wrong is a tad bit misleading, since someone else does the testing and interpretation."

"Yes, strictly speaking."

"And we are speaking strictly today, are we not?"

Giggles once again came from the gallery. Neither the judge nor Denise objected.

"And we also know from what we have heard here today that labs make errors, serious errors—errors that can set criminals free. Errors that can get an innocent man convicted." Palmer looked at David, sitting calmly at the defendant's table. "Errors that can ruin lives of families and friends. Errors that could happen in the lives of *anyone* in this courtroom—to *anyone* in this jury."

Denise could not let this go. "Is he summating, Your Honor?"

"Kindly bring this to a close. I think you've made your point," the judge said.

"Sorry, Your Honor." Palmer turned to head toward his seat. Parker was rising from his, when Palmer turned back toward him.

"One other thing."

Parker sighed audibly and sat back down.

"What was the source of the DNA at the crime scene?"

"The source was a strand of hair."

"And where was the hair found, specifically?"

"In a Bible."

"And how do you know this?"

"I heard it in the DA's office."

Palmer walked over to the evidence table and picked up a maroon Bible that had been placed in a clear plastic bag. "Number DB0220805, Your Honor," Palmer said, holding the Bible in the air. "This is the Bible to which we are referring—already entered into evidence."

Palmer carried the bagged Bible over and handed it to Parker.

"This is the Bible that was found at the crime scene, Mr. Parker. It was on the nightstand next to the victim's bed, and entered into the chain of custody by Officer Ray Mullins of the Spring Precinct Four Sheriff's Department. Officer Mullins also found the strand of hair—the source of DNA to which you have been testifying. He found the hair in the Bible. He also made a machine copy of a note handwritten on the flyleaf of the Bible, and attached the copy to the outside of the evidence bag."

Parker was examining the bagged Bible as if it had great interest for him.

"Your Honor, I would like to have Mr. Parker read the note to the jury."

Denise was on her feet in an instant. "Your Honor, I object. Mr. Parker is a DNA expert!"

"What?" Palmer interjected before the judge had time to reply. "What kind of expert do you have to be to *read a note?*"

"I strongly object, Your Honor," Denise said again.

"Your Honor," Palmer responded, "We can certainly locate Officer Mullins, bring him in here and have *him* read the note. I'm just trying to save the court some time, that's all."

"Yes, and the Court certainly appreciates your magnanimity Counselor. Slightly irregular, but I'll allow it."

"Your Honor…!" Denise was still on her feet.

"I said I'll allow it," the judge said, pointing his gavel handle at Denise.

Palmer turned back to Parker. "Kindly read the copy of the inscription to the jury, please."

Parker reached into his jacket, retrieved his glasses, cleared his throat and read,

> *Nov. 20, 2004*
> *Dear Summer,*
> *I thank God for you and for what you have meant in my*
> *life. It has been a real encouragement to me to see Him*
> *work in you. I have faith in you, but more importantly*
> *God has faith in you.*
> *I pray for your continued blessings and that you will*

clearly know His plan and purpose for your life.
Jude 2
David Baxter

Parker returned the Bible to Palmer. There were audible sobs from the jury box and the gallery. Had anyone looked closely, they would have seen the glisten of tears in David Baxter's eyes.

Palmer hesitated before speaking, allowing the moment to have its affect.

"So, we have, number one, the hair, the DNA, found at the crime scene. We have, number two, the Bible in which the hair was found; and we have, number three, the note that was written by the defendant, David Baxter. A note to a friend.

"We can say then—can we not, Mr. Parker—that the hair was naturally deposited in the Bible as a result of common handling by Mr. Baxter prior to giving it to Ms. Summers as a gift? Can we say that it would be absolutely normal for this hair, this source of DNA, to be found in this Bible?"

"Yes."

Palmer turned and walked toward his table.

"Thank you. No further questions, Your Honor."

TWENTY-NINE
The Present

Darrel sat before his TV, feet up on the hassock, beer in his right hand, retrieving chips from the bag on his lap with his claw-like left hand. His eye was intent on the screen.

"*Today, in the first day of the Summer Chase murder trial, defense attorney Palmer Hutchins made mincemeat of the state's DNA witness, casting doubt on the DNA testing process, and making it clear that the hair found in the Bible could most certainly have been left there by innocent means, since the Bible was a gift to Summer from the accused, David Baxter.*

"*I get the distinct feeling that the DA's office thought this was going to be a slam dunk, don't you, Stephanie?*"

"*I most certainly do, Clark. And that was clearly not how things went. I would have to say, 'Score one for the defense' wouldn't you?*"

"*Absolutely, but what I wonder, Stephanie, is why Palmer Hutchins spent so much time debunking the DNA testing system, which has not been getting very good press lately, why he did that, and then turned around and basically admitted that the hair was Baxter's and had gotten between the pages of the Bible quite normally and naturally.*"

"*I think he was simply sowing doubt, Clark. Making the statement that just because the state has a system and a process one doesn't have to just automatically conclude that the process is fault free—just because the state is doing it. He could very well have been setting things up for the state's next witness, their fingerprint expert."*

"Perhaps you are right, Stephanie. Well, in other news, police in Southeast Houston . . ."

Darrell clicked the TV off. He took a swig of beer. He was feeling somewhat anxious, so he got up, went to his bathroom cabinet and took two Clonazepan.

He was not anxious about the trial; he knew that. The trial was in fact benefiting his plan, which was to let David off the hook. David must be out of jail for the next phase of his program, which was to combine justice with the Light.

He had planned to begin sending clues to the police, to Parella, to let them know that they had the wrong man in jail. He would let David off the hook—get him out of jail. He may still send the clues, considering that it would be quite fun. Why not? If lawyer Palmer did manage to secure David's freedom, Darrell could still begin a dialogue with the cops. Certainly. It would be a hoot. What's his name, the BTK killer, had done it with the cops for years. His only stupid mistake was sending them a message on a floppy disk from his church's computer. He might as well have sent them his driver's license.

But that was not why Darrell's anxiety was building like steam in a blocked boiler. He needed a girl to minister to.

Patience, he heard, from somewhere near the ceiling above the refrigerator. *Have patience, my son.*

THIRTY

June 21, 1974

The fourteenth and final surgery was completed at 4:30 Friday afternoon. It had gone relatively well. Doctors Angus McWhorter and Lois Dryden could not see how they might have done better under the circumstances. Darrell had handled it well, with no ill effects. Both doctors were exhausted after the ten-hour procedure.

In the previous six surgeries Lois had replaced damaged bone with formed stainless steel plates in the boy's forehead, cheek and jaw. Then she had replaced the missing teeth in the bone and metal areas of the upper and lower jaw. She had attached custom molded silicone packets to those areas, and then she had put a glass eye in the left eye socket. Sadly, she and Angus had drawn the conclusion that Darrell's real skin would not work to cover the left side of his face. The area to be covered was too large and would not receive sufficient nutrients to remain alive and pliable. Instead, it would dry up and die. So, reluctantly, they had settled upon lambskin, similar to lambskin gloves except with a more refined process that would keep it pliable longer. Darrell would have to learn to deal with emollients for the rest of his life, developing a habit of applying a special cream to the skin so that it would not dry and crack.

Lois had done the best that she could do, with Dr. McWhorter's able assistance, yet she felt no sense of achievement. This boy would have to deal with things that she could not even imagine. He had done splendidly with the physical pain of his injuries. Everyone had marveled at the fact that Darrell complained so little. He was a wonderful little patient. After that early morning when he had screamed out the pain of his trauma, he had come out of his shell, talking and even joking some with the nurses.

But he had yet to see himself in a mirror. That would be the true test.

THIRTY-ONE

June 22, 1974

A commercial airliner rumbled overhead, turning westward toward California, as David and Birdy walked the path toward Hobo Jungle where they often spent their Saturdays together. It was already eighty-seven degrees and promised to be another boiling day in La Marque, Texas. Johnny Collingsworth and Herbert Carlisle, also members of the RAs, would be joining up later.

With Red Ryder BB guns dangling casually from their right hands, they kicked at the smaller rocks on the path. Both were wearing camouflage pants, tee shirts and ball caps. Their faces were smeared with brown, black and green grease paint. Birdy looked up at the plane.

"What're you going to be when you get big?"

David shrugged his left shoulder. "I dunno. An oil man maybe."

"I'm going to be a pilot—fly jumbo jets," he ran out in front, his arms outstretched, BB gun in hand, dipping and swerving with the noise of a jet engine coming from his throat. "I'm going to fly *around* the world."

He flew back to David and the wings dropped.

"Oil men make more money," David said, looking up at the plane disappearing into the western sky.

"Nuh-unh. Do not. Jumbo jet pilots make more money than anybody."

"Betcha not."

"Alright," Birdy said, looking at David. "A Whopper. Betcha a Whopper."

It was a wager among many wagers that would never be validated or completed.

The boys continued on without further conversation. Birdy practiced whistling, a newfound skill. They both kicked rocks. At seven years old their lives could not be more complete.

Hobo Jungle was a veritable paradise for the boys. It was a gravel pit, about five acres, abandoned years and years ago; sufficiently long enough ago that the pit was filled with full-sized trees; oak, mulberry, china berry, hackberry, Bois D'arc, and overgrown with underbrush and shrubbery. In some areas of the jungle wild Mustang grape vines had overtaken trees and underbrush. When in season, late July and August, the boys would cram the sour grapes into their cheeks like chipmunks. They laughed with tears rolling down their cheeks, because every time Birdy managed to get in at least one more grape than any body else. Every face would be pinched because of the sour juice.

"Man, that'll get your gizzard," David had said.

Once, Johnny's mom gave him a couple of pillowcases to fill with grapes, and she made some deliciously sweet grape jelly. Johnny later brought a paper bag full of wax paper wrapped peanut butter and grape jelly sandwiches to the Jungle, and they had gorged themselves, sitting Indian-style around a small campfire in a clearing.

"It don't get no better than this," Herbert said, holding his can of orange Shasta aloft.

The Jungle was many places for the boys—sometimes Viet Nam, sometimes WWII Guadalcanal or Iwo Jima, sometimes Pork chop

Hill in Korea, sometimes it was Venus or Mars. Today it would be Viet Nam—Herbert and Johnny would be the Cong. David and Birdy, the U.S. Marines, had decided that they would ambush the enemy from one of the several caves they had dug in the sides of the pit. They chose the Lava Caves, on the eastern rim, one with an old piece of vinyl flooring on the dirt. They had a clear view of the one entrance to The Jungle, although it was possible to enter by scaling down the walls on any side. If Johnny and Herbert came in through the entrance they would be seen and their movements tracked.

But Johnny and Herbert did not enter through the entrance, not in a normal fashion, anyway. Johnny, freckle-faced with a head of thick red—almost orange—hair, the smallest of the four boys, adjusted his amber-lensed shooters glasses as he crept into the brush at the right of the entrance to The Jungle. Herbert, with a mouth full of hardware and a dark crew cut, was the tallest of the crew. He followed Johnny into the brush. They were wearing their camouflage and paint as well, plus they had a secret weapon. Herbert had recently received from his uncle, a deer hunter, a pair of 20x-camouflaged binoculars. Creeping low, the two boys slowly duck-walked into the brush at the right entrance to Hobo Jungle and sat down. Herbert began slowly scanning the area with his binoculars.

"See anything?" Johnny whispered.

"No, shhh," Herbert admonished.

"I wanna see," Johnny said, still whispering.

"No, they're my glasses. I'll let you know."

"I'll stand up," Johnny said in his most threatening tone.

"What?"

"I'll stand up. They'll see me."

"I don't care," Herbert countered. "You'll get shot." He continued to scan. He was going in a counterclockwise direction around the pit, presently looking at the old dilapidated gray house on the southwestern rim. There was no glass left in the windows, and there was a gaping hole in the roof. Nevertheless, it was a good location to make a stand. Herbert could see no movement. Sometimes the enemy would get into the attic and shoot from the roof hole. Not today.

He scanned the south wall caves—there were three, two small ones and a very large one.

"C'mon, Herb. My turn," Johnny was almost whining.

"Just a minute. I think I see something." It was a ruse to keep the glasses longer.

"What do you see?"

"Something."

"Aw, bull. I'm standing. I'm standing."

"Crimey, Johnny, for Pete's sake. Here." Herbert thrust the binoculars toward the boy.

"What were you looking at?" Johnny asked, his heart thumping now that he had the binoculars.

"The Pirates Caves," Herbert said.

Johnny immediately trained the glasses on the three caves. "I don't see nothing."

"Me neither," Herbert said. "Be sure and look in the trees, too." Sometimes the enemy would put snipers in the trees.

"I am," Johnny said. "Don't see nothing." Then a slight movement. Johnny's heart jumped. It was at the left edge of the glasses. He moved the glasses further left. The Lava Caves. They were two caves, about the same size. He strained to see inside.

"Whatcha see?" Herbert whispered.

"Something—I dunno." He volunteered the glasses to Herbert. "I think the Lava Caves."

Herbert put the glasses on the two caves. Nothing. "Did you see something?"

"I'm not sure. I was . . ."

"Wait. There's Birdy. There he is!" Herbert could hardly contain himself. He handed the binoculars to Johnny.

"I see him." Birdy was at the mouth of the cave, shading his eyes with his right hand, he was gazing toward the Jungle entrance. "I don't see David. Maybe he's someplace else." He handed the glasses over.

"No. There's David, too," Herbert said. "They're both in there."

"What're we going to do?"

"Go around to the left, on top," Herbert said, the consummate general.

They crawled upon the northeast ridge and began circling clockwise toward the Lava Caves. Keeping low to the ground, they would not be seen by the enemy. They had not discussed what they would do once they got to the caves.

☆ ☆ ☆ ☆ ☆

"Where the heck are they?" Birdy asked David. "You think they're not coming?"

"No, they're coming alright. Just keep your eye out," David assured him.

"Maybe we should move some place else." Birdy was getting fidgety.

"No, if we go outside they'll show up the second we do and see us. We got to stay put."

"They're taking too long," Birdy said. "It's hot in here."

David and Birdy felt the thud of footsteps overhead first, and then they heard the yelling. Taken completely by surprise they instinctively retreated further into the cave.

In later years Herbert and Johnny would look back upon this day, asking over and over why they had done what they had done. It certainly was not out of malice. And they had certainly intended no harm. They were just seven-year-old kids, having fun. How were they to know?

In any case, Herbert and Johnny began to jump and dance wildly on the roof of the cave.

"We gotcha! We gotcha!" they screamed with glee.

Besides the fact that the caves had been dug with no reinforcement on the walls or ceilings, it had been raining steadily the two previous days.

Without warning the roof collapsed. At once Hebert was buried up to his waist; Johnny was in just above his knees.

Inside, the cave was instantly filled with thick, soft, damp earth. Everything became immediately black. David's first instinct was to cry out for help, but he dared not for fear his mouth would fill with dirt. He could feel the earth in his eyes and ears, unable to move either his arms or legs. He could manipulate his fingers slightly, with no possibility of extricating himself. Johnny and Herbert would dig them out soon. They needed to hurry because his chest and ribs were beginning to hurt. For some reason, the thought of death never entered his mind. Then, as the darkness began to become even darker, there was a sudden, brilliant light.

David's eyes flew suddenly open. Assaulted by the light he squeezed them shut again. He heard his mother's voice, drenched with tears.

"Oh, David, sweetheart," she said. "We're here. We're right here. You're okay. It's your mom and dad."

"We're right here, son." The mellow voice of his dad said.

Herbert and Lila Baxter had kept a twenty-four hour vigil since the accident at 10:30 a.m. yesterday morning. It was now approaching 11:15 a.m. Sunday morning.

David opened his eyes gingerly. His chest and ribs ached.

"What happened?" he asked, confused. "Where am I?" He could see his folks better now. They were at his left side. At the foot of the bed was a woman he did not know.

"You are in the hospital, sweetheart," his mother said. "This is your nurse, Ms. Hill."

Ms. Hill immediately approached his right side, took his hand and said, "How do you feel, David?"

He looked at her, his mind still foggy. "Okay, I guess."

"Do you hurt anywhere?" she asked gently.

David shrugged. "I dunno—I guess. My sides hurt a little. What happened?"

"You were in an accident yesterday, son," his dad said. "Do you remember anything?"

The nurse said, "In due time, Mr. Baxter. No need to rush."

But the door had been opened and David's mind began to churn. "An accident? Yesterday?" Suddenly the memories flooded in. Herbert and Johnny yelling.

We gotcha! We gotcha!

Instant darkness fell, with the smell of earth, cool and damp. Then there was the increased difficulty in breathing.

Birdy had grabbed him, before the dirt completely enveloped them, by the left wrist, so tightly that it had hurt at first.

"How's Birdy?" he asked fearfully, for he already knew the answer.

"Herbert and Johnny are doing fine," his mother said. "They are out of the hospital already."

David looked at his father. "Is Birdy . . . ?" Birdy's grip on his wrist had gradually relaxed until it was just a soft, feather touch.

His father shook his head, his eyes brimming. "Birdy didn't make it, son. They couldn't get to him in time. I'm so sorry."

Oh, no. Oh, no. David's young mind reeled with the enormity of it. *Birdy. I want to see Birdy. We weren't through with stuff. Birdy wants to be a jumbo jet pilot.*

He suddenly saw Birdy in front of him, arms outstretched, the sound of jet engines roaring from his throat.

The sobs came, hard and uncontrollable.

"Birdy wasn't ready," he cried. "Birdy wasn't ready."

THIRTY-TWO

The Present

"Have this stuff checked for trace evidence," Parella said, handing a manila envelope to Vincent. The entire team had been given a copy of the cryptic message with instructions from Parella to "Share your thoughts on this, no matter how ridiculous you might think it is."

On one sheet a message read:

> *Roses are red*
> *Bruises are blue*
> *Pay close attention*
> *Here follows a clue*

On a 5" x 7" pink sheet of paper was another note:

> *Gemini the younger held her*
> *In the night.*
> *Gemini the elder will lead her*
> *To the light.*
> *Without seeking she will find*
> *Things not meant for those behind.*
> *The galaxy's loss*
> *Will bear Gemini's cross.*

In brilliance so bright
She will join us in light
The elder will know the younger. Again—
Not in seeing or hearing, but in pain.
The finding is not hard,
Search near neighbor's yard.
In supple green grass,
See—fair white-ribboned lass.
Soon, Gemini One

The *white-ribboned* line sent a rush through Parella's body and lifted the hair on the back of his neck.

The envelope had been delivered by ordinary mail, addressed simply to John Parella, Precinct Four, Spring, TX.

"He's sparring with us," Parella said to Vince. He's laughing at us—at how stupid we are." Parella slammed his palm down on his desk. "'Just in case you idiots don't get it,' he says, 'I'm going to highlight the important stuff for you.'" Parella paced the floor of his office. "'And by the way,' he says 'My name is Gemini.'" Running his hand through his hair, Parella continued, "Typical smarter-than-your-average-cop serial killer. It's a game. Catch me if you can."

"Problem is," he continued, his right hand massaging his forehead "this doesn't do a thing for us, except confirm that we have the wrong guy in jail. It won't even get him out. It's not really *proof.* Any sick soul could've sent this, except for the *white ribbon.* Even at that—even with the white ribbon line it's not air-tight; it's not a key to Baxter's cell door."

"You've got to show it to Denise anyway," Vincent said. "You know that."

"Yeah, I do know," sighed Parella. "Maybe since she got hammered so badly on Friday she'll loosen up a little."

"You think?"

"No."

THIRTY-THREE
June 29, 1974

An army gathered in Darrell Phelps's room as he was being prepared for his first look at his refurbished face. Not one there expected it to go very well. Dr. Perkins, of Psychiatry, standing at the bedside to Darrell's left, held the mirror. On Darrell's right stood Nurse Margie Townes. Then there were Doctors Angus McWhorter and Lois Dryden, along with two orderlies the size of pro linebackers. They were there to hold the diminutive seven-year-old down just in case he went berserk and threatened to rampage the hospital. Next to the orderlies stood Marianna Parks, caseworker for Child Protective Services. She would take Darrell under wing as soon as he was released.

Darrell's little heart was thumping inside his chest like an animal trying to escape.

Though the staff had spent many hours of preparation, Darrell had no idea what to expect. Would he look like the person he remembered? Would he look better?

"Now before we take off the wraps, Darrell, I want you to remember what we said," Dr. Perkins began. We have done the best that we can do to repair the left side of your face, okay?"

"Okay," Darrell said. His fear was evident in his voice, and could be clearly seen in his right eye. His breathing was shallow and rapid.

"The left side of your face has been covered with sheep skin. It is soft and smooth, and it will last a long time if you take care of it. Okay?"

"Yes, sir," Darrell said.

"So the sheep skin does not *look* like your skin, Darrell. It's… *different*."

Darrell said nothing. His eye fixed with trust upon Dr. Perkins, making the doctor painfully uneasy. This was, far and away, the most difficult thing that he had ever done, even surpassing the day that he informed his mother that she had been diagnosed with lung cancer.

"So," Dr. Perkins cleared his throat. "You ready, Darrell? Everyone ready?"

The room was silent. No one was actually *ready*.

Finally, in a small voice, Darrell said, "Ready."

"Let's . . . ah . . . do it, then," Dr. Perkins said.

THIRTY-FOUR

June 29, 1881

There were two interrelated births on June 29, 1881. The births were intertwined because Marcus Hiram Waters was involved in both of them.

The first birth, of which Marcus had no knowledge, was that of his son, to be named Joseph Ezekiel Waters.

The second was the birth of the city of Temple, Texas.

On that day baby Joseph had signaled his early arrival while his mother, Trudy Lynne Waters, was hanging clothes on the back yard line at about 9:30 in the morning. Trudy knew immediately what the sharp pain meant. She calmly continued to hang the four remaining items on the line, set the straw clothesbasket on the back porch and went into the house to fetch her older sister, Ora Higgins. Ora was visiting all the way from Giles County, Tennessee, and had made the long journey to the cotton farm in Waco, Texas specifically to help with the impending birth. She planned to stay as long as necessary, which could extend to three or four months.

The birthing was unspectacular, but four hours after it started, when the exhausting event was over both women were reduced to uncontrollable sobs, which then ebbed into hysterical laughter. Ora handed Trudy the clean but bawling infant and collapsed into the small bed beside her, brushing away strands of blond hair from her face.

"Oh-h-h, he's so beautiful!" Trudy exclaimed. Her face, framed by raven-black hair, flushed with excitement, glistened with perspiration. "Have you *ever* seen so lovely a child, O'?" Her deep blue eyes glistened as well.

"Well," Ora laughed, "Considering the stock, how could he not be lovely?"

"I just so wish Marcus could have been here. He will be very disappointed."

"A disappointment which will soon be swallowed up by pride at the joy of being the father of a strong and healthy son," Ora said, tweaking her baby sister on the cheek. "And considering your wee frame, it was all somewhat of a miracle. He's monstrous. And two weeks early at that."

"How much?" Trudy beamed.

"Just a bit over eleven pounds."

"Oh, my," Trudy said. "He's a calf!"

"And what would that make you, my dear?"

Trudy playfully slapped her sister on the arm. "Oh, you," she said. "Sometimes, I swear, you're a caution. I don't see how Mum and Daddy ever got you past thirteen years old."

"I'm blessed," Ora responded. "I have a guardian angel."

"A very busy one, I might expect."

They both laughed. Trudy was filled with joy as she looked down at the contented infant at her breast.

Marcus Wilby Waters had felt a tingle in his spine when he stepped down off the train into the melee of a party that had started the night before. Had he known this would be the day that he would kill a human being for the first time he would have immediately gotten right back on the train.

At twenty-three he was a man filled with dreams for his growing family. He was soon to be a father, and he planned to see to it that his wife and future children fared well. He had decided that continuing solely in the line of cotton farming would not get the job done. He would be a landowner. Real estate was the path to independence.

The farmer in him generated a reflexive look to the sky. Clear blue and not a cloud to be seen, it was a perfect day for an outdoor party. Dressed in brand new Levi-Strauss coveralls and a tan cotton twill shirt, with genuine calf leather travel bag in hand, Marcus was ready to go. The clothes were loose fitting, and belied the wiry strength in the body underneath. Marcus was not a man of quick temper, but neither was he known to back down when confronted. He was quick to defend his own honor and that of his wife, whom he deeply loved and cherished above all things. Seldom a day went by that he did not marvel that she should choose him to be her own. And now she would soon give him a child, a fact that he still found difficult to comprehend.

Marcus' tawny hair blew in the steady breeze as he took in the sights around him. There were two other trains, letting steam, sitting on the tracks. The bulletins which had plastered store windows and walls all over Waco for the past three weeks had said that there would be trains from five cities—Austin, the farthest; Belton, the nearest; Salado, Groesbeck, and Waco. He assumed the remaining two trains would arrive soon.

The bulletins had said

> *Come one, come all! To the largest auction of them all!*
> *Free beer and free BBQ! Free carbonated beverages!*
> *Saturday 29th of June, 1881*
> *The Gulf, Colorado, & Santa Fe railway company will*
> *auction off parcels of land in the heart of Bell County to*

the highest bidders. All transactions will be completed
at the day of auction. Please do not bid without the
wherewithal to complete the transaction.
The railway will refund the price of train tickets to all
buyers of land!
Auction Begins 2 p.m. Promptly

Mr. Jonathan Ewing Moore, also a man of vision, had purchased land near the center of Bell County for just such a time as this. The Santa Fe railroad had approached him a month ago. They needed a community near the central Texas junction to provide services to the railroad and its passengers. Jonathan had sold them 181 acres at $27 per acre. Some in the Santa Fe thought this was an exorbitant price to pay. The property would be parceled out to new residents, and the town would be founded the very day of the auction. It had already been determined that the new community would be named Temple, Texas, after Bernard Temple, the engineer who had laid out the railroad lines.

Oddly, the property on which the infant city of Temple would dwell is divided almost precisely through its center from the southwest to the northeast by the Balcones fault line. Running through Texas west from Del Rio, the Balcones escarpment winds its way through the hill country to San Antonio, then eastward to Austin where it bends northward on up through central Texas to the Red River and Oklahoma. On the eastern side of the fault the land is known as The Blackland Prairie, comprised mainly of Houston Black Clay, a rich, black clayey loam, most suitable for farming—especially cotton farming.

To the west of the fault the soils are mixed, light to dark with shallow, limey sub surfaces, and large areas of stony soils. Such a mixture does well for ranching, supporting tall grasses for cattle grazing and for hardwoods and pines.

Marcus had determined that he would acquire at least one parcel of good farming land to the east. He had $500 in crisp bills in his well-broken-in Justin boots. He did not want the land for himself for farming; he simply felt that this land would appreciate more quickly. He would be able to sell it sooner for a greater profit.

Hundreds of men and women were milling about, with children of every age scurrying everywhere. Many of the youngsters licked on "snowballs," paper cups filled with scooped balls of crushed ice covered with liquid flavors of all colors. These were folks and their children who worked hard every day but Sunday, who suddenly found themselves freed for a time from the cage of necessity. No one would blame them for acting like the puffer-bellies on the tracks, letting off a little steam.

Marcus noticed a handful of Indians sauntering about, mostly Lipan Apaches, he thought, and some Kiowas—it was hard to tell them apart in their white-man's clothes. White immigrant settlers and the decimation of the buffalo herds nearly forty years ago had driven the Indians from their hunting and camping grounds in this area. Now the sons and their sons were beginning to return to a land that the old chiefs had spoken of with reverence and respect. It would be a good way.

Marcus decided to take a stroll. The air was filled with the pungent smell of pecan and mesquite coals. A southerly wind blew thick, white smoke from open bar-b-que pits across the open countryside, obscuring the groves of oak and pecan trees in the short distance. In a line about fifty yards from where the trains had stopped were eight pits, each about six feet long and three feet wide, heaped with glowing coals. Above each pit was a pole that spanned the length of the pit and was nestled in the Y of a pole at either end. Attached securely to the pole above the fire was either a side of beef, two pigs, a row of chickens, or three cabritos, the Mexican name for baby goats.

The meat juices and sauce dripped liberally from the meat onto the burning coals, filling the air with such sweet aromas that the crowd wondered if they could wait for the noon dinner bell. Many had had the foresight to bring a snack of fruit or sandwiches, and could have sold them for a handsome profit had they been of a mind to.

Marcus wandered over to the row of buckboards where the beverages were being handed out. Several buckboards in a row were filled with blocks of ice that cooled kegs of beer and barrels of soft drink.

A short, fat man wearing a black bowler hat cocked to one side greeted him as Marcus arrived to the front of the line.

"Name ya poison," the man said, in a high-pitched voice. Were Marcus' eyes closed he would have thought the voice's origin to be a woman. "Beer or a soft drink?"

"I'll have a soft drink, please."

"What flavor will it be? Strawberry, ginger, lemon or . . . ? "

"I'll try a strawberry."

The little man filled a paper cup with the strawberry drink.

"You want ice in it, or straight?"

"No . . . no ice, just straight please," Marcus said, taking the drink and walking away.

The drink did in fact taste somewhat like strawberry—a bit too sweet for Marcus' taste. It was refreshingly cold however, and bubbly. He finished it in two swallows. Strolling over to a nearby buckboard he saw a tall man dressed in black top hat and tails, standing in the back of a buckboard addressing a collecting crowd of the curious.

The man looked like Honest Abe without a beard. On the side of the buckboard was a colorful sign with a picture of a rearing palomino stallion. Stenciled in black letters over the stallion was the message:

Dr. Stanley Philmore's Bottled Medicine
A Wonderful Pain Destroying Compound

Strongest and Best Known Liniment
For the Complete Cure of All Pain and Lameness
Get Your Free Bottle

The man was holding aloft a bottle of the medicine, speaking persuasively to the gathering.

"Why, ladies and gentlemen, this is the elixir of kings—of heads of state. Rulers of countries all over this world use this wonderful potion.

"Ladies and gentlemen, please, step right up. You do not want to miss a single word of what I am about to say about this astonishing cure. Step up now, and hear for yourself. If you hear your ailment or disease mentioned then you need to purchase your bottles of Dr. Stanley Philmore's Bottled Medicine. Only seventy-five cents a bottle. And today only, ladies and gentlemen, you can buy five bottles and get one bottle free. So make sure that you are within earshot. Listen to what this marvelous liquid cures, and buy your bottles from my colleague just behind me here. Don't be shy—just step on up to my assistant any time you're ready to make a purchase, and he will be glad to assist you. Listen closely to what this balm of Gilead will do.

"It will eradicate abscesses, ague, apoplexy, bad blood, black fever, black pox, black vomit, blood poisoning, brucellosis, bule, cachexcy, cacogastric, cacospysy, caduceus, camp fever, childbed fever, chin cough . . ."

Marcus heard "childbed fever" and immediately thought of Trudy. She would be delivering in a couple of weeks. He should get a bottle—or two bottles—for her—just in case.

" . . . coryza, costiveness, cramp colic . . ."

Colic . . . Marcus knew that all babies came down with colic. Maybe he should buy the five bottles and get one free. If not for now then for later additions to the family.

" . . . cynanche, day fever, debility, delirium tremens, dengue, dentitum, deplumation . . ."

Dentitum—dentitum . . . all babies teethed, so, all babies got dentitum. He would definitely buy five bottles. A line had already formed at the buckboard, and a fifty-cent helper was taking money and handing out bottles as fast as the exchange could be made. And the medicine man had only reached the *Ds*.

Checkered tablecloths covered fifty wooden picnic tables that were set up in the shade of the grove. There were an additional three tables laden with bowls of corn on the cob, pinto beans, potato salad, cole slaw and homemade rolls. Another two tables held plates of pecan, cherry and apple pies; chocolate and lemon meringue pies; bowls of peach cobbler and banana pudding; chocolate cakes, German chocolate cakes, white cakes and yellow cakes. There were sugar cookies, chocolate chip cookies; oatmeal and ginger snap cookies.

Benches were at each table, and Marcus set his piled plate of food and Mason jar of iced sweet tea with lemon on the table at the end of one of them, removed his straw cowboy hat, sat it on the bench to his left and began to eat. Shortly, a gentleman in a dark suit, dark gray Fedora, beneath which grew thick white hair that curled down over his collar, and sporting a white handlebar mustache, sat next to him.

"Mind if I sit here?" the man said, removing his hat.

"Looks like you already are," Marcus smiled.

The man offered his hand and said "Horace Greenway."

"Howdy," Marcus shook the hand, "Marcus—Marcus Waters."

Horace Greenway selected a pork rib and began to strip the tender meat off the bone with his teeth. Rapidly going through several of the ribs, he started a pile of bare bones next to his plate.

"My, my—this is *good*," he said with a mouthful, the bottom edge of his mustache tinged red by the secret sauce.

Taking a swig of tea, Greenway asked, "You here buying?"

"I'm seriously thinking on it, yes sir. And you?" Marcus spread some fresh-churned butter on a roll and ate half of it with one bite.

"Haven't decided. I'm from nearby over at Belton. There is a lot of good-priced land hereabouts, some of which I already own, so I'm thinking I'll hold back a little to see how the bidding's going." Greenway kept his head down toward his plate, scooping in a mouthful of beans. "Where *you* from?"

"Up east of Waco," Marcus said. "I grow a little cotton, got a few head of cattle, a pig or two and some chickens. Not much. What keeps you occupied, Mr. Greenway?"

"I practice law out of my little office in Belton. Somebody is always getting crossways with somebody else and needs a lawyer and judge or jury to help sort it out," Greenway replied. "If you end up down this way, keep me in mind."

They ate in silence for a while. Six others, who apparently knew one another, making no attempt to engage Marcus or Mr. Greenway, had occupied the table.

"Well, I enjoyed your company, Mr. Waters," Greenway said, rising, ignoring the others at the table. "Perhaps I will see you around."

"Yes, good to meet you, Mr. Greenway," Marcus offered his hand with a smile, but he was thinking about the chocolate meringue pie.

THIRTY-FIVE

June 29, 1974

Darrell was trembling like a baby bird that had fallen from its nest as Dr. Perkins began to unwrap the bandages that covered most of his head. Nurse Townes came over and took his right hand in both of hers. Darrell's left hand and forearm were still in a cast after the last of eight surgeries performed by Dr. McWhorter.

"You can do this," Nurse Townes whispered over and over as Dr. Perkins loosed the layers and layers of bandages. He was nearly finished when he quietly looked around the room into the eyes of each one there.

All knew what the look meant. Dr. Perkins had prepped them in a group meeting before going to Darrell's room.

"I have to warn you," he had said, "There can be no gasps or sudden intakes of breath, or fainting on the floor, or turning away of the heads. I want you to be unemotional when the wraps come off. If you don't think that you can do that, then please, don't come in. We're all professional—we need to act like it for Darrell's sake. Any questions?" He was really only admonishing Nurse Townes and the two orderlies, since Drs. McWhorter and Dryden had performed the surgeries that had resulted in what Darrell's current appearance was. They certainly wouldn't gasp or turn their heads, but it was nice of Dr. Perkins to include them in on this meeting.

"How do you think Darrell will react?" Nurse Townes asked.

"I don't really know. I can't imagine being in that boy's place—I can't imagine how *I* would react, really."

"What if he goes kinda coo-coo? What do you want us to do?" one of the orderlies asked.

"I'll let you know what to do. It depends upon the seriousness of his response. I will try to sedate him first if necessary. If that doesn't work we will strap him down. I seriously pray that that won't be necessary because that will add untold time to his emotional recovery. To be strapped down like an animal will only reinforce his feeling that he *is* one. If it does come to having to physically restrain him, just remember that he is a seven-year-old. Don't break a bone, or dislocate something. Okay?"

Both orderlies nodded, trepidation on their faces.

Perkins removed the last layer of wrapping. Drs. McWhorter and Dryden smiled slightly. Nurse Towns smiled her broadest smile. Both orderlies had their best Marine Corps guard-faces on.

"There we are," Dr. Perkins said. "It's off. You ready to take a peek., Darrell?"

"I dunno," he said in a tiny voice. "I reckon." He removed his hand from Nurse Townes' and took the mirror. Slowly he brought it before his face. His first look was one of puzzlement as he tried to adjust the mirror in and out as though he couldn't focus properly. The look changed to horror, and he turned to the two surgeons.

"That's not *my* face," he shouted. "That's *not* my face. Why didn't you do my face? I don't know what that is! It's not me. It's not me." He flung the mirror, the glass crashing into pieces against the wall.

Dr. Perkins nodded to the nurse, and she immediately pushed the plunger on the syringe in the IV.

Darrell continued to rant, but gradually his words began to slur. Finally he laid his head back and closed his eye.

Dr. Lois Dryden was silently weeping.

"This boy's going to need lots of help," Dr. Perkins said, running his hands through his hair.

THIRTY-SIX

June 29, 1881

The auction began precisely at 2:00 p.m. There were approximately 500 prospects in attendance, for which the Santa Fe Company was extremely grateful, since they had predicted an attendance of 300.

A stage had been constructed in the shade of the grove, where some folks had brought in folding canvas and wooden chairs. Others spread blankets in the lush grass. Marcus got as close to the front as he could and sat on the ground. He could feel the excitement building.

A dignified gentleman dressed in a white Havana suit with a red carnation in the lapel, sporting a straw Panama hat, and a gigantic smile, stepped to the podium with the aid of a black ivory cane with golden handle. He waited a few seconds for the buzz in the group to quiet down, and then began.

"Good afternoon, ladies and gentlemen." The man had a baritone voice that carried like an opera singer's. "Can *anyone* hear me? I'll try once more. Good afternoon, ladies and gentlemen."

This time there was a rousing "Good afternoon!"

"Ah—much better," he laughed, much at ease with himself and the audience. "Can everyone hear me in the back there? Raise your hands back there if you can understand me."

Several hands were raised, and there were a number of "Yeahs" and "We can hear you."

"Good. Okay, well, let's begin then. My name is Harold Beckett, Vice-president of Operations for the railroad. On behalf of our great railroad company, I want to welcome you all—or should I say 'Ya'll'? We hope that you enjoy yourselves today, whether or not you lay any money down. I expect that you have some idea why we are here, but perhaps not the reason behind the why. The reason that Santa Fe is doing this is, very simply, we need you. We need your partnership in our endeavor. We have the five lines coming into this area right here where we are. This is what we call a major junction. At a major junction a railroad needs more than trains and tracks. It needs people—that's you folks—and it needs service capability. We need to be able to service the arriving trains with water for the steam engines, coal re-supply, parts for the trains, and mechanics to replace those parts. We need to service the train personnel. They need food, drink, recreation, places to shop, places to sleep, to recuperate for a day or two. And we need to service the passengers. Depending on their schedules they may have time to do some local shopping, or to grab a meal at a nearby café or restaurant. As a minimum they will have an opportunity to stretch their legs."

Beckett paused to take a sip of water from a cup. Marcus' heart was beating so hard he was sure it was visible through his coveralls. He needed no more sales pitch; he was ready to buy some land.

"Any questions to this point?" Beckett looked about the crowd. "No? Okay, so what we are about to offer is a prospect for both yourselves and the railroad. You folks find yourselves with a golden opportunity here. You will be afforded the chance to bid for land parcels of various sizes. Today we are limiting the number of parcels that any one person or partnership or corporation can acquire." Beckett turned to someone in back of him on the podium for a brief interchange.

"We are limiting the number of parcels today to three per individual," he said. "Eventually the property that you are acquiring will be zoned—some of it residential, and other areas will be zoned commercial. As a rule, the properties nearest the tracks will be commercial properties. Are there any questions to this point?"

A gentleman near the middle of the group raised his hand. Mr. Beckett pointed to him and said, "Would you mind standing, sir, and speak loud enough for all to hear?"

"Alright," the man said, standing. "What if I buy a parcel, and it's residential, and later on decide I want commercial. Can I swap with the railroad?"

"Good question," Beckett said. "Let me make this very clear to everyone before anybody lays down their hard earned cash. Once you have purchased a parcel and signed on the dotted line, you are a landowner. You have all the rights of a landowner, within the law. The railroad will be out of the picture at that point. You can put your property up for sale, you can exchange it with someone else, and you can just sit on it. It's totally up to you, okay? Make sense?"

There were several nods and mumbles of assent in the crowd. So far it was going very well.

Marcus just wished it would go faster. He was ready to buy some land.

There were several vendors walking through the crowd, selling boxes of taffy candy with prizes inside, popcorn and lemonade. Marcus bought a cup of iced lemonade for five cents. He was still stuffed from lunch.

After about thirty more minutes Beckett completed his instructions to the audience, fielded a few more questions, and finally brought the auctioneer to the podium.

"It is my pleasure, ladies and gentlemen, to bring to the podium the man that you have been waiting for. He is renowned for his cattle-auctioneering prowess throughout Texas; allow me to introduce to you, from the Tall Mountain Auction Company in Ft. Worth, Texas, please welcome Sir Stanley Christie." Beckett began to clap and the crowd quickly followed, standing to their feet, whistling, shouting and clapping.

Sir Stanley approached the stand with both hands in the air, flashing bright, large teeth. He exuded a powerful presence, dressed in cowboy regalia, complete with ten-gallon hat, a red shirt with buckskin vest, leather chaps and pointed boots. He sported a red mustache and beard, with red hair flowing to his shoulders, reminiscent of Wild Bill Hickok.

"Good afternoon," Sir Stanley shouted. "How're ya'll doing? You ready to get going?"

The shouting and whistling increased in volume.

"Alright then," he continued. "Here's how it works. See these two gentlemen down here in front of me with the bowler hats on? They're my helpers, my spotters. They'll point out bidders to me that I might miss. Now the important point—you will bid by giving me a sign, or giving a spotter a sign if you can't catch my eye. So, raise your hand, give me a nod. If you are the high bidder you have bought yourself some property. We also have folks who will come out into the audience to write down all the necessary information. They will then bring the information back upstage where they will give it to the county clerk, Miss Tanner or one of her assistants, who will record everything in the county record books."

Sir Stanley paused and looked around. "Ya'll are staring at me like a calf looking at a new gate." The crowd laughed. "Am I making any sense?"

"Yeah—keep on going," someone shouted.

"Please don't bid if you don't have the cash to back it up, alright? So, let's get started. We are going to start with parcel number one and go right on through to parcel number 100. The smallest acreage in any parcel will be two and a half acres. The largest will be five acres." Sir Stanley produced his pocket watch and flipped it open.

"It is 2:30. My guess is that we will finish up about 10:30 or 11:00 tonight. Alright with ya'll?"

Again, everyone shouted in assent.

A large white board was produced with the layout of the parcels outlined on it. The junction of the railroad tracks was near the center. Sir Stanley took a pointer stick and indicated land parcel number one, located in the northeast corner of the properties. Marcus' heart sank a little. If the auctioning continued on the eastern side it would be several hours before he would bid on anything.

"All right, then," Sir Stanley stroked his mustache. "Let's get rolling. We will be bidding dollars per acre. If you bid one hundred dollars for this two and a half acres you will be paying two hundred and fifty dollars. Okay? If you can't cipher don't bid. I have parcel number one, two and a half acres. What am I bid for it? Who'll gimme a hundred? Do I see a hundred? Can I see seventy-five? Somebody gimme seventy-five."

Finally, Sir Stanley said, "What will you give me for it?"

Somebody in the audience shouted "Thirty-five!"

Sir Stanley backed by years of experience jumped on the bid like a duck on a June bug. He knew, both, that it was an icebreaker, and that he could boost it.

"Thank you, sir. I have thirty-five who'll gimme forty? Thirty-five, who'll go forty? I have forty right over here—can I see fifty? Yes, fifty right here—somebody give me sixty. Can I see sixty? Fifty-five? Somebody give me fifty-five for this fine parcel. No? Alright—going once, twice, going three times—parcel number one is sold to this gentlemen to my right for fifty an acre."

The crowd shouted and clapped at the first sale.

The second parcel went for forty-five dollars an acre, the third, which was three and a half acres, and went for fifty-five dollars per acre. Things were going very smoothly when suddenly there was a commotion over to Marcus' right.

"May I inquire as to what is happening over there, gentlemen?"

One of the spotters said, "This Comanche placed the winning bid for parcel number eight and ain't got enough money to pay for it. He wants it for half what he bid for it."

The Comanche, black hair flowing half way down his back, stood and raised a fist full of money. "I am called Pocowatchit," he shouted. "Of the Penatekas. I will buy this land. "

"Not for half what you bid for it, you ain't. You have to pay what you bid, Mr. Poco whatever," Sir Stanley shouted. The Indian had not understood that he must multiply what he bid by the number of acres.

"Folks," Sir Stanley continued, "We have lots of dirt to plow, and we can't afford these kinds of interruptions. This happens again, *by anybody,* and we will escort the culprit off the premises. We will re-auction parcel number eight soon's we've completed number eleven. Now, where were we?"

The auction soon became routine, and after awhile longer a little dull. Folks who had acquired property and those who had decided they would not participate were drifting off. Sir Stanley promptly addressed the issue.

"Folks, let me remind you, there's plenty more to happen. Once we finish auctioning we are going to have a special ceremony. A brand new town will be birthed here today. You will be a part of it—a part of the history of this great land. If you feel that your business is finished for the day there's still a wagonload of food over at the tables; they's lots of beer and soft drinks. You can catch a buggy over to Belton or down to Salado—maybe a thirty-minute's ride. Any case, they leave every hour straight up. Or, you can bed down for a nap on your train, or under a tree if you like. Point is, it ain't over yet. We'll be finishing our business about 10:00 or so." For farmers and ranchers who didn't stay up much past sundown this was an adventure.

Sir Stanley pointed to the board with his stick. "Parcel thirty-two. Four acres."

Marcus had determined from the board that there were forty-two parcels on the east side of the tracks and fifty-eight on the west. He would have plenty of time for a break. He stood, stretched and headed for the outhouse latrines that had been placed upwind to the northwest side of the grove. He thought of Trudy as he walked—dark hair, bright, blue eyes and the baby rolling and kicking in her belly. He missed her dearly.

Just as Marcus was opening the latrine door he heard the snap of a twig to his left rear. He turned to see what had made the noise, and in turning saved his own life. Instead of entering his back between the shoulder blades, most likely puncturing his heart, the knife sliced between his left arm and armpit with a searing hot flash of pain. He continued to turn to see the Comanche, preparing to strike again. Marcus' instant instinct was to fling the door open with his right hand with all the strength he could muster. The door caught the Indian by surprise, striking the knife first where it stuck into the wooden door, yanking it from his hand. In the same movement Marcus stomped the Indian's left foot, clad in soft moccasin, with the hard heel of his Justin boot. Slamming the door shut again, Marcus grabbed the knife as it went by, and without a single thought thrust it into his attacker's neck.

Pocowatchit of the Penatekas stood there with a bewildered look on his face, then, oddly, pulled the knife from his throat, from which a gout of blood sprayed in a long arc, then he dropped like a sack of flour. Marcus fell backwards against the latrine, feeling sick and dizzy.

"What in heaven's name . . . ?" Attorney Horace Greenway said, exiting the latrine next door and hitching up his pants. He quickly surveyed the spreading puddle of blood beneath the Indian, and Marcus' bloody armpit, and said, "We need to find you a doctor right now. Let's go."

Marcus placed his right fist in his left armpit and clamped down tightly to staunch the flow of blood, which had soaked the left side of his cotton twill shirt and the left front of his coverall bib. He struggled to remain conscious as Greenway helped him toward the picnic tables, where he was laid down.

Gathering quickly, a crowd circled the table to see for themselves firsthand what had rapidly spread by word of mouth. In just moments, faster than the wind strips a dandelion, there were a number of disparate stories of what had happened, and how that young farm boy had killed that uppity Comanche in self-defense. The savage was no doubt trying to hijack the youngster, but obviously done picked on the wrong subject this time. Someone brought a quilt and laid it over Marcus, who had begun to shiver. The donor cared not that the quilt might come back with bloodstains on it—in fact that might even be desirable. *This is the quilt that covered that boy who killed the savage on the day that Temple was founded. Being a smaller man than the Indian, the boy struggled desperately for forty-five minutes before finally getting the upper hand and dispatching the redskin with his own knife. Why, it's evident the lad almost expired in the ruckus, having lost copious amounts of blood, much of it you can see with your own eyes right here on this quilt that my grandmamma made.*

A doctor was soon found; he set his black bag on the table, gave Marcus some bitter tasting liquid, stitched and taped him up, and told him to keep an eye on the wound for infection. The doctor was Arthur Carroll Scott; born near Gainesville, Texas, recently educated in Bellevue Medical Hospital in New York. He and his partner Dr. Raleigh R. White would, in later years, found the prominent Scott and White Hospital, in which Marcus' great-great-grandson Darrell would one day be a patient.

Marcus had become an instant celebrity in the crowd and would become the subject for various future legends; first because no one cared for Comanches much, even the few other Indians in the throng; and second, it was a good killing. It would prove to be first of many in this area, and the new little town of Temple would soon acquire a reputation for being a rough and tumble community. In a brief span the town gained the nickname of Tangle Foot for its calamitous activities. In turn this proved to be a draw for many a young man looking for adventure, and whose mother's had warned them, "Stay away from Temple."

In spite of his injuries Marcus purchased three parcels that day, two adjacent and one near the two. His notoriety proved to be an asset in his purchases because nobody wanted to bid against him. He bought one three acre parcel for thirty-five dollars an acre, a four and a half acre parcel for thirty-two dollars, and a five acre parcel for thirty dollars. There had been a great cheer each time he had won the bid. After it was said and done he had $101 in paper money remaining. He used four dollars of it to buy a hand made cradle from down in Salado. He was eager to get home and tell Trudy everything and show her the cradle.

What he would never tell Trudy, or anyone else, was what had happened to him when he had killed the Indian. It was something he could not put words to even if he did want to tell some one. He dreamed of the event often, mostly late at night, when he would awaken with the sweats. Even in the daytime, while plowing or slopping the pigs, he thought of the thrill of it—seeing the Comanche's eyes, life slipping away—and he would catch himself. Guilt would immediately flood in.

But the guilt did not do away with the feeling. It had a life of its own and would come when unbeckoned and linger when reprimanded.

On occasion, during moments of brutally honest personal vulnerability, he admitted to himself that the act charged him, electrified his spirit as nothing else. At other times he caught himself feeling as though it were something that he wanted to do again if he could. Invariably he would catch himself, and do something like pound himself forcefully in the chest with a closed fist.

Get a hold of yourself, Marcus. But the cycle never stopped. Finally, needing the thrill more than he needed anything else, he killed again. He could not stop himself. The second victim, he told himself, would not be missed. He had cut the throat of a whore one moonless night in a back alley in downtown Belton.

Marcus' feelings of guilt were minimal. He was not "a religious man." He thought little about God, believing that God thought little of him as long as he minded his own business and stayed out of the way. So, Marcus knew nothing of supernatural things, and therefore had no basis by which to understand this thing that grasped his mind like a giant claw, and electrified his spirit in a way that nothing else came close to. No one ever suspected his dark secret, and before breathing his last, a multimillionaire on his deathbed near Waco, Marcus had killed seven humans. Only the first was justified; the rest were a vain attempt to satiate the unbearable hunger that only grew with each killing.

So, not being acquainted with things supernatural, Marcus had no idea that he could have stopped his mania in its tracks. Unknowingly, he would pass it on to his son, Joseph Waters, who in turn would pass it to his son Hiram Waters who would then send it down through Jolene Waters, who died in prison while giving birth—but not without first passing it to her sons, Darrell and David.

THIRTY-SEVEN

Present Day

Denise Nichols answered her cell phone on the first ring.

"Denise Nichols."

"Denise, hi. This is Palmer."

"Why am I not surprised?"

Palmer did not beat around the bush. "I am assuming that Detective Parella has shared the interesting little missive that he received today?"

"My, that's a big word for a Dallas boy," Denise said. She was obviously still stinging from her "whupping"—as some had called it—in court.

"I'm a Plano boy—big difference—and it means letter."

"*I know* what it means, Plano Boy. Just didn't know if you did. And yes, of course, Parella has shared the *missive* with me. You know he doesn't let any grass grow under *his* feet."

"Well? What's your response? What do you think?"

"Frankly, I don't think it means much of anything yea or nay, Palmer. Anybody could've written the thing."

"Oh, come on, Denise. Good grief," Palmer exclaimed, exasperated but not surprised by her hardheaded response. "No body knew about the white ribbon except the perp and the police. You know that."

"No, I don't *know* that Palmer. There could've been a leak. There could be any number of explanations. Besides, there's . . ."

"There's the fingerprint."

The phone was quiet for several seconds.

"What?"

"A fingerprint—Identical to the others—smack dab in the middle of the note." Palmer waited for the explosion. Finally it came.

"Then why in heaven's name was I not notified? I can have you up for withholding—for not following proper discovery . . ." her voice was gaining volume with each word.

"We just got it, Denise. I'm telling you as soon as I found out. Call it 'stupid'—call it whatever you want to call it, but the investigators were so into the note, especially the white ribbon part, they just didn't dust for prints until later, okay?

There was silence on the line for several seconds.

"The same fingerprint," Denise said. It was not really a question.

"The same."

"It could've been prepared beforehand. An accomplice could have delivered it."

"Yeah, and I flapped my arms and flew to work this morning to avoid traffic."

Exhaling a long deep breath, Denise asked, "What do you want?"

Palmer could sense Denise's shoulders drop over the phone.

"You know what I want, Denise. I want David at the dinner table with his wife and daughter. I want a clear public statement from you that he is exonerated, and that he is no longer a person of interest."

"No way, Palmer. He *is* a person of interest." Denise's jaw was set.

"I want him whole, Denise. This has damaged his name, his reputation and his business."

"I will let him go, Palmer. He is free. I will make a statement that we are dropping all charges, okay?"

"Okay," Palmer's heart was racing. He couldn't wait to tell David. "Just don't *say* that he's a person of interest, even though he is."

"I can live with that." Inexplicably, Denise was feeling lighter. "And Palmer?"

"Yes?"

"You did a great job in court."

THIRTY-EIGHT

July 4, 1974

It was no surprise to anyone that Marianna Parks had chosen social work as her career—indeed, her life. Her uncle Michael had first spoken it when Marianna was three after she had applied the last in a box of fifteen band-aids to her dolly.

"This girl's going to be a nurse," he guffawed from behind a cloud of cigar smoke during their weekly Friday night Spades game. It was Mitchell and Joyce Parks' night to host Michael and Peggy Parks for their regular game.

"Or a social worker—the way she found someone to adopt all them homeless kittens," Michael concluded.

"She certainly has a big heart of compassion for such a little girl," Joyce smiled.

Someone had left a cardboard box of six kittens on their front porch on Fenno Street in Quincy, Massachusetts. Marianna had been instrumental in finding homes for each of the fortunate orphans. Two had been given away door to door in response to Marianna's plea, "These kitties don't have a mommy. Will you be their mommy? Please?"

Marianna and her mother had taken the remaining four kittens to the A&P supermarket. Mrs. Parks had asked the store manager if they could set the kittens near the doorway so that patrons going in and out could see them, and he had said okay. Joyce had put pink ribbons around the kittens' necks and matching ribbons in Marianna's dark hair. They had found homes for each kitten in less than thirty minutes.

Marianna left Quincy for the University of Texas in Austin in 1966 where she obtained her Bachelor of Arts degree in Social Work in 1970 and her Masters in Psychology in 1972.

When arriving in the spring of '66 Marianna found Austin to be like a foreign country. The food, the geography, and the people, the way they dressed and spoke (she could hardly understand the Texas drawl), it was every bit foreign to her.

She had the most trouble adjusting to the menu. There was bar-b-que, chicken fried steak, and the spicy Mexican food. Tex-Mex it was called locally. She missed her lobster and clam rolls, and baked beans with franks each Friday night. The only thing that might be close to her accustomed fare was pizza. Even that was not done right in Texas, but it was the easiest to adjust to. So she ate lots of pizza and salads.

Already diminutive at 5'1" and 112 pounds when she arrived; she lost eight pounds in the first month.

But she was not deterred by these changes in her life. She was driven, knowing without a doubt that she was on the right path. In her heart of hearts her desire was to help wounded and damaged children. She had given herself to that end.

And she had never seen any child as damaged as Darrell. No matter what, she would help bring healing into the boy's life.

Marianna had introduced Darrell to his first foster parents, Mark and Tina Williams, just the day before. They had invited Marianna to a July 4th party at their home to celebrate with them their newly formed family.

Marianna could smell burgers cooking on the grill as she approached the Williams' home on Berrywood Lane, just north of Austin's city limits. She was a little early, just a little before 4:30.

The home was a snug bricked one-story, tastefully landscaped with purple sage and clumps of marigolds, with cedar trees on either side shading the roof. Across the street were undeveloped woods, filled with Cedar trees and scrub Oak. It was a relatively mild mid-summer day in the low eighties. Overhead was a cloudless sky.

Tina answered the doorbell with a bright smile. She opened the door wide.

"Come in. Come on in," she beamed, standing aside so Marianna could enter.

Seeing Tina, Marianna felt a little overdressed. Tina wore khaki shorts and a white sleeveless blouse. Her short blond hair was loose and unfettered. Marianna wore a yellow flowered skirt, light blue short-sleeved blouse, with her dark hair in a tight bun. She wore tan pumps while Tina sported shower clogs. Marianna had not yet acclimated to the casualness of Austin. It was sort of like the laid back atmosphere of the oceanside towns in Massachusetts.

"Mark and Darrell are out back cooking burgers. Would you like something to drink—tea or coke?"

"I'd like some tea please."

"Okay—sweet or non sweet?"

"Sweet, please. Not much ice."

"Okay. Come on back, we can see the boys through the window."

Marianna had been in the Williams' home several times previously when she was evaluating prospective fosters and had been instantly impressed. The décor was bright and lively, but not gaudy. She would have to call it eclectic, with some antique, some traditional and some western pieces. There was art on all the walls, some original, some reproduced. There was the warmth of plants, some real, some artificial. There were personal touches everywhere in the accessories. The décor had been instrumental in Marianna's decision.

Marianna sipped her tea and sat at the breakfast table so that she could see out back.

The yard sloped away from the house, cedars on both sides. A covered outdoor "kitchen" was at the right, with a flagstone walkway leading to it. The St. Augustine grass was a lush green. Plumes of smoke rose from the cooker.

"The boys" were standing with their backs to the house. They were looking at the cooker, Mark's right hand on Darrell's shoulder; Darrell's hands hanging loosely to his side.

"How was his first day?" Marianna asked.

Tina shrugged slightly. "There's not much to say either way. We all know that it's going to take some time. Darrell is pretty much in a shell. Sometimes he will give a word or two response to a question or comment; sometimes he just gives you a blank stare."

Marianna nodded and said, "We're praying for a miracle."

"It was good timing on your part, to put Darrell in our home yesterday. Mark has a long four-day weekend off, so all of us will get to spend a good bit of time together."

The back door opened and closed and the aroma of cooked beef filled the air. Mark entered with a tray of cooked patties. Darrell carried the cooking utensils.

"Hi, Mark. Hi, Darrell. How are you?" Marianna smiled at Darrell who looked straight at her with his good eye.

"Have you been cooking?"

Darrell turned and put the fork and tongs in the kitchen sink.

"Would you guys like a drink?" Tina asked.

"You know what?" Mark said, "I forgot my coke out by the cooker. Would you go get it for me, please, Darrell?"

Darrell left the room. All eyes were on him as he walked toward the still smoking cooker.

"You guys have a formidable task ahead of you," Marianna said. "I can't imagine anything more horrible than what Darrell has to deal with."

"Well, Tina and I have both eyes open," Mark reached across the table and took his wife's hand. "We believe that Darrell wants what everyone else does, love and acceptance. We are committed to giving that to him."

"Some have more difficulty receiving than others," Marianna said. "They believe themselves unworthy to receive anything good. It will take a lot of good to balance out all the bad in Darrell's life." Marianna looked out the window. She could no longer see Darrell.

"As you know," Tina said, "we have a lot of support."

"I know, you have a great network through your church, and I want you guys to know that I really appreciate you, and what you are doing. I believe that Darrell will appreciate it as well."

She looked out into the yard again. "Where did Darrell *go*?"

"Ah, he's just goofing off," Mark said. "Let's give him a little space."

They talked for perhaps five more minutes. Marianna could feel the tension mounting in her stomach.

Finally, Tina said, "Honey . . . ?"

Mark glanced out of the window again. "I'll go get him. He just got preoccupied, I'm sure."

Marianna sipped her tea. It had a little more ice in it than she cared for.

Mark came in, half running, heading for the door to the garage.

"He's not back there," he said breathlessly, as he hurried through the kitchen.

"What?" Tina said. "What? But where . . . ?"

Mark popped back in from the garage. "His bike's gone," he said, his hands hanging to his side. They had bought Darrell a nifty yellow Schwinn DeLuxe Stingray with the high handlebars as a welcome home present. It was the one and only time they had seen a smile from him, however brief.

"What should we do?" Tina asked in a shrill voice, her eyes wide.

"Let's stay calm," Marianna said, her own voice was a higher pitch than normal. "How long has he been outside?"

Mark shrugged, "Maybe ten, twelve minutes. He must be close

by somewhere. I'll get the truck."

Mark backed the green '71 Chevy pickup into the driveway.

"Get in," he said, "Quick."

The women clambered in, and Mark backed out of the drive-way. They slowly cruised up and down Berrywood, looking for the yellow bicycle; looking between houses. They drove over to North Oaks Drive and cruised it; then over to Oak Trail, then to Oak Haven.

At first Mark was confident they would find Darrell. He couldn't believe that Darrell really wanted to hide from them.

"I can't believe it," Mark said, stopping the truck, his hands draped over the steering wheel. "What now?"

"Go back to the house," Marianna said. "I'll call the police."

THIRTY-NINE

July 4, 1974

The fourth of July was not the same without Birdy. Nothing was.

It had been less than a month since the accident, and David often forgot, thinking he would see his friend walking down the street toward his house.

David and his dad were on the patio out back, cooking a brisket on the grill. They had started at 9 a.m. that morning. It was now 3:30.

Mr. Baxter raised the lid of the cooker, and peeled back the aluminum foil covering the pan.

Smoke, steam and a mélange of delicious aromas swelled out of the pan. Mr. Baxter cut a slice off the top of the brisket.

"Here, try this." He handed the sliver to David.

The meat was deliciously sweet, permeated with the Baxter secret sauce.

"Mmmm," David said, "Really good."

"Is it ready, you think?"

"Yes sir," David said. "I think it's done."

"Okay, then. I'll put it on the platter. Go tell your mom."

David ran into the kitchen where Mrs. Baxter was taking the bowl of baked beans out of the oven. The potato salad and cole slaw were already on the table.

"Mom, five minute warning."

"I'm ready," she smiled. "Are you hungry?"

"Yes ma'am. I am."

"Good. Put some ice in some glasses, would you, please?"

"Sure."

David ate, even though he didn't have much of an appetite.

Were Birdy still here they would be at one or the other's house. They would gorge themselves on brisket, ribs and sausage. Then they would go to Hobo Jungle and shoot off fireworks. There would be bottle rockets, canon balls, black cats and smoke bombs.

But Birdy was not still here, and it was almost beyond comprehension.

The funeral was less than a month ago. More than 200 were in attendance. David had not remembered much of the service, his mind fogged by the heavy weight of sorrow, but the Spirit of God was there, and one thing that the minister said stuck in David's mind.

The pastor had read from the book of Job. "I know that my Redeemer liveth… and though after my skin worms destroy this body, yet in my flesh shall I see God."

David couldn't let settle the thought of worms eating Birdy. But the idea grabbed him that even though our body might be destroyed, we can still see God in our flesh. It had the ring of truth to it, and it settled like a seed in his spirit.

He had taken Birdy's wallet sized photo and written the verse on the back.

Both he and Birdy would see God.

And he *would* see Birdy again.

FOURTY

The Present

Lillian and Meredith Baxter waited outside with eager anticipation for the door to the Harris County Spring Precinct Four Holding Station to open. Reporters, videographers and photographers were everywhere. Police surrounded Lillian and Meredith to keep them from getting mauled. It didn't stop the cameras and microphones from being poked through the barrier, nor the constant questions.

"Meredith, how do you feel?"

"Mrs. Baxter, it looked pretty desperate for awhile there. Did you ever lose hope?"

"My hope is in Jesus Christ," Lillian responded. "He cannot fail."

"Lillian, what are your and your husband's plans?"

"Meredith, what is your life like at school now?"

"Mrs. Baxter, this must've been a strain on your family. How do you plan to recuperate?"

Then the doors were opened. The cameras and reporters surged in that direction.

David Baxter exited the door with Palmer Hutchins close at his elbow. David seemed rested and relaxed and looked like he was dressed for a round of golf. He was wearing a maroon polo shirt with khaki trousers. He was also wearing a giant smile.

Palmer on the other hand was dressed to the nines in a lightweight dark gray Armani three-button suit, Versace plum striped floral silk tie, white pinstriped pointed collar Balenciaga shirt, and black leather buckle shoes by Prada. The whole ensemble cost almost $2000.

"You look like you're dressed for court," David had said. "The Supreme Court."

"You know the old saying," Palmer replied.

"You mean, 'Clothes make the man?'"

"No, I mean, 'If you've got it, flaunt it.'"

"Or you might say, 'Conspicuous competitiveness confiscates.'"

High-fiving each other, they headed for the door to a free and normal life.

David immediately spotted Lillian and Meredith and, with Palmer's assistance, began to wind his way toward them. The police helped.

When David was just a matter of feet from his wife and daughter a reporter thrust his microphone in David's face.

"Do you have any idea who the real culprit is? Who is the real child-killer?" he asked, his face in David's, looking him straight in the eye.

David met the stare directly for a long three seconds, then said, "No, of course not."

A policeman forced the reporter to the side. David reached out toward Lillian and drew her to him, passionately embracing and kissing her, not caring what anyone photographed or thought. Meredith tried to embrace them both, laughing ecstatically. Palmer found himself weeping for joy.

Thank you, Lord, he thought over and over. *Thank you, Lord.*

Ah, such a sweet reunion, Darrell thought, looking on nearby. *Such blissful joy, David. Too bad, so sad. So sad, my lad. The latter grief must needs be worse than the first.*

But none of your pain, little brother, will be close to the pain that I have known.

But that won't keep us from trying, will it?

FOURTY-ONE

July 7, 1974

Darrell had grabbed his new bike and hidden in the thick woods across the street from the Williams. As soon as he had seen them drive off in the pickup to look for him he scrambled up and headed toward Interstate 35, two blocks west. He didn't know his way around, so on a whim he elected to turn south, staying on the service road. Less than two miles later he arrived at the intersection of IH35 and Highway 183. On the northeast corner of the intersection was the *Tres Hermanos* Mexican restaurant. On the northwest corner was a small strip mall with several specialty stores. At the southwest was a Waffle House Diner. What had caught his eye was the large Shell truck stop at the southeast corner of the intersection. It appeared to be very busy. Waiting for a clearing in the heavy highway traffic, he had pushed his bike across the four lanes and went immediately to the five dumpsters behind the truck stop. It had been broad daylight still. He knew that he would attract attention if he were seen. Because of his grotesque face he would be easily remembered.

The dumpsters had been overflowing with plastic garbage bags. He leaned his bike against one of them and piled several bags on it to hide it. He hadn't ridden it since.

It had been three days since Darrell had taken up residence by the dumpsters. He had been lifting candy, cookies and sandwiches from the truck stop convenience store. He would simply put a candy bar, cookies or sandwich in each pants pocket; or a can of something to drink in one pocket, and walk out the door.

He sat on a bag of trash in the shade of a dumpster, eating a Baby Ruth and sipping a can of Coke. He had found a June issue of National Geographic. Since he couldn't read very well he just looked at the pictures. There were colorful photographs of Nevada and Yosemite Park, a story about oil exploration, and some pictures of England.

The magazine reminded him of his mother. She subscribed to it and used to read articles about colorful faraway places to him as far back as he could remember.

Invariably he would fall asleep while she was reading.

Immediately the memory brought to his young mind the scent of her body and its comfortable softness. Tears began to flow out of his right eye. He missed his mother terribly. But she would not let him grow up, and that was why she was not here anymore. She wouldn't let him grow up. He could do lots of grownup things, and she wouldn't let him do them. It was her fault that she was not here because she would not let him grow up.

He could tell that the Williams were not going to let him grow up either. That's why he left. They had too many rules. He had been there only one day and already they had begun. They told him that he would be expected to help around the house, that he would have chores like doing dishes, and helping with the laundry, or taking out the trash. His mom never told him to do any of that stuff. So he left.

At the early age of seven years and four months, Darrell Phelps became entirely convinced that he was in need of no one. He would do perfectly well all alone in this world.

His determination of self-sufficiency was cemented on his outing just prior to his release from the hospital.

Two days before he was to be released from Scott and White Hospital in Temple, Nurse Margie Townes and Marianna Parks drove him to Austin.

It was a clear, bright morning for the drive down, not much traffic. Darrell looked out the window at the countryside, the cotton fields, the cows on the dairy farms, the sparse oak trees, a buzzard gliding lazily in circles overhead.

"Are you happy to be out of the hospital, Darrell?" Nurse Townes asked from the front seat.

The question stunned him as if he had been struck by lightening.

Are you happy, Sugar?

Are you happy . . .

His mother had asked him that question while they were driving home from the movie.

Are you happy, Sugar?

Are you . . . ?

And then she had died.

He would never be happy again.

Darrell began to cry uncontrollably.

It had taken thirty minutes to calm Darrell down. Pulling over and stopping at a roadside gas station, Margie and Marianna tried to persuade the boy to talk to them, tried to encourage him to share what had set him off

But he would not.

"Well, then," Marianna said, looking at Margie. "Shall we continue?"

"You bet," Margie said. "Let's go have some fun at the mall. Okay, Darrell?"

"Sure," Darrell sniffled.

On the way Margie began to bounce up and down in her seat.

"Oh, look, look," she cried. "It's a Waffle House! I love Waffle House. Let's stop for breakfast."

It began immediately as soon as they walked into the crowded diner. The hubbub of conversation, and the clicking of utensils on plates slowly ebbed to a painful silence as the waitresses and patrons alike stopped in mid-sentence and mid-action to look at Darrell and his peculiar face.

"Mommy, look," said one little girl, loud enough for everyone in the small diner to hear. "Is he a monster?"

"No, honey. Shhh."

"Bad idea," Margie said. "Maybe we should go."

"No," Mariana said in a whisper. "No, we must stay."

They sat in the only booth available, one next to the counter.

It was an inordinate amount of time before one of the waitresses approached them, an older woman. They had seen her and a younger waitress speaking animatedly at the other end of the counter, each of them shaking their heads vigorously, with pieces of the conversation drifting their way.

" . . . I can't . . . too scary . . . you're older . . ."

" . . . to do with it? . . . just go . . ."

Finally, they broke off the conversation.

"What will you have to drink?" the older waitress said.

"Coffee," Margie said.

"Coffee as well," Marianna said. "What would you like to drink, Darrell?"

Darrell said nothing, but sat with his head down, staring at his menu. He kept his left two-fingered claw-like hand in his lap, under the table.

"Does he talk?" the waitress asked.

"Yes, he *talks*," Margie said with crisp shortness. "He'll have a chocolate milk."

"Coffee," Darrell said.

"I don't think . . ." Margie began, but Marianna quickly raised a hand.

"Three coffees," she said to the waitress.

Margie wanted to choke the woman, and scream to everyone in the restaurant. *There is a little boy in there—he has feelings, you idiots!*

The tension remained in the diner throughout their breakfast. Darrell ate little of his pecan waffle. He drank all of his coffee, plus a second cup. He was growing up.

The stares and whispers had not been lost to Darrell. They were like needles in his heart.

They went to Highland Mall, and it was the same there. Children stared unabashedly. Some pointed their little fingers. Some adults averted their eyes. Some looked and could not conceal the horror on their faces.

Darrell wanted to ask them, *How would you like it if the left side of your face got smashed off? How would you like that? How would you like it if you only just had one eye?*

Thus started the wall that Darrell began to construct, founded upon anger and resentment toward the terrible things that had happened to him. Thus began his determination that he would isolate and insulate himself. He would need no one.

The mall trip had been cut short, and Darrell had been returned to Scott and White Hospital. He remained completely withdrawn on the drive back.

Dr. Frank Perkins, the case psychiatrist discussed the incident with the two women, and tried to discuss it with Darrell. But Darrell remained in his shell.

Dr. Perkins called the two women back to his office. He sat behind his dark pecan desk and before his vanity wall, which bore several lavishly framed diplomas bearing witness to his many degrees. He was chief resident of the Child and Adolescent Psychiatry Program at Scott and White Hospital. He graduated with a B.A. in Psychology from Rice University in Houston, then a B.S. in Biology from Texas A&M University at College Station, finishing his Medical Degree at the University of Texas Medical School in Houston, then his residency training in psychiatry at the Baylor College of Medicine in Houston, and finally he completed a fellowship in Clinical Brain Disorders at the National Institute for Mental Health.

On occasion, when he found a small break in his hectic schedule, he would stand before the wall and reminisce. His favorite diploma was his first, for a couple of reasons, first: he met his wife, Patricia, at Rice. They were married eighteen months later. Second, he was the fifth in a family of five sons, born and raised in Ardmore, Oklahoma, the first and only to graduate from college.

"We have to discharge him," Dr. Perkins said to Margie and Marianna.

"What? We all know he's not ready," Mariana said. "There are too many issues."

"Issues are not the issue," Dr. Perkins said, intertwining his fingers on his desk. "The insurance has bottomed out."

"Come on, Doctor," Marianna pleaded. "Get the hospital to write it off."

"I asked already. Lily says 'No.' Our budget is busted."

Dr. Lily Turner was the hospital's Health Plan Coordinator. She coordinated insurance with finance and had a widespread reputation for being tough. Some said she had no soul.

Marianna stood and walked to the window looking out onto the main parking lot, and beyond that, 31st Street. "This is a small boy, doctor. His life has been smashed. To smithereens. He has no mother. He never knew his father. We don't even know who his father is. He has no choices, doctor. He has known nothing but pain this last year, physical and emotional. You are telling me that the hospital is washing its hands of Darrell. Which means I am going to have to find someone who will foster him, someone who is not repulsed by his face, someone who can give him something of what he needs. It won't be easy, and Darrell will suffer some more. You need to write this off. Four more weeks. Give Darrell a chance to be with some people who accept him the way he is."

Dr. Perkins kept his fingers interlocked. "I completely concur, Marianna. It's not my call. But listen, what seven year old has choices? I mean choices like where they're going to live, and who they're going to live with? And, really, we're not washing our hands of the boy. If he had an infection, a broken leg, he would be right in there, receiving the best treatment we could give him. Plus I would be happy to see him from time to time if you want—or assign one of my staff."

Finally, Dr. Perkins unlocked his fingers and placed his hands flat on the desktop. The meeting was over. Nurse Margie stood.

"I'll let you know if CPS needs your services, Doctor," Marianna said, heading for the door. It had been a long time since she felt so depressed.

It was as though Darrell were outside himself, watching the events.

The crowd was huge, cheering wildly. Darrell was about to be awarded his trophy. He was standing in the middle of the stage. The lights were blinding, but he could see someone approaching from his left. It was his father, and he had a huge trophy. He didn't know what his father looked like, but he knew this was his father. He looked a lot like Gerald Ford, the president.

"Darrell," his father said, "this is your first place award for being the best looking boy in the world. Everybody says 'Thank you!'"

With a giant, gleaming smile, his father handing him the giant trophy. It was as big as Darrell.

Darrell was so happy. He held the trophy in the air. The roar was deafening.

Then, suddenly, there was complete silence. What was happening?

Darrell could see the left side of his face. It began to crack. Wide fissures began to form. Large chunks of flesh slid to the floor until the left part of his face was a skeleton.

The crowd began to scream in terror, pushing and clawing at one another, scrambling over each other to get away.

Then his left eyeball fell out, hit the stage and bounced, then rolled out of sight into a hole in the stage.

Suddenly, Darrell's eye flew open. Where was he?

It was early morning, the sun not up for long.

He couldn't breathe. Who was that? Someone had him by the shirt collar, twisting it tightly, choking him. Who ever it was stunk. He tried to focus.

"Ah, he's awake," a raspy, guttural voice said. "It's alive. The monster's alive."

The man's big hands were hurting him.

"But maybe not for long, huh? I'm thinking something as ugly as this don't deserve to live. But then again, here's someone uglier than me. Maybe I should keep you around. I could teach you a few things, yes sir."

The man pulled Darrell up to a sitting position by the collar, and propped him against the dumpster. He didn't let go, holding Darrell at arm's length.

To Darrell he looked old, very old. He had a long, scraggily beard, most of which was yellow with brown stains on it. A constant leer revealed yellow, crooked teeth, some were missing.

"What's your name, boy?"

Darrell was silent.

"Come on, what's your name?"

Darrell remained silent.

Frustrated, the man moved to stand, and to haul Darrell up. In doing so, his twisting grip on Darrell's collar slipped away, and he stumbled backwards.

Scrambling to his right, Darrell grabbed an empty beer bottle by the neck, broke it on the cement, and swung it in an arc, aiming it at the man's left eye.

The man was at a great disadvantage. He was much older, he had cataracts, he was beset by arthritis and his blood-alcohol level was almost always well above legal limits. He didn't see it coming. The jagged glass struck him square in the left eye, sending a paroxysm of pain throughout his body. He fell backwards, grabbing his eye with both hands, screaming horribly. Bright red blood gushed between his shaking fingers.

Dropping the bottle, Darrell ran as hard as he could. A loud blast of an air horn to his left startled him. Scrambling around the chrome bumper of the eighteen-wheeler, Darrell streaked on.

"Hey, kid, watch where you're going!"

Darrell ran through the parking lot, turning south on the service road. He saw a motel about a block away. He could hide behind it.

Darrell heard the *whoop* of the siren before he saw the patrol car.

The black and white car, red, white and blue lights flashing, pulled around in front of him, blocking his way. Two policemen got out.

Darrell tried to turn and run, but one of the policemen reached out and grabbed him by his right arm.

"Whoa, cowboy, where you going?"

Twisting Darrell around, the officers reacted to what they saw simultaneously.

"Oh, man!" one of them said.

"What the . . . ?" the other exclaimed.

They quickly tried to recover their professional demeanor.

"Ah, what are you running from so fast? "

Darrell lowered his head and said nothing.

"This is the runaway CPS kid," one said to the other. He opened the rear door.

"Scrammy on in," he said. "We need to get you home."

I don't have a home, Darrell thought.

The police radio suddenly crackled, *All units northeast quadrant, 11–8 at 35 and 183 Shell station.* 11–8 was police code for "man down."

"Watch your hands and feet there," one of the policemen said to Darrell. "We've got to go. I'm closing the door."

They both got in and the siren was switched on. The one on the passenger side spoke into the microphone.

"Dispatch, 25. ETA one minute."

"10–4, 25. An ambulance is in route."

"10–4."

Darrell found all of this exciting. The patrol car peeled off in the direction that Darrell had just come from.

FOURTY-TWO

The Present

Darrell sat on the plush sofa, with his feet on the hassock watching the wide screen TV. With beer in hand and chips at his side, he giggled in anticipation of the moment he knew would come.

Aha, aha, there he was on TV. Right there, right in David's face

"Hooahhh!" he shouted. Right in his face. Right in baby brother's cheeky little pink face. He could have reached up and pinched it. Matter of fact, if he had it to do over again, he would've.

With his DVR remote he paused the picture and rewound it to the spot where he and David were eyeball to eyeball. Darrell looked closely at his disguise. He couldn't see a flaw.

He appreciated his latex mask and makeup and wig. When he took the two hours to apply the disguise it changed his life immediately in so many ways.

It gave him freedom to move around in public.

It gave him freedom to be anonymous. No one even noticed him. He could mingle in a crowd, or he could walk alone on the sidewalk.

It gave him freedom to approach someone—to approach them without watching their features morph into a face of horror, and begin backpedaling, barely suppressing a terrified scream.

It gave him freedom to ride in an elevator.

The only problem with his disguise was that it was hot and sweaty to wear, and he could only wear it for about four hours before the liquid latex that he used to blend around his mouth and eyes and neck began to peel away around the edges.

Then Darrell noticed something. There—in the bottom right corner of the screen. It was Detective John Parella.

Darrell rewound the scene several seconds and played it forward in slow motion, watching Parella. Yep, he was being the cop. He was scanning the crowd, looking for unusual or strange behavior. He knows that perps often mingle in crowds like these, for the thrill of being close to the action.

He was right, too. It was a thrill.

But nothing like the thrills that were coming up.

"Everybody hold on," Darrell said, in just above a whisper. "We are going for a ride."

FORTY-THREE
The Present

Lillian had David's favorite meal ready and waiting when they got home. Everything was in the oven, which was set on warm. She insisted that David sit while she and Meredith moved the food to the table.

In moments there appeared a platter full of chicken fried steaks, a bowl of mashed potatoes accompanied by a gravy boat full of brown gravy, a bowl of black-eyed peas, a bowl of fried okra, yellow squash, and a green salad. To drink, there was a cold pitcher of iced raspberry tea.

David ate with relish, gorging himself.

"I didn't know if I was going to ever eat home cooking again," he laughed.

"Well, we knew," Meredith jumped in. "We never doubted did we, Mom?"

"No, we didn't," Lillian smiled. "You had quite an advocate in Meredith, Dave."

"We had a prayer chain going in the youth group, Dad. Someone was praying twenty-four hours a day."

"Obviously it worked, Meredith. I'll have to tell the kids 'Thank you.'"

"Okay," she beamed.

Lillian had made strawberry shortcake, which they all enjoyed with coffee.

Lillian had also made arrangements for Meredith to spend the night with her best friend, Carol Lewis, who lived around the corner from them on King Arthur Court, so that she and her husband could get reacquainted.

"Welcome home, sweetheart," Lillian said in David's ear later that night.

"Thanks, Lill," David laughed. "Now I feel officially at home."

That night they both slept the deep sleep of the innocent.

"Great coffee," David said next morning. "The stuff at precinct four was real muck."

"I'm thinking, based upon last night, that you have a new, or renewed, perspective on lots of things," Lillian laughed, and hugged her husband's neck.

"I'm thinking you are right on," David laughed with her.

Lillian had placed a pile of his mail beside the coffee cup, which he was taking his time to open. Lots of it was letters from well-wishers proclaiming their belief in his innocence.

He picked up a red envelope that had his name and address printed on a computer label. There was no return address.

A white ribbon fell from the envelope.

Mmmm, David thought. *What's this?* He assumed it to be a symbolic ribbon from a supporter, similar to the yellow ribbons that people displayed to show support for our military in Iraq.

Then the next item that he removed from the envelope caused the hair to stand on the nape of his neck. It was a digital photograph of Meredith walking through the neighborhood.

"What is it?" Lillian asked, apparently noticing some sort of reaction in him. His first thought was not to alarm his wife.

"Some kook," he said. "Not what you might call a well-wisher."

He pulled the note from the envelope. It, too, was computer printed.

> *He learned obedience through suffering. Hebrews 5:8*
> *Geminis cross and the sparks fly,*
> *Iron sharpens iron,*
> *Someone will cry.*
> *The answer my bro is in her hand.*
> *Receiving the light will complete the plan.*
> *I know where you live, and more's the shame.*
> *It's that you do not know the same.*
> *One small clue as we begin,*
> *It is the Pale Horse who rides again.*
> *Soon, Gemini One*

"David? You look as white as a sheet." There was the tenor of alarm in Lillian's voice. "What is it?"

"Call Meredith. Tell her I am coming to pick her up right now."

"David, tell me, for heaven's sake."

"I think the killer is targeting Meredith."

Lillian's hands flew to her mouth. "Oh, dear God keep her safe," she whispered.

The heavy lead ball that had resided in David's stomach the last three weeks swiftly returned. This time it felt even heavier.

FOURTY-FOUR

The Present

Palmer Hutchins stirred in his bed, having slept better than he had in days. He had had an interesting dream, which already was eluding his memory as he rose to consciousness. He stretched and allowed one eye to open just enough to see the digital clock at his bedside—7:26 a.m.

There was plenty of time before his 2:20 flight from Houston to DFW airport.

He would stop by to say a quick goodbye to David and Lillian, check in his rental car and be on his way.

Things could not have gone much better really. Palmer was pleased with his efforts. The only thing that remained in this whole affair was for the police to capture the real killer.

Incongruously, a shadow passed between the morning sunlight threading through the window and across Palmer's face.

Had his mind not been still wrapped in the fading fog of sleep Palmer may have had more of a chance. As it was he had none.

He felt the sharp burning pain across his throat and was immediately aware of what was happening. He opened his eyes and briefly saw the face of a repulsive monster with a grotesque smile. Then his vision faded.

At once he began to slip into a deep abyss, then suddenly he sensed his direction reversing and he began to fly, increasingly faster. Euphoria engulfed him as a great dazzling light exploded before him. Immediately he was filled with its brilliance and warmth.

A voice spoke to him with incredible, overwhelming love.

"Well done, Palmer. Well done, my good and faithful servant."

Darrell stood at Palmer's bedside, smiling at the growing flower of crimson on Palmer's pillow.

It had not been difficult for Darrell to get an electronic key to Palmer's hotel room. He had simply followed Palmer to the lobby, ascertained his room number, and when he knew that it was safe, and the receptionist was busy and distracted, he boldly asked for another key, and was given it.

Arriving about 7:00 a.m. he took the elevator to the third floor, carefully avoiding being seen.

Inspecting the room one last time, leaving the note on the nightstand, Darrell quickly checked the hallway to see that it was empty.

He left, filled to overflowing with satisfaction.

FOURTY-FIVE

February 13, 1983

David Baxter ran as hard as his legs would allow, bitter tears stinging in his eyes. He prayed hard that Lillian would be home.

He just could not get his mind around what was happening. Why hadn't his parents mentioned his adoption before now? Had his real parents done something terribly wrong? Was he taken from them—what was his life all about? Who was he?

As he passed Fire Fighter Park a black cat ran across his path, causing him to stumble and nearly fall. The cat stopped and looked up at him with wide yellow eyes. David had an urge to kick it like a football. Unchecked anger welled up inside him.

Kill it, a voice inside him said, clear as a bell. *Kill it with a rock.*

The cat showed no intent to budge. David pulled the collar of his jacket up around his neck. It was getting colder. He looked around. There was a softball-sized rock near his right foot. He reached down and picked it up, testing its weight in his right palm.

It's easy, the voice cooed. The cat meowed, the noise irritating in David's ears. *You can do it.*

David drew his arm back, the rock poised.

You can do it, David.

David began to weep. He *couldn't* do it.

"Get!" he yelled to the stupid cat. "Get outta here!"

He kicked at the cat, which scurried off, and he flung the rock into the park.

Again he ran down Nadeau Street toward 29th Street North where Lillian lived. He bounded onto her porch, ringing the doorbell, laboring for breath.

Lillian answered the door.

"David?" she said, reaching for him. "Your parents called. Are you okay?"

"I don't know," he said, winded. "Did they tell you anything?"

Lillian's parents were standing in the entryway.

"They told us everything, David," Lillian's mother said. "They are concerned about you, sweetheart."

"Lillian, can we go outside?"

Lillian nodded, took his hand and led him to the swing on the front porch.

By the time Darrell Phelps was sixteen years old he had lived in five foster homes, this one was the sixth. Three of the homes had had children; two had been childless. They all had meant well. At first they would try their best to love Darrell and to provide whatever it was that they had determined that he needed. But he was adept at finding their irritants, and he would push those buttons incessantly, until they would cry *uncle* and raise the white flag, letting it be known that they wished to turn him back in.

Marianna Parks, his CPS caseworker, was the only constant in his life. She believed that all mankind tended toward good, and that Darrell had a good heart—he just needed the right environment to bring out his goodness.

She had placed Darrell in the home of Carl and Betty Morris, who had a sixteen-year-old son, Willy. Although sixteen chronologically, Willy had the mental capacity of a ten-year-old. The boys had been together for four months now.

Carl and Betty's belief system was akin to Marianna's. They were firmly convinced that inside Willy was some goodness somewhere—it just needed the right circumstances and environment to bring it out. All of this in spite of constant reports from Pflugerville High School that Willy was truant, a distraction to other students, arrogant toward teachers, and the school bully. The police had warned the Morris couple on more that one occasion that they were responsible for their son, and were very close to being fined for his less than acceptable behavior.

On the surface the boys got along just fine. Behind the scenes it was all out war; no quarter asked, none given. Willy constantly taunted Darrell with, "Freak face, freak face, Darrell's got a geek face."

The problem was that Willy had six inches in height and 108 pounds on Darrell. Willy was six feet three inches tall and weighed 223 pounds. Darrell was left with his wits, which he put to good use.

On this particular weekend, the Morrises were away; Darrell had caught Willy the Whale napping on the couch with the TV blaring. Quickly scurrying upstairs he returned, huffing and puffing with two fifty-pound barbells from Willy's room, and a blanket from his bed. Darrell placed one edge of the blanket on the floor behind the sofa and laid the barbell on it, wrapping the blanket's edge around it. Next, he threw the blanket over the couch covering the entire length of his tormentor and placed the second barbell next to the sofa, wrapping it as well, trapping the blanket beneath.

Stirring only slightly Willy continued his long, laborious snoring.

Darrell, taking his baseball bat, whacked the boy across the shoulder, not too hard.

"Hey—what . . . ow!

Darrell hit him again, harder this time.

"Ow! What are you doing, you freak!"

Willy began to struggle under the blanket but was effectively immobilized.

"Be quiet!" Darrell shouted. "Be quiet—and be still. If you move again, I *will* crack your head open," Darrell hissed, jerking the cover down so that he could see Willy's face. It was red and covered with sweat. Willy's eyes were wide as a terrified calf.

"Don't hit me no more," Willy said in a whisper.

"I'll think about it," Darrell said. He reached down next to the sofa and picked up the large, pre-placed butcher knife. He placed the point against a fat, wet cheek.

"Now, listen up, you barrel of blubber," Darrell whispered in the shivering boys ear. "If you so much as touch me on accident whenever I walk by, I swear you will wake up one day with this knife in your throat."

Darrell pressed the point until it penetrated the skin. A thin trickle of crimson ran down, mingling with the sweat.

"Ow—ow—ow! Don't, please," the boy began to cry. "I promise, I promise."

"You promise what?"

"I promise I won't hit you no more. Please. I won't do nothing."

After that the boys got along as well behind the scenes as they did publicly.

That same evening as Darrell was walking along Railroad Avenue North by Pfluger Grove Park a black cat scurried immediately in front of him and stopped just off the sidewalk. The cat's stare was direct and unwavering, and somehow malevolent, his round yellow eyes unblinking.

Freak face.

The statement was as plain as if the cat had spoken it aloud.

Darrell had first killed a cat when he was nine, choking it to death, watching closely as life ebbed from the eyes. This night he would kill his fifth by smashing its head with a rock.

Two months later Darrell lured Willy to that same park by telling him that he had a six-pack of beer stashed on ice in the trees. Taking a large rock, Darrell crushed the left side of Willy's face. He then took Willy's left eye and dropped it down a storm drain.

Inexplicably, witnesses reported seeing a black man in his forties in the area the afternoon of Willy's murder. The police questioned Darrell only briefly. He never even became a person of interest.

In their grief the Morrises could no longer care for Darrell, and he was once again placed in the Helping Hand Home for Children in Austin until Marianna Parks could find him another foster home.

FORTY-SIX

The Present

David Baxter's heart raced as he sped through the neighborhood to the Lewis's to retrieve his daughter, calling John Parella in route.

"John, David Baxter here."

It was 7:30 a.m. David reached Parella on his cell.

"David, what's going on?"

"I got this scary note with Meredith's photo in it. I'm sure she's being stalked by the killer."

"Are you at home?" Parella asked.

"No, I'm on my way to Meredith's friend's house to get Meredith." David gave him the address.

"I'll meet you there, ten minutes," Parella said, finishing his coffee, pushing back from the breakfast table.

Annie Louise entered the kitchen in her bathrobe, hair damp from the shower. She could read her husband's face like a large-print book.

"What's going on?" she asked, toweling her head.

"The serialist is at it again—no body, just stirring things up. He's apparently stalking Baxter's daughter. Where's Jenny?"

"She's upstairs getting ready. I'll be so glad when you catch that scumbag."

"Myself," Parella said, kissing his wife on the lips. "Later. I'll call you. Tell Jenny I said to have a good day."

"Thanks, Hon. Be careful."

Parella holstered his Glock 19, adjusted his sports jacket and walked out the door.

David pulled into the Lewis' driveway, hurrying to the front door.

Carol answered the front door. Complete bewilderment covered her face.

"Mr. Baxter, did you forget something?" She paused, looking at David as if he had a horn growing out his forehead. "What happened to the bandages on your face?"

"What are you talking about, Carol? Where's Meredith?" David peered over the top of her head into the foyer.

"That's what I'm talking about, Mr. Baxter. You picked her up at 6:00. You said you'd had a fire at your house and you'd burned your face, and that Mrs. Baxter is in the hospital, and you were taking Meredith there to see her. The left side of your face was all bandaged up."

David struggled to comprehend. "What do you mean *I* picked her up? What is going on, Carol? Was Meredith with you last night or not?"

"Yes sir, she was here. All night, then you came by about 6:00, all out of breath, and she grabbed her stuff, and ya'll left real fast. In your car." Carol pointed toward the driveway.

"You said *bandages?*"

"Yes sir. The whole left side of your face—it was from the fire."

David heard a car pull up and spun around, hoping somehow to see Meredith. It was John Parella.

Parella, seeing the look on Baxter's face knew that something was dreadfully wrong.

"Baxter, what's up?"

"I think," David said, ashen-faced, "that he has Meredith."

FOURTY-SEVEN

February 13, 1983

The air was crisp and unusually dry. Lillian hugged herself and shivered as she and David sat quietly in the porch swing, their breath making small clouds in the cold air.

Staring intently at him, registering deep concern in her eyes, she said, "Are you okay?"

"I don't get it, Lill. It's like I've been living a lie. "

"That's not it at all, Dave. A lie is when you know something and you tell it differently than what it really is—on purpose."

"Then my parents lied."

"How do you figure?" Lillian said. "Your folks didn't lie. They just waited till now to tell you that you're adopted. Tomorrow's your sixteenth birthday. I think they figured you're mature enough now to handle it, you know?"

David could not express how he was feeling, but it felt like he was about to explode. "I don't know, Lill." He squeezed his temples between the palms of his hands. "I feel like I'm stuck out here all alone."

Lillian took his hands in hers. "David," she inched closer to him. "Look at me."

Her eyes were the deepest, clearest blue, with no trace of guile. Looking into them warmed his insides. He just wanted to be with her, and no one else. The touch of her hands was exhilarating, her nearness making him giddy.

"They are *your* parents, David. *Yours*—no one else's. They love you. They've provided for you—everything that you could want or need. You are their child David. They chose you. Most parents are stuck with who they get. They picked *you, David.*"

Her words and voice helped; the storm inside him abated somewhat. This was why he had run to her—he knew that, of all people, Lillian could help.

"David—look! It's snowing!"

David looked out across the front yard darkness, toward the yellow shaft of light from the street lamp. Fat flakes of snow glistened in the light, lazily swirling to the ground.

"Wow," David said. "Look at that!"

It never snowed in La Marque, Texas.

FOURTY-EIGHT

The Present

Waking slowly from her drug-induced slumber, something akin to reality suddenly exploded upon Meredith. Her mind struggled to make some sense of what was happening. She felt as if she were on the *Serial Thriller* ride at Astroworld, a coaster ride that flung its captives into inversions, sidewinder half-loops, corkscrew spirals and a double spin. Feeling nauseous she closed her eyes again and took slow deep breaths.

She had been kidnapped—by someone who looked just like her *father?* He, whoever *he* was, had jabbed her in the thigh with a needle. It still hurt.

Wherever he had taken her, it was dimly lit, and it smelled funny. She was bound to a wooden chair, in the corner of what appeared to be a horse stall. Angled beams of sunshine crisscrossed through the shadows, highlighting lazily drifting points of dust. The dirt floor was smattered with bits of hay, wooden shavings and other debris. Her arms were tied behind her and ached from her shoulders down to her wrists. Several flies flitted about her.

Listening intently, she heard nothing but a breeze blowing through some trees outside.

"Help!" she yelled as loud as she could. "Somebody help me!"

She knew instinctively that there would be no one within earshot to heed her cry.

She tried to stand, to lift her chair, but it was attached to the wall.

Surveying her surroundings, she noted a large wire-framed fan up in one corner of her stall. The roof was tin, sloping down to the outside wall. The window in the wall was screen-less but shuttered, with numerous cracks of light coming through. A metal half-wall stood, forming the stall, about four feet high, with vertical metal bars standing an additional four feet above it. There was no door to the stall, simply an opening in the middle from the floor to the top of the bars. All of which mattered little, since she was secured to the chair and to the stall wall.

It appeared that there were similar stalls on either side of hers. They were empty.

The whole place smelled moldy and damp.

Across the breezeway from her was an open door to a tack room where she could see dust-covered saddles, halters, helmets, a shelf of spray bottles and various supplies, and an old rust-pocked refrigerator. Rays of sunlight angled down from somewhere behind the wall and across the doorway.

Two other doors, to offices or some such, were closed. The doors at either end of the breezeway were also closed. Nevertheless, an occasional whistling breeze came through the many cracks, sufficient to stir up strands of hay, sending them, sometimes, swirling around her face.

She ran the recent, puzzling events through her mind, trying to discover some semblance of sanity. Her father had appeared at Carol's door, all out of breath, the left side of his face covered in bandages. There had been a fire—her mom was in the hospital, he said. Seriously injured.

The alarming news had disoriented her, but something about

her "father" was just not right. She studied him intently as they sped along in the Tahoe. It was his voice, his mannerisms, his *spirit*.

Finally she said, "You're not my dad. Who are you? What are you doing?"

It was then, suddenly out of nowhere, his hand flashed toward her leg, and she felt the hot sting of the needle. The next thing she remembered she was waking up in this place.

She prayed, *Jesus, help me.*

She said to herself, *Don't be afraid. Be calm, be calm.*

Then she thought of Summer Chase. Then she knew with lucid clarity, *This man, who looked like her father, had killed Summer Chase.*

Immediately the dam burst, and she began to weep.

Would she ever see her parents again?

FOURTY-NINE

June 20, 1983

After four months, Marianna Parks had not been able to locate another foster home for Darrell. In just a couple of years he would be released into society. She so wanted him to be ready, and it was obvious to her and everyone that he was not. No matter how much she wanted it, he was not capable at this juncture to function as a contributing member of society, nor would he be, if things continued at this pace, when he turned eighteen.

Feeling often as if she were the only one in Darrell's corner, she pondered how she might be able to secure his future. One evening, in the early twilight of sleep, it exploded upon her in a burst of brilliance. It was right there in front of her all along. How could she have missed it?

The reason that Darrell was the way he was was because of his face. If people had not shunned him all of his life since he was seven he would be normal—as normal as anyone. She could not imagine living life in his body—the averted eyes, the looks of revulsion and loathing, the whispers, the giggles and the finger pointing. She just knew that if it were not for all that Darrell would be confident and strong, full of self-esteem. So, a different face would have meant a different boy.

And who was to blame for his face? Who indeed, but the two

doctors, Angus McWhorter and Lois Dryden? They had, in Marianna's opinion, botched the entire thing.

And then of course there was Scott and White Hospital. They were certainly liable as well.

She would contact Steve first thing in the morning.

"Casey, Strong, Garner and Whitten," the operator answered the next morning, precisely at 9 a.m.

"May I speak with Steven Casey, please? Tell him it is Marianna Parks."

"One moment, please."

Marianna and Steven had dated a handful of times at the University of Texas in the early '70s. It had been just a long enough relationship for Marianna to discover that L. Steven Casey was a self-centered, self-serving, self-aggrandizing individual, whose sole desire was to be the best tort lawyer in Texas. He was just what she needed at the moment. And if he had not yet achieved his goal he was very close to it. She had followed his career through the media. He was well known, loved by some, hated by many, and he had won 95% of his cases.

"Marianna? Is that you?"

"In the flesh, Steven. How are you?"

"Doing great—couldn't be better. Still wondering why we never got married. How's CPS?"

"I wonder the same sometimes, Steven. CPS is fine. You know—overworked, underpaid."

"Hey—my own self. How can I be of service, M?"

It irritated her that Steven so easily reverted to the familiar—and once intimate—nickname. And that he would even imply that he was in a similar financial boat as she—with him being a three-quarters of a billionaire, lacking for nothing, while she wondered occasionally if spaghetti was in her budget.

Nevertheless, she proceeded.

"I have a case—a sixteen year old boy who has gotten the short end of the stick for most of his life, Steven. I have handled his case since he was six. At that time he and his mother were in a terrible car wreck—she was killed instantly. He was terribly disfigured. The left side of his face was basically torn away. He lost his left eye. His left arm was majorly damaged. The foster mother's meager insurance and the state, of course, handled his medical, which, in my opinion, was a total botch. I have reason to believe, based on some of my own research, and discussion with other doctors, that the attendant cosmetic surgeons did not use the best medical practice known at the time for such injuries. The facial reconstruction was just horrible. It has ruined his life. I believe that he is in a good position for reparations. I thought that you might be interested in looking at his case."

"Well, my only question to you, M, is why have you waited until just now to contact me?"

"When can we meet?"

"I assume by 'we' that you are including the boy?" Steven asked. "Can you make it tomorrow? 9 a.m.?"

"I absolutely can," Marianna said, elated. "I'll bring Darrell with me."

"Good. I look forward to it. Plan on lunch afterward. Great Tex-Mex."

The defense assembled three powerful teams: a team of five for Dr. McWhorter; a team of seven for Dr. Dryden, and a team of seven for the hospital.

The Scott and White team caved first. When they first saw Darrell in the "flesh" it was clear to a man that there was no way on earth that they would be able to avert the tidal wave of sympathy that would swell forth from the jury box were this to go to trial.

They offered Darrell $1.5 million.

L. Steven Casey choked on the glass of water he was sipping, composed himself and laughed aloud in the direction of the seven attorneys plus staff assembled across the meeting table from him.

"I assume," he wiped his lips with a napkin. "That you are beginning the process of negotiation. If so, your first offer should be in the realm of reasonable, not ridiculous. Understand? Because if you persist in remaining in the realm of ridiculous, my team and I will stand up, walk out of here, and the next time you hear my voice will be in court. By the way, reasonable is in the vicinity of thirty million."

There was a collective intake of breath from the other side of the table.

After some rapid huddling and whispering, one of the hospital attorneys said,

"We need to make a quick phone call." He arose to leave the room.

"Wait, wait, wait, wait, wait," L. Steven said.

The defense attorney stopped, looking quizzically across the table.

"I thought that I was speaking with decision makers here. If I am not talking with decision makers we are wasting our time." L. Steven Casey played poker twice a week with two different sets of players, each group with its own style of playing. Steven remained single, which allowed him to play whenever he desired. He used the games to hone his skills in the tort business. He loved poker, and he loved tort negotiations. To him there was not a lot of difference between the two. One could either have a winning hand or one could bluff. In this instance he was certain of a winning hand.

The object of course was to get the pot as high as possible before raking it in. He preferred that his opponent fold after the pot was sufficiently fat, but if the other guy wanted to play the hand out, so be it.

Another attorney on the other side said, "We do, indeed, have the right people at this table. Just give us ten minutes, please, to discuss this."

Steven's team emptied the room and gave the other side fifteen minutes to decide their answer.

When they returned they were barely seated when the spokesman for the hospital said, "We are prepared to offer Darrell Phelps forty-two and one half million dollars for general damages for pain and suffering, and against future earnings. Final offer." The gentleman slid some papers across the table, as casual as if he were offering a newspaper article to Steven to read.

Steven looked the man in the eye for several long seconds, looking for a "tell"—a poker term meaning a sign, nervous habit, twitch, anything that would indicate that one's opponent is bluffing. In any case, tell or not, if one has a winning hand, one should play it accordingly. Steven continued to stare at his adversary who stared back, until finally the man pulled at his ear. Steven pounced.

"Tell you what," he said softly, "that's a very generous offer. There might have been a time when I would have jumped on it like a duck on a June bug. Not today."

A joint sigh of disappointment rose from the other side.

"And I'll tell you why," Stevens said. "I mentioned $30 million before. You came back with forty-two and one half. I'm figuring that you split the difference between my thirty million and your cap that your management gave you. Which would make your cap somewhere around $55 million." Steven leaned back slowly in his chair.

The other side fidgeted nervously. The papers were retrieved from the center of the table.

"So, here's the deal," Steven said. "Everyone needs to go home with something. We will settle for $50 million. That will give you about $5 million to take back to your hospital."

"Done," the hospital attorney said, scribbling on the paper and sliding it back toward Steven.

To L. Steven Casey's chagrin he would discover five years later through an attorney who had been an aide for the hospital legal team that the other side was willing to settle for at least $100 million. Texas juries were notorious for handing out huge settlements, which the hospital attorneys estimated could be as high as $200 to $400 million. Maybe more. The legal team for the hospital reported to their bosses that they had saved them $150 to $350 million. They had done their jobs well, basing their strategy on the premise that the whole tort system was driven by one thing—pure, unadulterated greed. And greed fogs the brain.

Nevertheless, Darrell ended up with a hefty sum. Dr. McWhorter's malpractice insurance went to court, but settled during jury selection for $150 million. Dr. Dryden's attorneys did not want to go it alone, so they settled as well. Not knowing the bottom line of the other settlements, L. Steven was able to jack them up to $220 million.

When it was over, Marianna Parks sighed with relief. It had been a good idea. When all was said and done, Darrell received $84 million after the government and the law firm of Casey, Strong, Garner and Whitten had taken their piece of the luscious green pie.

Darrell's money was installed in a trust fund upon which he could draw when he turned eighteen.

"Thank you for everything you did," Darrell told Marianna after the tort proceedings were over.

"You're so welcome, Darrell," Marianna smiled. "We are glad that everything worked out."

"I want to give you a million dollars," Darrell said.

"Oh, no," Marianna said quickly, holding up both hands. "I couldn't—it wouldn't be proper."

"Can't I do what I want to with my money?" Darrell asked.

"Well, you can when you reach eighteen, sure—but . . ."

"Okay, I'll pay you then—when I'm eighteen. It won't be like I'm just *giving* it to you. I want you to do a job for me. I want to hire you, and it would be worth a million dollars to me for you to do it."

"Oh?" Marianna's curiosity was certainly stimulated by the request. "What would you like for me to do for you?"

"Would you find out who my real parents are, please?"

FIFTY

May 16, 1966

Jolene Waters had taken $236 from the coffee can in the kitchen and run away. Her $18 bus ticket would take her from her hometown and birthplace of Brownsville, Texas northeast to Houston. At sixteen-years-of-age she had never been away from home. Looking out the bus window into the dark countryside speeding by, she was terrified. But the fear of leaving was less than the fear of staying home.

She remembered, trying her best to get Faye, her sister, older by two years, to go with her. But Faye would not.

"We have got to get out of here, Faye," she had whispered in the dark. "Can't you see? This is crazy. Mom and dad are crazy. They're going to kill us, can't you see?"

But Faye just whimpered.

Suddenly, light had burst into the room.

"Are you brats *talking*?" their mother screamed, storming into the room. "What did I tell you?" She whacked Faye across the face with a flyswatter, simultaneously thunking Jolene on the top of her head with the back of her hand.

"What is it, Thelda?" their dad stomped into the room.

The girls were in the center of the barren room, tied back to back in their cane-bottomed chairs, each clad only in a white, over-sized t-shirt.

"Nothing, Jim. I heard the girl's whispering s'all. I don't need nothing from *you*."

The shadow of Thelda Water's large frame filled half the room.

"So, I told ya'll," she continued with the girls, "that I was going to give you some supper tonight. Didn't I?"

"Yes ma'am," they responded in unison.

"So now what?" She stomped over in front of Jolene. "What?" she shouted.

Jolene jumped, startled. "I don't know, mama. I don't know what you're asking."

"You've got to be dumber than a sack of rocks, Jolene. I want to know what you would do if you was me."

Jolene was dumbfounded. She still didn't know what her mother was fishing for. She sat, silent until her mother swatted her with the fly swatter.

"What should your punishment be? What would you do?"

"I would not—give us anything to eat."

"Well now, there you go," the girl's mother puffed. "Just shows you what a better mother I am than you would be, 'cause I ain't try-ing to starve you girls to death, just showing you who's the parent here. I'm going to give ya'll some bread—just not cornbread—and some chicken soup. So get ready for dinner. Wash up."

Thelda Waters turned to get dinner. "Get the girls ready, Jim."

Jim Waters brought in a pail of water and a tin pie pan. It would be filled with food for them to share. Then he removed the coil of rope binding them together.

"Chew your food well, girls."

Thelda brought in the food and dumped it into the pie pan.

The bread was three weeks old, splotched with bluish-gray

mold. The soup was thin and watery, bearing little resemblance to chicken soup.

The girls were hungry, however, and wolfed the food down in short shrift, being careful to share equal amounts between them. Also being careful not to spill any on the bare, wooden floor, else they should be swatted.

They had no sooner finished eating when Daddy Jim returned to rebind them. Jolene tensed her arm muscles as tight as she could while he, once again, placed them back-to-back, winding the rope around them from their shoulders to their wrists. His credo was the more rope the better. Tying it off at their wrists, he stood and brushed off his hands.

"Night-night, girls," he smiled, flicking on the night light at the baseboard near the door. He closed the door, believing it unnecessary to lock it, since he had tied them up so well.

Jolene had relaxed her arms as soon as Daddy Jim had left the room, providing some small slack in the rope. After a brief period a duet of loud snores emanated from their parents' bedroom. Waiting a while longer, as quietly as possible, Jolene and Faye began to wiggle their shoulders—twisting their arms back and forth as spirals of rope began gradually inching down until it reached their wrists.

Shaking her hands vigorously, Jolene was able to free herself from the coils, and then she did the same for her sister.

"Faye," she whispered very quietly. "You've *got* to go with me. You've *got* to." Jolene hissed the words between her teeth.

Eyes glistening with tears, Faye said, "I can't, Jolene. I'm scared."

"Faye, listen to me," Jolene took her by the shoulders. She would have shaken her, but she didn't want Faye to start crying aloud. Faye was right on the brink as it was. "It is more scary to stay here, don't you see? Mama's going to kill us if we stay, Sugar."

But Faye just hung her head, tears streaming from her eyes. "I love you," she sniffled quietly.

"I love you, too. I've gotta get my stuff and go. I'm sorry, Faye."

Jolene crept quietly into her and Faye's bedroom. She had not been inside that room for six months, since her mother had started "home schooling" the girls. Peering through the darkness she had difficulty seeing their bed and chest of drawers. Hoping her mother had not rearranged things she groped toward where she remembered the chest to be. It was still there.

She opened the second from the bottom drawer, her clothes drawer, trying to identify by feel what she would wear. Her underwear and socks were in the bottom drawer. She grabbed some tennis shoes next to the dresser and tiptoed from the room. She would dress when she was well away from the house.

The coffee can was still in the cabinet next to the refrigerator. She carefully removed it, not wanting the change to rattle. Hurrying outside, tears streaming, she would not go back into the room to see Faye. It was too risky.

After running about a block from the house, staying in the shadows Jolene quickly donned her clothes. She removed the bills and change and stuffed the money into her jeans. She had no clue how much she had.

Living in East Brownsville all of her life Jolene had learned her neighborhood well, having walked it and played in it until just six months ago when her mother's weird time had started. Walking briskly, she quickly covered the eight blocks to East 9th Street where she turned left onto East Charles. The bus station was just two blocks down.

It was crowded with travelers, mostly Hispanic, sitting on the benches and lying on the floor, bags acting as pillows. Cigarette smoke hung in layers in the waiting room.

There was no sitting space available on the benches, so Jolene went into the ladies room. There was a line of three women waiting for a stall. Jolene knew enough Spanish to know that they were not talking about her.

Finally her time came. Entering the stall she quickly sat, mainly wanting to count her money. She had $236 and some change. She had no clue how much a ticket would cost.

At the ticket window she looked at the schedule on the wall behind the ticket master. The clock on the wall said 10:15. The next available trip was to Northwest Houston. It would leave at 11:45 p.m. and arrive at 8:00 in the morning.

"May I help you, young lady?" the ticket master asked. He was thin and bald, peering at her through thick glasses that made her imagine that he was peering through a fishbowl.

"How much is a ticket to Houston?"

"The 11:45 to Northwest Houston is $18 with tax. Is that what you want?"

"Please," she said, sliding a twenty dollar bill beneath the cage bars.

Exhausted, peering out the bus window at the occasional lights streaking by in the darkness, Jolene fell into a fitful sleep, to be suddenly jolted awake by the bus pulling to a stop, brakes screeching.

"Okay, ladies and gentlemen," the bus driver shouted from his seat. "You have a twenty-five minute rest stop, with food if you want it. The bus will pull out precisely at 4:35. Get on or get left. I will honk the horn twice to give ya'll a five minute warning."

Many of the passengers were filing down the aisle. Many remained in their seats, either sleeping or trying to.

Jolene was famished. She did not know how much weight she had lost the last several months, but she knew that the clothes that she had put on were inches too large.

She ordered a hamburger, fries and a strawberry shake. She ate slowly, relishing every bite, not remembering anything ever tasting so good. Then she thought of Faye who would be stuck with stale bread and watery soup and began to cry quietly.

"Are you okay, Shug?" a woman sitting at the counter next to her asked.

"Yes, ma'am," Jolene responded, wiping her eyes. "I miss my folks, is all. I'm going to Houston to visit my aunt while my mother's in the hospital. She can't take care of me right now."

"Oh, dear," the woman fluttered her hand to a rouged cheek. Her face was wrinkled and powdery white—a stark canvas for her lips, vivid scarlet, and her eyes, a shadowy jade. "What is the matter with your mother?"

"She is dying of leukemia."

"Oh, dear," the woman said again, her eyes widening. "You poor thing. My late husband, Harmon, died of congestive heart failure, so I know how you feel."

Jolene had no idea what the comment meant, but she said, "Yes, ma'am," and put another French fry into her mouth.

L.J. Wade knew exactly what he was looking for as he watched the bus from Brownsville, precisely on time, pulling in to a stop near The Box Store. Today was the eighteenth, which meant that he had only two days to complete his assignment. There would be a full solar eclipse the day after tomorrow, and it was Wade's task to see that everything about the ceremony was ready on that day, including the most important central figure—the beneficiary.

He had been watching for three days, with no luck. He had a sense about this morning.

And he was right. There—just stepping down off the bus was a girl. Young, emaciated, and frightened. She stood, looking around quizzically, until someone said something to her, and she moved out of the way of the other passengers. She started in one direction, stopped, and then headed in another.

"Do you have some bags?"

Startled, Jolene looked up to see a striking young boy with blond hair, sparkling green eyes, and a large, disarming smile.

"What?" she said, completely off balance.

"Luggage," his smile broadened. "You got any luggage in there?" He nodded toward the lower compartment of the bus.

"Oh, ah—no," she replied nervously. "I'm . . . ah . . ."

"No problem," he laughed. "Where you staying?"

"Ah—I'm staying with my aunt."

"She picking you up?"

"Yeah, she's picking me up," Jolene looked all around. Hoping the boy would give up and leave.

"My name's Leon," he said, holding out a hand. "Everbody calls me L.J."

She took his hand. It felt strong.

"Hi," she said, attempting a smile. "I'm Jolene."

"Listen, Jolene," L.J. said. "I don't mean to pry or anything, but when I saw you get off that bus I said, 'There's a pretty girl who could use some help.' I'm going to assume that I was right and just go ahead and tell you this. I have a friend, a girl about your age; she's eighteen, who lives near here—in a little community called Decker Prairie—with her parents. They are great people. They would be happy to put you up for a night, or ten—depending on what you need. If I'm way off base just say, 'No thanks, Leon,' and I'll be on my way." He continued to hold her hand.

No matter how hard she tried, Jolene could not prevent the pain from boiling up, overflowing into racking sobs. She hated herself for it.

L.J. cradled her in his arms, and, finally, she let him. She needed it. She had been the strong one, not Faye. She had carried them both through six months of the worst kind of hell. Their parents, instead of providing comfort and a safe haven—a place where they could discover themselves and plan for the future—their parents had become their tormentors, their adversaries, their removal of hope that there might even be a future. Now she needed someone, L.J.—anyone—on whose shoulders she could cry. And cry she did.

Without her realizing it, L.J. inched them closer to his car, a bright new red 1966 Chevy Nova. When they got to the car, L.J. opened the passenger side door.

"Here," he said. "Crawl in. You need a hot bath, a hot breakfast and about ten hours sleep. Then we'll go from there. How's that sound?"

"Okay," Jolene said. She no longer had a will of her own. She was just too tired. And a hot bath sounded better than anything.

It was about 9:15 in the morning when they arrived. A sprawling single story ranch house sat at the end of the winding gravel road, which curved from the entry gate to the top of the hill. The gate was open, overarched by the large curved sign that identified the property as the Pale Horse Ranch. A large tree-lined pond nestled in a vale down to the left of the mansion, with one enormous tree, a weeping willow, stealing the show, dipping its leaves into the dark green water. White-faced cattle casually grazed throughout the lush green pastures, along with a couple of horses. A substantial red barn settled in the valley in the near distance. Perhaps 200 yards to its west was a stall for the horses. Three cars, all black, were parked at various angles around the manor.

The Smiths immediately proved to be great people. Mr. and Mrs. Smith treated her better than her parents ever had. It was almost like arriving just in time for Christmas. Mrs. Smith took her to a Houston mall to shop for some great new clothes, had her hair and nails done, and then they had enjoyed a great salad together.

The Smith's daughter Iris was a different story. She had not joined them on the shopping excursion. She had not welcomed Jolene as if she were a long lost family member, as had her parents. She had, on the other hand, shown open resentment toward Jolene.

Jolene could describe Iris in a word—*vivid.*

Everything about eighteen-year-old-Iris was beads, bangles and color—tie-dyed colors of orange and red and yellow stripes, swirls and splashes on her crinkled dress; with blues, greens and purples spiraled on her hoody pullover. Braided with smoky quartz and agate beads, her long corn silk hair fell well below her shoulders. Atop her head sat a crushed green wool flare bucket hat. Iris jangled with necklaces, bracelets and anklets when she moved.

Her first words to Jolene when the two of them found themselves alone were, "What are you doing here?"

Bewildered, Jolene responded with her new-found story, "My mother's dying of leukemia." Her hope was to elicit some sympathy.

"So?" Iris shrugged. "What's that got to do with anything? What are you *doing* here?"

Jolene could not answer.

"I think you are stupid for coming here. I hope you are not sorry for it."

The words greatly puzzled Jolene. How could she ever be sorry for coming to such a nice family? She couldn't be made to feel more welcome by Iris' parents.

Just as puzzling was a conversation overheard later by Jolene. It occurred not far from her bedroom door late the second night after she arrived. They must have thought she was sound asleep.

"Just what do you think you are doing, young lady?" It was Mr. Smith, speaking in a harsh whisper.

"I'm not doing anything, Henry. Let go of me." It was Iris' voice.

"I'll let go when I'm ready to let go. Understand?"

"Ow, that hurts."

"If you mess this up it will be your hide, darlin.' You might think you're exempt, but don't kid yourself. You could end up being the beneficiary in this thing. It's that important to us. Just don't kid yourself."

When Friday the twentieth arrived there was palpable tension in the air at the Pale Horse Ranch. The usual banter around the breakfast table was greatly diminished, plus there were six people that Jolene had never met, sitting and eating at the massive table. No one bothered to introduce them either, and they stared at her as if she were some prize specimen. Jolene thought it a little strange that they did not seem to be the least bit embarrassed to stare at her so openly.

During a long pause in conversation Mrs. Smith said, "Jolene, I have a special surprise for you, dear." She reached down beside her and brought up a garment box from the floor. "Here you are," she beamed.

"Oh, dear," Jolene said, definitely embarrassed now. "What is this for?"

"Remember, I told you?" Mrs. Smith asked. "Today is a very special day for us here at the ranch. We're having a party to celebrate. This is your party dress."

Jolene remembered no such thing. "But why *me?*"

"Because you are our special guest. Come get it now, and try it on. You must model it for us."

Jolene took the box. She knew that her face must be bright red.

"Open it, open it," everyone said in chorus, except, she noticed, Iris, who was sitting back, her face sullen.

Iris is jealous, thought Jolene. She opened the box and lifted the dress out of it. It was the most absolutely beautiful garment that she had ever seen—white and lacy, covered with pearls and sequins. And it came replete with a veil.

"This looks like a . . . wedding dress," Jolene said in amazement.

"Yes, it does, doesn't it," chirped Mrs. Smith. "Quickly, go try it on."

Iris hastily jumped up and said, "I'll help." Mr. Smith shot her a look but said nothing.

Jolene and Iris went into an adjacent sitting room to try on the new dress.

Iris wasted no time, "You have got to get out of here!"

Jolene looked at Iris closely. She seemed to be sincerely concerned, fear in her eyes.

"Why, Iris? Why should I leave? I like it here."

"Put the dress on, Jolene," Iris said nervously. "If we take too long they'll come check on us." She looked out the window. "Oh, jeez."

"What?" Jolene said and looked out on the front lawn. Six more people were arriving, all were dressed in black.

"It's *The Third Six,*" Iris said in hushed tones. "The First and Second Six are in there." She nodded toward the dining area.

Jolene slipped the magnificent dress over her head. "What on earth are you talking about, Iris?"

"I'm not supposed to be telling you this, Jolene. I could get in trouble—*big* trouble."

"Tell me what? Just tell me."

"These are all Satan worshippers. They are all witches."

"What are you talking about? There's no such thing as . . ."

"I'm telling you," Iris hissed. "They are witches. *I'm* a witch. The guys are Warlocks." Iris was speaking rapidly now. "Mr. Smith is not my father. He's not even Mr. Smith. And Mrs. Smith is not his wife. I don't even know their real names. I'm a runaway, Jolene. Just like you. L.J. picked me up just like he did you. Eighteen months ago. My folks don't know and don't care where I am."

Jolene was almost dressed. Her fingers trembled so that she could not fit the veil over her head.

"You're making me scared, Iris." Jolene's eyes were wide. "What should I do?"

"I don't know. You can't run, they'll catch you for sure. There are people all over out there."

"What is happening? What are they going to do to me?"

"Smith is the Grand Master of this coven—this congregation of Wiccans, or witches. He has been talking for years about this day: the 20th of May, 1966. He's been teaching us about the Descent of the Queen of Heaven. Today is when it happens—there's a complete solar eclipse today, and that's when it happens. The Queen of Heaven will come down, and she and Satan will make a baby. The baby is supposed to be revealed in thirty-nine years—for some reason, one year less than forty."

"So what are they going to do? What has it got to do with me?"

"*You* are the Queen of Heaven, or at least you will be the beneficiary of the spirit of the Queen of Heaven. Smith, the Grand Master, will receive the spirit of Satan."

"This can't..." she said, teetering on the threshold of hysteria. "I don't believe this!"

Mrs. "Smith" opened the door and gushed, "Oh, deary. What a lovely bride you are! My, my!"

"What are you people doing?" Jolene could not help screaming. She backed up against the couch, her arms outstretched. "Get away from me!"

The woman turned a contemptuous look upon Iris. "You told," she spat. "We'll deal with *you* later. I just hope you haven't ruined everything." She stuck her head back outside the room. "L.J., bring a rag."

L.J. appeared, a folded handkerchief in his hand, slowly approaching Jolene like a cat stalking its prey. She had nowhere to run, so she screamed, but it didn't help. L.J. grabbed her and spun her so that he was at her back, able to reach around and hold the handkerchief to her mouth and nose. She pulled and scratched at his arms to no avail.

The chloroform stung in her nostrils and eyes. Suddenly there was the greatest moment of clarity where she seemed to understand everything, her surroundings, the sky, the entire universe, but in a flash it escaped her, and all was blackness.

Time came and went—and Jolene could see and hear some things in a dense fog. It was as if she were connected to nothing, then she would retreat to darkness, to solitude and to peace. But each time she returned she was more lucid.

They were doing things to her, things that they should not be doing. There were smells, and flickering candles. Everyone was in black robes with chalk-white faces and obscene grins, and they were around her, looking down at what was happening. They were on her where they shouldn't be, and there was strange music and chanting in a bizarre language.

Her arms were stretched above her head. She looked down. The dress was no longer there. There was blood—she was covered in blood.

Oh, Lord, I'm bleeding to death.

Suddenly a shot exploded, reverberating throughout the room. Initially there was silence except for the music, then pandemonium. Screaming and crying, there was a blur of bodies scrambling in all directions.

Iris was at her side, slapping her face hard. "Jolene, you got to wake up!" Iris yelled in her ear.

"I'm dying," Jolene mumbled. "Blood."

Iris slapped her again. "It is pig blood, not yours. You got to get up." Iris fumbled with the bonds that bound Jolene's wrists and arms above her head. She got one of them loose, then the other. She was waving a gun wildly.

"Get up. Get up." She gave the gun to Jolene. "Here, hold this while I untie your feet."

Suddenly there was L.J., his face filled with rage. A knife flashed through the air, and Iris went down. Jolene shot him in the forehead, and he slumped to the floor. She removed the loose ties from her feet and looked around for "Mrs. Smith" and saw "Mr. Smith" on the floor, propped on one elbow, his arm outstretched toward her. His black robe had fallen open, revealing dark blood oozing from his stomach. Iris had shot him in the midsection.

"Please," he rasped to Jolene. "Help me."

Jolene approached him, her entire body shaking, looked him straight in the eyes and shot him in the sternum. Screaming erupted behind her, and she stood, turned, and shot "Mrs. Smith" in the chest.

Immediately, the gun dropped from Jolene's hand, and she collapsed to the floor, slipping into darkness once again.

Police cars were all over the Pale Horse Ranch. By the time they had been called, and had arrived to investigate four homicides— the murder of Mr. And Mrs. Smith, their adoptive daughter Iris, and their close family friend L.J.—all of the trappings of The Sacred Magick of Abramelin the Mage, and the special Descent of the Queen of Heaven ceremony had been erased from the ranch house.

By all accounts, except Jolene's, the teenager had rebelliously run away from home, and had been befriended by a loving couple and their daughter. Through the process of her dysfunctional thinking,

Jolene believed that she was not being given her rightful position in her newfound family. Only Iris stood in her way, so Jolene stabbed her in cold blood, then shot Mr. and Mrs. Smith when they came to help their daughter, and then, finally, she had coldly murdered L.J. All of it was without remorse.

Jolene's story, on the other hand, was bizarre. All of her newfound friends were witches, and her parents were animalistic abusers. The police in Brownsville were asked to talk to Jolene's parents. They found nothing to corroborate Jolene's story. Even her sister Faye reported that all was fine at home and that Jolene was a rebellious teenager who had run away.

The jury trial was swift, her public defender totally inept and uncaring, and sentencing was immediate. Jolene, having been tried as an adult, received four consecutive forty-year consignments to Halbert Substance Abuse Felony Punishment Facility in Burnet, Texas. It was not clear how she ended up at Halbert since Jolene had not been determined to be a substance abuser. In any event, that is where she met Dr. Ethan Chesnee, a kind and gentle man who would listen attentively to her wild and crazy stories when no one else would. In the midst of it all, though no one would believe her, she felt strangely comforted that she had killed those people. She came close to allowing herself even to believe that she had enjoyed it.

She had been at Halbert for two weeks when the doctor had called her into the clinic.

"I have some news, Jolene," he said, pausing for a response.

"Okay," she shrugged. "Good or bad?"

He shrugged in return. "Up to you, I guess. You are pregnant."

Jolene's face drained of color. *It was like a physical blow to her stomach. Mr. Smith, or L.J. or who?*

The next morning, eyes puffed and red, Jolene greeted first light through her cell window with the satisfaction that she had made a decision. It had taken a night of sobbing and crying out to God, if He was really there. Nevertheless, she had decided. She would keep the baby, and she would determine that he would be placed in a good home, with solid, loving parents.

Jolene collapsed on her bunk, exhausted, and went to sleep.

As she drifted off in the arms of some measure of peace, she had not a clue that she was carrying, not one, but two identical boys. They would be, what science terms: mirrored twins.

FIFTY-ONE
The Present

Standing in her doorway, Carol Lewis was the embodiment of complete befuddlement as she looked from David Baxter to Detective John Parella. Mr. Baxter had, about an hour and a half ago, picked up her best friend Meredith. But it wasn't Mr. Baxter. Who was it? It looked like Mr. Baxter, at least the part of his face that she could see, because the left side was covered in bandages. Had someone kidnapped Meredith?

Oh, please, God, she prayed. *Make her safe.*

Just as David was about to hand the note that he had received, probably from the killer, to Parella, the detective's walkie-talkie chirped.

"John, you there? This is Vince."

"Yeah, go ahead."

"We've got a Henry at the Hanesworth Suites on 1960. A cutting."

"10–4," Parella said.

"Who's Henry?" Baxter asked.

"'Henry' stands for homicide. Police talk."

"You coming over?" Vince asked.

"You handle it; I'm tied up right now."

"Roger, that," Vince came back. "By the way, the victim is that attorney from Plano. Hutchins. Palmer Hutchins."

Oh, merciful Jesus, Parella's brain shouted. His eyes darted to David Baxter's face. Though Baxter stared at him, his eyes were focused yards beyond him. Baxter's bottom lip began to quiver uncontrollably.

"Oh, please, not Palmer. It can't . . ." Baxter's legs no longer supported him. He teetered back against the doorframe and slid to the porch, Parella attempting to help ease him down.

Carol, seeing Mr. Baxter like this could not control her emotions. Everything was piling up. Weeping wildly, she turned and ran into the house.

"Mom, hurry. Come quick, something has happened!"

Parella drove like a wild man; siren blaring, and lights flashing. Occasionally he glanced at Baxter who was shaking violently, ashen-faced; gray lips quivering.

God, help me. God, help me, ricocheted in David's head. He did not know if he could bear this. The load was too great. His dear good friend was dead, apparently violently, and for all he knew his daughter might be dead as well. *Had they told Doris, Palmer's wife? God, help her. And she would have to tell Ricky and Tatum, the son and daughter.*

Where was Meredith? Oh, God, protect Meredith.

"I want to see him," David said, tears streaming, clenching Parella's shoulders with both hands. "He's my friend." Instantly, the image of Birdy, arms outstretched, flying down the path toward Hobo Jungle and his own demise, appeared before his eyes. Neither Birdy nor Palmer was ready. It wasn't time. What was the matter with God? Didn't He know that they were not ready?

Meredith was not ready.

Please, dear God, David prayed. *Not my Meredith! Not Meredith!* This was more than he could endure.

"You *can't* see him, Baxter," Parella said, resisting David's attempts to push by him. "First, it's a crime scene. We have to preserve evidence. Secondly, you don't really want to see him. It is not how you want to remember your friend."

David relaxed suddenly. He looked imploringly into Parella's eyes.

"We've got to find Meredith. We've got to find her. Help me, detective."

Sitting in the foyer of the Hanesworth, David could not control his shaking. Holding a cup of coffee with both hands, he had sloshed some of it onto the shiny marble floor. Parella was doing his best to console him.

"We will find Meredith, David. You have my word." *Of course,* Parella thought, *we prefer to find her alive.*

Hearing the pneumatic hiss of the lobby entry doors opening, both men looked up to see Lillian crossing the lobby, sheer terror filling her eyes. David rose quickly to meet her halfway across the lobby floor, where they clung to one another desperately.

"Oh, David, what are we going to do? Our baby, our sweet baby," Lillian's body quaked with sobs. They clung to one another for several long moments. "And dear, dear Palmer," Lillian gasped, "How are Doris and the kids?"

"They are devastated, Lill," David began to sob openly again.

"Doris knows about Meredith. She said . . . she said," David tried vigorously to catch a breath so that he could finish the sentence. "She said that she understood; that we need to concentrate on finding Meredith, and that she would be praying for her safe return."

"What are we going to do David?"

"I don't know anything to do right now but pray, Lill. Just pray—for Meredith's safety, for the police—for wisdom for them. All I know to do is put her in God's hands—I feel so helpless. I keep thinking, God says He does not allow more to come into our lives than we can bear—but this, this is . . ." David could not finish.

"I know," whispered Lillian, "I know."

A uniformed policeman approached Parella and handed him a piece of paper with gloved hand. Parella quickly reached into his jacket pocket and donned latex gloves.

"Vincent said to give you this," the officer said.

"Thanks," Parella said, and began to read the note. In a moment he looked over at David and Lillian still standing in the middle of the foyer. "You guys need to hear this," he said. They approached, and he said, "This will probably be alarming and disturbing to you, but I think you need to hear it."

"We fully understand," David said. "Read it, please."

"This is from Gemini," he prefaced, and began to read.

> *Dearest Brother Davey,*
> *If you think this is pain,*
> *You must think, Bro, again.*
> *What is to come is straight from perdition,*
> *'Twill give a small glimpse of the human condition.*
> *For just as a lamb that is destined for slaughter,*
> *This is the way you will see your sweet daughter.*

Your task is to find her, dear Davey, of course,
Before she rides off upon the Pale Horse.
But please be assured, 'twill be my great delight
to introduce Meredith to the wonderful Light.
Gemini One

"You mean that this is...? David exclaimed, his face a mask of confusion.

"You got it," Detective Parella said. "Palmer's killer is our serial killer—Gemini One. And it would seem clear now that all of this is some sort of vendetta aimed directly at you—the frame up for the other killings, Palmer's murder, your daughter's kidnapping. You have somehow made Gemini very angry, Baxter. By the way, you never mentioned that you had a brother."

David Baxter looked back and forth between Parella and Lillian.

"I don't have a brother," he said.

FIFTY-TWO

The Present

Darrell had found none of it to be very difficult.

Marianna, his one true friend, had used her position in CPS to uncover things that would have taken him years to unravel. She had provided him with copies of all the records.

He discovered that he had been born to Jolene Waters who had died giving birth at age sixteen in the Halbert Substance Abuse Felony Punishment Facility in Burnet, Texas, where she was incarcerated for the heinous murders of four innocent victims. His mother's story had been that she herself had been a victim, that she had suffered some sort of satanic ritual abuse at the hands of the people that she had killed. No one believed her story, and there had been numerous eyewitnesses for the prosecution who had testified to her cold bloodied murders.

Darrell had done the math. The day of the killings, May 20, 1966, was almost nine months to the day of his birth, February 14, 1967. It struck Darrell intuitively. Something *had* happened on that day, May 20th, just like his mother had said. That's why on the copy of his birth certificate where there was a space for the name of his father it said *Unknown*.

The transcript of the trial had shown that his mother Jolene Waters had stated that Iris "Smith" had told her that May 20th was a special, high day to the Satanic group, that Satan, during a total eclipse of the sun on that day, would indwell the High Priest, and that the Queen of Heaven, the Goddess of Light would descend from the sky and indwell Jolene and the union of those two spirits would result in the birth of a baby who would be revealed to the world in thirty-nine years. All of the madness had occurred at the Pale Horse Ranch, near Decker Prairie, Texas, just northwest of Houston.

Surprisingly, Darrell had discovered that his mother had given birth to another son, an identical twin brother, later named David Baxter, who had arrived two and one half minutes after Darrell. The nurse who had attended his birth, Darlene Phelps, had adopted Darrell; his brother had been adopted not many days after birth to Herbert and Lila Baxter in La Marque, Texas. David had graduated law school from Baylor, and had married Lillian Jean Hansen, with whom he had had Meredith Loraine, whose destiny was now in Darrell's hands. David had not been difficult to locate. Interestingly enough, he did not live far from where they had been conceived and from where Darrell was now holding Meredith at the abandoned Pale Horse Ranch. Not long now and all of this would rush to the final conclusion, and his dear brother would finally know just some of the pain and anguish that Darrell had suffered most of his life. It was almost time for the true son to be revealed; it was thirty-nine years now.

The plan had been ingenious from the beginning. It had evolved, of course, as Darrell had grown, as he had understood more and more. Darrell had ultimately conceived it all with just one aim in mind. He would bring it all full-circle. It had not been about the girls. Not about them at all. They had been only a means to an end. He was the chosen purveyor of light. He and his brother had originated from the Queen of Heaven, the Goddess of Light. The return path was by way of the road of suffering. Darrell had suffered dutifully. His brother had now begun to suffer, but not yet

252

sufficiently. Soon, Darrell would usher them in together, and they would finally enter the light to be with their mother, the Queen, the Goddess.

Marianna had delivered the last of the information to him when he was eighteen years old. He had told her that he was living in the Home and Hearth Suites on Austin's west side. In fact he had checked in that day, head swathed in bandages to hide his battered face, under the name of Toby Tyler.

Marianna had expected one million dollars for her efforts. She had already committed $330,000 of it on a new house.

Darrell had, instead, given her much better. He had introduced her to the Light with a baseball bat. That next morning, around 3:00 a.m., he had discarded her body in some deep wooded property north of Highway 183. To his knowledge her remains had never been discovered; and the police had never approached him about it.

The FBI would soon be involved because of Meredith's kidnapping. Surely, one of them, the police or the FBI, would be able to decipher his coded messages. He would hate to have to just come right out and tell them where Meredith was being held in reserve. There would be no predominance in that. It was the way the world was. Once you accepted that, everything else fell into place. The cat knew its place and accepted it. The mouse knew its place and accepted that as well. The cat taunted the mouse, played with the mouse, tormented the mouse—he would even let the mouse go— seemingly, within a prescribed sphere of reality. But the end would always be the same. Always. The cat killed the mouse. Always. The mouse never killed the cat. Never. If so, it would have made major headlines. It would rock the world: *Mouse Kills Cat.*

Strange how that works, Darrell mused. *It seemed that the recipi-*

ents that he had ministered to over the years always somehow understood this principle. Usually just before the end. He could see the conversion occur in their eyes. It would occur as a final epiphany.

"Hey," they would seem to say to themselves, "I'm a mouse!"

Then the final realization, "And I am in the presence of a Cat!"

FIFTY-THREE

The Present

Both David and Lillian responded to the doorbell. Detective Parella stood at the entryway with another man. There were several men and women strung down the sidewalk. To David's relief there was no sign of the media.

"Mr. And Mrs. Baxter, this is Special Agent Michael Grant with the Bureau here in Houston," Parella gestured to the dark suited man next to him. Both men were the presence of utter solemnity. Agent Grant was a shade taller than Parella. He was unquestionably government, evidenced by his standard issue brown crew cut, dark suit, white shirt, dark tie, and brilliantly polished black shoes. He was not, however, wearing sunglasses. Baxter assumed they were tucked away in his jacket.

David offered his hand and said, "We're glad that you are here, Agent Grant."

Grant's handshake was strong and filled with confidence. "We are here to see that your daughter is returned home safely, Mr. and Mrs. Baxter." He turned and nodded toward the group lined up on the walkway. "This is our Kidnap Recovery Team, along with some of Detective Parella's team. We fully recognize that this may be somewhat invasive for you, Mrs. Baxter, but we will need to set up in your home.'

"Please," Lillian smiled weakly, "Do what you must. This house is not what is important at the moment."

"Good," Agent Grant said, returning the smile in kind, not too broad. "Our goal is to be here for the shortest possible time." He turned and nodded toward the waiting team, and then, returning his gaze toward Mrs. Baxter, he gestured toward the interior.

"Shall we?" he said.

The teamed filed in after them, laden with boxes of equipment, cables, power cords and power strips, printers, notebook computers and light stands.

"Typical home circuit breakers can't handle the power that we will be needing, Mr. Baxter," Agent Grant said. "So we bring our own power generator. It will be in the front yard, but it's very quiet. You may hear it inside the house, but only slightly."

"Please," David responded, "As my wife said, don't worry about the house—or us, either. Feel free to do whatever you deem necessary. You don't have to check with us, okay?"

"Yes, sir," Grant said.

"And one other thing," David said.

"Yes, sir?"

"Call me David."

"Yes, sir."

"Ah, the cavalry has arrived," Darrell chuckled aloud. "And none too discreetly."

He drove slowly past David's house in his rental, yellow Ford Ranger pickup. He was following three other rubberneckers, so he would not attract any undue attention. Besides, his credo usually was, *The best place to hide is in the open.*

He had no idea what progress, if any at all, had been made with his clues. The latest note should arrive soon. Plus, there would be the added information provided by his phone call.

He would just let them set up all their tracing gear and snooty gadgetry before he made the call.

Meredith was cycling through peaks and valleys of peace and terror. Her mind would race through various scenarios of terrible possibilities, then she would pray aloud, beseeching God for His supernatural peace. She recalled the verses that she had memorized from Philippians chapter 4: "Be anxious for nothing, but in everything by prayer and supplication with thanksgiving, let your request be made known to God, and the peace of God, which passes all understanding, will guard your hearts and minds in Christ Jesus."

"Thank you, Father for Your peace," she said aloud. "Thank You, Jesus for guarding my mind and my heart." Tranquility would settle upon her, and she would relax, at one point she even fell asleep for a brief period.

During interludes of calm, she would try to review what she had learned at the self-defense classes that her father had encouraged her to attend. She and her best friend Carol had attended together, and had practiced with and upon one another. She ran through the techniques, wondering if she could bring herself to attempt any of the procedures if she had a chance.

The first rule was to always find a weapon if possible; a pole or stick, preferably one that was sharp on one end, and long enough to use for jabbing. The primary objective was to deliver a disabling puncture wound to the attacker; to the eyes, neck, upper torso, thigh; anything that would allow you to run, and prevent him from chasing.

A larger board or pole would also work, something that could be used as a club. One could also throw heavy objects, such as a reasonably large rock or brick, lamps, small pieces of furniture—any heavy object. The main point was that one must think clearly and fast; potential weapons could be within easy reach. In the absence of something heavy, dirt or flour could be thrown to cause temporary blindness.

In the absence of anything that could be used for a weapon, Meredith tried to remember the next steps. One's fingers, hands, arms, legs and feet were the next available weapons if used properly. Finger jabs to the eyes could immobilize an assailant, a sudden palm thrust at the end of the nose upward, breaking the nose, could discourage an attacker.

She went through the various steps as best as she could remember them, still wondering if she could employ any of them given the opportunity. She remembered something her instructor had said, "Heaven forbid, there may come a time when you have to make an extremely difficult decision. Will I survive or will I die? The basis for self-defense is founded upon your attitude toward this question. The answer will be in your hands; *you* must reconcile yourself to the premise that you will live, regardless of the consequences to your attacker."

Meredith's heart began to race when she heard the vehicle tires crunching on the pathway outside the stables.

Footsteps approached and stable doors creaked open, flooding the interior with light. More footsteps. Meredith seemed powerless to make a sound.

"Hello, Meredith. Hello-o-o-o."

The man standing in the stall entry did not look like her father. His face was not bandaged. He had shoulder length, sandy hair and a mustache. He wore a white T-shirt, jeans, and tennis shoes. Strangely, he wore a black leather glove on his left hand. His left arm was shorter and smaller than his right, and it appeared that he could not seem to straighten it out. He carried a bag in his right hand from which wafted the odor of French fries and a hamburger.

"How are you, Meredith? Are you reasonably comfortable, child?" She was very pretty with those freckles splattered across her nose, her red hair pulled back in a ponytail, and those crinkly green eyes. *My goodness. You've done well, David. Very well, indeed. Ah, well, my dearest brother, that's all starting to change, isn't it? And how does it feel? Not so hot, huh? Well, don't worry, Davey. It'll get worse.*

"Let me go, please," Meredith pleaded in a whisper.

Cat and mouse.

"Okay, here's how it works," the man said, squatting on his haunches just inches from her. "I talk first. You respond. I ask a question. You answer. Okay?"

Meredith remained silent.

"Now, that was a question, Meredith. *Okay?* was a question." He grabbed her jaw in his left hand and squeezed until it hurt. Tears formed in her eyes.

"Okay," she whispered.

"Good enough," he said, standing.

Meredith had noticed two things. One, the man smelled like rubber. Two, his left eye looked weird, and never moved, regardless of what his right eye did.

"Hungry?" the man asked, holding the white paper bag near her face. Her nostrils filled with the blended, rich aromas of ¼ pound of beef, chopped onions, mustard and pickles.

"No," Meredith answered. She was too frightened to be hungry.

"You must be hungry," he said, pushing the bag into her face. "It's been at least twelve hours since you ate last. I don't want you to be all woozy on me. I'm going to untie you so you can eat. Okay? That's another question."

"I have to go." Meredith was embarrassed to say it.

"What?"

"I have to go to the restroom."

"There is no restroom," he said derisively.

"Well, I have to go real bad."

"This place is shut down." He was becoming agitated. "There is no running water, no electricity. It's abandoned."

"I don't care. There has to be some place I can go. Hurry." She looked at him with pleading eyes.

"Alright, alright. I'll see what I can find. I'll be right back." He left abruptly.

Meredith was having trouble controlling her breathing; it was too shallow, and she felt light-headed. She remembered her self-defense instructor emphasizing the importance of breathing deeply—slowly and deeply. Her head needed to be clear. Her main objective now was to escape—to get away. There was no question in her mind that this man could do her great harm.

She prayed again, *Lord, help me. Lord, help me.* It was all that she could think to pray at the moment.

"You're a pain, you know it?" the man said as he came striding into the stall. "A real pain. I hope you're not this much trouble to your folks."

He began fumbling with the rope that secured her chair to a cleat in the wall. She could see that his left hand didn't provide much help.

You can bite a nose off, you can bite an ear off, or you can bite a lip off. Any of these things can slow an attacker down long enough for you to run away. You have to be reconciled within yourself that you are willing to inflict pain upon, and do damage to the one who threatens you. You must be committed. If you do it half-heartedly you will do nothing more than make your assailant mad. Say to yourselves, and to me, "I can do it!"

I can do it, reverberated in Meredith's mind. *I can do it. Lord, help me.*

"Alrighty, then," the man said, standing up. "You're all set." The ropes dangled from his right hand.

She tried to stand, and crumpled back into the chair. She could not feel her legs. There was no way that she could do anything in this condition, she couldn't even walk, much less run. She tried rubbing feeling into one arm and hand, then the other.

"C'mon, c'mon," he said brusquely. "I have places to go, people to see."

"I'm sorry," she said, as meekly as she could. "I can't stand up."

"Well, you'll figure it out if you have to go bad enough. Meanwhile, I'm going to eat this hamburger since you don't eat."

"I am thirsty," Meredith said.

"Hmmp," he grumped, and pulled a cup of coke out of the bag. He flipped the lid off, took a long swig and handed her the cup. "I don't have any germs," he smiled crookedly.

"I can't hold the cup very good," she said, trying to take the cup in both hands. "My fingers aren't working right."

"For Pete's sake," he groused. "Are you helpless?" He bent over and placed the cup to her lips, his face within inches of her own.

FIFTY-FOUR

Present Day

It had been three hours since the FBI had completed their equipment setup. There had been only two phone calls—one, a friend of Lillian's, Janice Peters; the other from Evan James, David's mentor. Janice had called to say that the church was praying for them and for Meredith. Evan had offered to come over to be with the Baxters, and David had welcomed him.

As soon as Evan had arrived, he gathered whoever desired to join him in a prayer circle. The Baxters and five of the police/FBI team clasped hands around the room and prayed for Meredith's strength and safekeeping, for wisdom and insight for the investigators, for supernatural peace for the Baxter's and the intervention of the Spirit of God in this whole heart-wrenching affair.

As they were saying "Amen" the doorbell chimed. Agent Grant went to the door and greeted a female agent, who offered him a large white envelope. The woman spoke rapidly and quietly. Grant kept his head down, scanning the contents of the envelope as he listened to the woman.

Evan was speaking quiet words of encouragement to David and Lillian as they were seated on the family room couch, but David's focus was on the entry door, anticipating news of Meredith, not hearing anything that Evan was saying. Lillian was fidgeting with a handkerchief, her knees bouncing up and down at a rapid pace. David noted that Grant had nodded Detective Parella over and had begun to speak in low tones to him, their backs to David.

"David," Lillian said, touching his forearm. "Evan asked you a question."

"Oh, sorry, Ev," David said, shaking his head. "I'm a little preoccupied." David was about to excuse himself to go see what news there was at the front door, when Grant and Parella turned toward him.

"David," Detective Parella said, "Could you come over here for a moment, please?" Baxter rose and went to the door, his eyes asking the two lawmen the unspoken question.

Parella answered the question, shaking his head. "There is nothing new on Meredith, Dave."

"Mr. Baxter," Agent Grant said, motioning to the newly arrived agent. "I'd like you to meet Special Agent Colleen Merick. She is an analyst with the Bureau. She and her team have been analyzing the notes from Gemini."

Agent Merick offered her hand to Baxter. "Mr. Baxter," she said. Her grip was firm, her gaze level and self-assured.

"Whatever you have to say," David said, turning toward Lillian who was still seated at the sofa, "I would like for my wife to hear it as well."

Although David had directed his comment to Agent Merick, Agent Grant responded.

"Certainly," he said. And then over to Lillian Baxter, "Mrs. Baxter, can we meet at your breakfast table, please? This is Agent Merick. She has some new information that we want to share with you and Mr. Baxter."

Agent Merick slipped a black computer bag off her shoulder and laid it on the table as everyone found their seats, except for Lillian Baxter, who busied herself serving up coffee.

"Please, go ahead," she said. "I can listen while I'm getting the coffee."

Agent Merick began speaking as she readied her notebook computer.

"First, I have some documents, Mr. and Mrs. Baxter, that are very important to you and this investigation. Plus, we would also like to share with you some of our thoughts regarding the clue-notes that Gemini sent to you and Detective Parella. The Detective's team had also been working the notes, and gave us a good head start with some of their insights." She nodded toward Parella and smiled slightly.

Adjusting the angle of the computer screen she asked, "Can everyone see okay?"

Anticipating what was coming, Baxter interrupted. "Agent Merick, I don't want to seem rude, but if you have a lot of documents scanned in there that you want to show us, please just give us a verbal summary." He smiled. "I'm wired so tight I can hardly sit, and I would guess that my wife is pretty much in the same shape."

"Certainly," Agent Merick said. "I brought hard copies that I can leave with you, Mr. Baxter." She closed the display on her computer.

"The primary thing that stood out in our initial look at Gemini's notes was his multiple references to you Mr. Baxter as 'Bro' and 'Brother.' We have investigated and determined that, rather than the references being just a euphemism, you and Gemini are in fact brothers."

China cups and saucers rattled on the tray as Lillian Baxter almost dropped the five cups of coffee she was bringing to the table. "Oh, my!" she exhaled in a loud whisper. Looking over at her husband, she saw the incredulity on his face, and she felt the love that she had for this man sweep over her. He seemed even more vulnerable than he appeared when he was incarcerated. At the same time she knew that there was an undercurrent of strength that emanated, not from her husband, but from the Lord. She sat the tray of coffee and accoutrements on the table.

"Please help yourselves," she said, and walked around behind her husband, placing her hands on his shoulders.

Agent Merick continued. "Mr. Baxter, our investigation has showed that you and Gemini are not simply brothers, you are identical twins. Gemini was born first, and then a few minutes later you were delivered."

"Identical . . . ?" David said.

"That's correct. He signs the notes *Gemini One,* which means, of course *Twin One.* He came first, so you are no doubt *Gemini Two.* In going back over your records, including addendums to your birth records made by the attending nurse, we determined that you are not just identical, but you are among a small group of identical twins known as mirrored twins. This is a phenomenon that is not fully understood by medical science, but it is just what the term implies. If you were to stand in front of your twin brother, it would be more like looking into a mirror. If you are right-handed he is left-handed. If the hair on the crown of your head swirls clockwise, his will swirl counter-clockwise. Even your brains are organized opposite from one another. Some say that the fingerprints of mirrored twins are very close to identical, except on opposite hands. The fortunate thing about your birth is that you were born as separate individuals. A large percentage of mirrored twins are born connected—conjoined or Siamese Twins."

"Why am I just now—why was I never told? Why didn't someone tell me I had a brother early on? Maybe I could have—maybe things would have been different. What happened?" David looked from Merick to Grant to Parella.

"Your adoptive parents never knew that you had a brother, Mr. Baxter," Agent Merick said. "It was not their fault." She studied him carefully. "Would you care to hear more, Mr. Baxter?"

"I don't know," David shook his head. "I can't imagine

what might come next. So, go ahead, I guess. I'll stop you if I've had enough."

"Your mother died giving birth to you and your brother. The attending nurse adopted your brother. Her name was . . ." Agent Merick consulted her notes. " . . . Darlene Phelps. Your brother's name is Darrell Phelps."

"Darrell Phelps," David repeated. "Darrell Phelps," he said again, as if testing the name in his mouth. "My brother. The one who has brutally murdered six people, including two of my good friends. The one who now has my daughter, heaven knows where . . . and heaven knows how she's doing!" David shouted, standing abruptly, slamming both fists onto the table, causing five cups of coffee and their saucers to jump into the air, sloshing coffee every-where. Agent Merick quickly lifted her notebook computer off the tabletop, while Parella grabbed the hard copies of the records. Lillian hurried to get paper towels.

David walked in circles, both hands to his head. "Meredith . . . Oh, Meredith."

Lillian left the towels on the table and went to her husband, encircling his waist with her arms. They held one another quietly, while the others silently honored their moment of intimacy. Agent Merick quietly busied herself by wiping up the spilled coffee with the paper towels.

"Sorry, guys," David said after a time, both hands lifted in sur-render. "I'm just . . . I don't . . ."

"No, no," Parella said. "It's okay."

"We don't have to continue right now," Grant said. "We can wait."

"It's okay," David said. "Let's go on." He remained standing.

"These are just the highlights," Agent Merick said. "You can get the details from the hard copies. Anyway . . . your brother, Darrell's adoptive mother was killed in an automobile accident when he was six. He barely survived and was severely disfigured on the left side of his face. He bounced from foster home to foster home until he was sixteen, when he ended up in an orphan's home in Austin. He won major suits against the doctors and the hospital that performed reconstructive surgery on his face. He became an instant multi-millionaire. He apparently was able somehow to convert his settlement from a trust fund to a lump sum, since we no longer see him on paper after eighteen. We have not yet determined what his identity was from then until now. His money bought him a new identity. Our thinking is that this was about the time that Darrell discovered that he was adopted. He went looking in the records and discovered his real mother. And, what's more important, he discovered that he had a twin brother."

"Who is she, my mother...and who is my real father?" David asked.

"Your mother's name was Jolene Waters. I'm sorry to say that she died at your birth. Your adoptive parents adopted you when you were five days old. You will see on your copy of the records that your biological father is listed as 'unknown.'"

"How could my brother do all of these horrible things . . . *Why* would he do all of these things? How can he be so evil?"

Agent Merick folded her hands, resting them on the table. Pursing her lips she pondered for a moment. "We believe that your brother has fixated on you, Mr. Baxter. What seems likely is that when he discovered his birth mother, and consequently discovered you, he set out to find you. He probably had no idea what he would do when he found you. We do not know when that happened—when he actually found you. It is possible that he has been stalking you for a number of years."

Lillian shivered visibly at the frightening thought.

"What Darrell discovered is that you have what he has always wanted and has never had. He found you surrounded by friends and family, living the good life, peace and tranquility were yours, and he resented it. What he discovered fueled the anger that was already at the combustion point.

"Serial killers live some large part of their lives in a fantasy world, Mr. Baxter. Like children. Darrell's world probably started when he was six. There were some photographs in his medical records—his injuries from the car wreck. It was terrible. The left side of his face was pretty much destroyed. He looked like a monster before his cosmetic surgery. He looked like a monster *after* his surgery. It is probable that he isolated himself in his self-fabricated world. If he is typical, he sees himself as a super-hero. He is special. He may even think that he is God. He no doubt has a messianic complex. He speaks in his clue-notes of leading his victims, or introducing them, to the light.

"We believe that Darrell devised an elaborate plan just to get to you—the homicides, the fingerprints, certainly your daughter's kidnapping—all of it has been designed to culminate in a confrontation with you, Mr. Baxter. He wants you to suffer just as he has suffered. It is not fair that he has suffered so much, and you have not. He references a scripture verse in his note to you . . ." Merick again consulted her notes.

"'He learned obedience through suffering—Hebrews 5:8.'"

"He is referring both to his past suffering and the future suffering that he has planned for you. In one of his notes he writes:

"'The elder will know the younger again—Not in seeing or hearing, but in pain.'"

His perspective is that he can validate himself and his world by controlling others in their world, and now more specifically, you and your world. To cause you pain, or to give you relief from it is his prerogative. It starts with him at a distance, looking on. Eventually, he will want to see you suffer up close and personal. He will want a one on one with you, Mr. Baxter."

Agent Merick paused, gazing at David, then towards Lillian.

Both of them looked as though a slight nudge would send them over the threshold into a catatonic state.

"So, I know this is a lot like getting a drink with a fire hose, Mr. and Mrs. Baxter, but we thought it might be helpful if you had some idea about what is going on. Do you have any questions?"

After a period of awkward silence, David finally said, "Before I knew that this . . . murderer is my brother, I had everything somewhat neatly packaged and gift wrapped. This was a cold-bloodied killer that, I had no doubt, could do harm . . . could murder our Meredith. He was not human, not a person." David's face contorted into a mask of grief momentarily. Then he regained control. "And this was very difficult—it is something that your mind simply does not want to accept, to realize—that someone wants to kill your child . . . is actually plotting to kill your child. In my mind he was nothing more than an animal—a predatory animal. This is what predatory animals do—they hunt and kill. You can expect nothing else from them. They are wired to kill." He massaged his forehead, not able to look into the eyes of anyone at the table for fear he would lose the bit of composure he was clinging to. He was pacing back and forth now.

"Now," he continued, voice cracking slightly, "Now I find that this is my brother doing these reprehensible things, my flesh and blood, my family, for heaven's sake and I . . ." He began shaking his head vigorously. "I can't comprehend it. I can't fit that into a neat little box. It is just . . . how is he able to do these things to his *niece*? How is he able—what is in him, or *not* in him that allows him to do such things?"

Before anyone could respond, David's cell phone rang.

FIFTY-FIVE

Present Day

"Is this David Baxter?"

The voice was calm, little more than a whisper, and extremely chilling to David. These were the first words from a brother that he had not known—had never known—even existed. These were the first words that he had ever heard from the mouth of a wicked, psychopathic killer.

"Is this Darrell Phelps?" David queried back.

Agent Michael Grant, who had donned his earphones, as had practically everyone in the room, flashed a thumbs up to David.

There was a pause before Darrell responded. "I see that the suits have been busy. What have they told you, David? What have they said about me?"

"How is my daughter? I want to talk to Meredith."

"Ah, feisty little Meredith. She's quite lovely, you know. You and Lillian outdid yourselves, Dave. Anyway, your little girl's fine. Don't worry about her. We have some business to attend to first, you and I."

David's voice rose, "I want to speak to Meredith! I'm not doing a thing until I know that she's alright."

"Tch, tch, tch, David. No need to be melodramatic. Did the FBI tell you to say that? Or did you get it from a movie? Because in real life it doesn't work that way. Why? Because you're not going to abandon your daughter, regardless of her condition. You will do as I say, David. You have no choice but to cooperate with me—that's the only way that you will *ever* find her. Understand?"

David nodded. "I understand. I don't like it, but I understand."

"You don't have to like it. You need to understand as well," Darrell continued, "that we have to keep the authorities out of this. If you can't do that, then Meredith is, shall we say, in real jeopardy. So is Lillian, and ultimately, so are you."

There was the sudden, sharp intake of breath from Lillian. Agent Grant shook his head and waved his hand before his face to signal: *Don't worry, everything will be alright.*

"And by the way," Darrell continued, "John Parella, your dear wife Annie Louise, and your own sweet daughter Jenny Marie would be in the same kettle of fish. Not to mention your own pathetic self."

Jumping to his feet, Parella slammed his palm on the table. "Why, you miserable . . ."

Agent Grant and another agent grabbed Parella by each arm.

"Whoa!" Darrell yelped on the other end of the line. "Struck a nerve, did we? I bet if Deputy John could come through the phone he would be here right now with his hands around my throat."

Parella held up two fingers to a uniformed policeman. "Two cars to my house, now! If Jenny is not home find her and fetch her there. Let me know as soon as everyone's in the house, safe."

"Face it, John," Darrell said. "You haven't done so hot on this one. You finally found the prints and hair, and you would have gotten nowhere without the notes. But, *C'est la vie,* I reckon."

Parella did not respond. Instead, David said, "Let's get back to Meredith, Darrell."

"Right," Darrell said. "We have established that you will cooperate, and there will be no police. It is necessary that it is absolutely clear to everyone within hearing distance of my voice; if I so much as get the slightest hint that there is a cop or an agent within sniper's range of me, then you can be guaranteed that you will never see the girl again. Understood? Everyone around the room, say 'We understand, Darrell.' One—two—three . . . say it."

Everyone in the room looked around awkwardly.

"Say it!"

Agent Grant stood, and counted, "One, two, three . . ."

The room shouted, halfheartedly, "We understand, Darrell."

"Good. Okay, here's how it is going to work, David. The objective is to get you to me without, as I said, any interference from anyone else. I want you to go to the Baskin-Robbins Ice Cream Store at Louetta and Stuebner Airline. Be there by 3:00. You will get your next instructions there."

"How will I know . . . ?" David began, but there was a dial tone on the other end.

"Did you get him?" Agent Grant asked his tracking team.

"He's on Lyons School Road. Not moving," a young agent, seated before a bank of high-tech equipment which included LCD monitors displaying a histogram of signal strength, another showing real-time waveforms of the cell phone signal, and a map with a blinking red dot in the middle of the screen, situated on Lyons School Road just south of Louetta Road.

"Gemini's 20 is Louetta Road and Lyons School Road," agent Grant said into his lapel mike, speaking to thirty-four field agents comprised of a five member SWAT team, two negotiators, fifteen plain clothes, and six two-man surveillance teams. The FBI was using a classified frequency that would not be on Darrell's scanner, if he had one.

All eyes expectantly turned to Grant, who shook his head and said, "All agents standby."

"Loss of signal," the operator monitoring Darrell's cell phone said. "He's powered down his phone."

"Or destroyed it," Parella said.

"Never mind," Grant said. "Mr. Baxter—David, we have just a few minutes to get you ready for your meeting."

David could only nod. His face and palms were dripping with sweat. Lillian clung to his elbow. Her daughter was in the hands of a killer, and her husband was about to be. It occurred to her that perhaps staying behind, not knowing, feeling helpless, was perhaps the most difficult part. She tried to control the trembling in her body but could not. All she could pray was *Jesus.*

"Remove your belt and put this one on, please."

"What is it?" David asked.

"It serves a twofold purpose," Grant said. "One, it has imbedded in it a micro-miniature transponder. A transponder does not transmit, but reacts to an incoming signal. It rebounds a signal, so to speak, responding to an incoming interrogation or ping by turning it around and sending it back to the transmitter. We can know where you are at all times so long as you have this belt on. Number two, it has a radio transmitter in it which will transmit every word you say, or anyone else says, who is within ten feet of you."

Smiling slightly, Grant said, "I need you to remove your shirt, please."

"Okay," David complied quickly.

Grant showed David a four-inch square flesh-colored patch. "This is a hot-patch. It won't be hot to you, David; it is hot to our FLIRs—our Forward Looking Infrared equipment. We will see a thermal image of you and those with you. This patch will let us know which target is you."

So the snipers know whom not to shoot, David thought. Aloud he said, "I'm assuming this infrared stuff is on a helicopter. How will Darrell not know? Won't he hear or see the chopper?"

"We have advanced technology in that area as well. Stealth technology. Trust me, David, Darrell will neither hear us nor see us. But we will see and hear him."

David rebuttoned his shirt. "I appreciate your prayers, folks. Any final words?"

Agent Merick spoke up, "Very briefly, Mr. Baxter, I know it's time for you to go, but we didn't have an opportunity to discuss the notes—just one thing; the notes refer more than once to the 'Pale Horse.' Now, we know that in the Bible in Revelation the rider of the pale horse is Death. Typically we find that persons who commit multiple homicides, and send written clues to 'help' the authorities in their efforts, most often apply double meanings to their clues. We are still researching, but I was wondering, does 'Pale Horse' mean anything to you?"

David let the name roll around in his head. *Pale Horse.* He recalled the verse: "behold, a pale horse: and he that sat upon him, his name was Death; and Hades followed with him. And there was given unto them authority over the fourth part of the earth, to kill…"

David shook his head. "Sorry," he said. "I can think of nothing. Sorry. I guess I had better go."

Lillian embraced David and kissed him on the lips. "I'll be praying every moment, Darling, for you and Meredith. I love you."

"I love you, Lill. I *will* see you soon. Meredith and I will see you soon." They embraced for a long moment.

John Parella shook David's hand. "God speed, David."

"Good luck to you, Mr. Baxter," Agent Grant said with a firm handshake.

Everyone in the room stood. "God bless you…Good luck, sir… God bless, Mr. Baxter . . . Go get 'em Mr. Baxter." The room was filled with well wishes.

David stepped outside, surveying the sky. Not a cloud was in sight, and the temperature was in the low seventies. It couldn't be nicer.

And he was going to meet his brother.

✳ ✳ ✳ ✳ ✳

David struggled to focus as he drove the short mile and a half to the meeting with Darrell. His stomach was in turmoil and his palms damp on the steering wheel as his mind wrestled with what was happening. He was finding it more difficult to breathe.

All of these years have gone by, and I had a brother and didn't know it. How is it that he has become what he has become? What was he doing when I was playing with Birdy and Johnny and Hebert? What was he doing when we were camping? How can a brother do this to another brother? He's my flesh and blood for heaven's sake. He's my brother—my identical twin brother My mirror twin brother.

What was he doing when I was playing football . . . baseball . . . ? Did he not have many friends? When did he first kill someone? How long has he been watching me? What was he doing when I got married . . . when Meredith was born? What has he done to Meredith? Is she okay? What can I do? Meredith, sweetheart, stay strong. God, strengthen her with Your strength.

David turned into the strip center parking lot, parked in front of the Baskin Robins Ice Cream Store, and went in. The shop was empty of customers.

"May I help you?" the young clerk asked, curling her hair around a finger. She stood expectantly behind a display counter of gallons of ice-cream-filled buckets.

"Small Diet Coke," David answered, noting that it was 2:55 by the clock on the wall. He looked around the shop. Where were his instructions from Darrell?

"One dollar seventy nine," the girl said, handing him the cup of cola. She was not much older than Meredith. And she was in this shop, safe, innocent, and no idea of the horrors out there. No idea of what his little girl was going through right now. He handed her a five-dollar bill.

Immediately a cell phone rang somewhere in the shop. The ring tone was Beethoven's Fifth Symphony. Da-da-da-dum. Death, knocking at the door. Da-da-da-dum. Following the sound, Baxter looked under the table. Nothing. He turned over the chairs, one by one.

"Sir?" the girl said. "What are you doing?"

There it was, a cell phone taped under the chair. He ripped it off and put it to his ear.

"Okay, Darrell. I'm here."

"Good. Remember what I said about law enforcement."

"I'm alone."

"Alright then. Remember this. Go west on Louetta to 249. Right on 249 through Tomball to Decker Prairie. Turn left at the intersection of 249 and Decker Prairie Road. Stop and wait there for instructions. Do you have it?"

"Why are you doing this?"

"What? Come on, David. Didn't the FBI shrink tell you? What were you doing the forty-five minutes you were with those kooks? What do they know anyway? I'm doing this, David, because I am the only one who *can* do it. It's exactly 13.4 miles to your destination. You have twenty-five minutes. Don't be late."

David was about to close the cell phone when he heard, "And David?"

"Yes?"

"Destroy the phone."

David recalled two other brothers as he drove west on Louetta Road. Two brothers who had conflicts with one another. Biblical brothers. Cain and Abel. Cain's jealousy toward his brother Abel prompted him to murder his brother. Then Cain's great great grandson, Lamech, murdered a man whom he felt had done him wrong. Somewhere in the book of Numbers it said that the iniquity of the fathers is visited upon the children to the third and fourth generations. It was often referred to as a generational curse. And a curse could be dealt with; a curse could be broken.

Turning north on State Highway 249, David could see that traffic was moderate. Reaching Decker Prairie on time should not be a problem. He strained to hear sounds of a helicopter overhead, but could hear nothing.

Entering the little city of Tomball, David could see people going about their daily routine, taking the moment for granted—taking life for granted. On the left was a marquee advertising current running movies: *End of the Spear, Glory Road, Chronicles of Narnia, King Kong*—people were going into the theaters to escape. David prayed to God that Meredith could escape, that he could escape. The word had a whole new meaning to him.

"Hello, David."

David Baxter's heart lurched. Reactively swerving he barely missed making contact with the adjacent car to the right. Darrell had stowed away in the back seat. He must have gotten into the SUV at the ice cream shop.

"Sorry for the scare, David."

David looked into the rear view mirror but could not see his brother.

"Don't turn around. Not just yet. We will meet more formally shortly."

"What if I had locked my car, like I usually do?" David asked.

"Then we would have gone to plan B. But you didn't, so, here we are. Just keep driving. Nothing stupid."

"You don't have to do this, Darrell."

"Shut up, David, you have no idea regarding what I have to do."

David heard for the first time the anger resident in his brother. He prayed, and decided not to shut up.

"There is a solution to all this, Darrell. There is an answer in the person of Jesus Christ. An answer to all your pain, your . . ."

"Shut up! You don't know what you're talking about. I am unique. So are you. I am an envoy, a messenger of light from the One on High. Didn't the Feds tell you about the circumstances of our birth?"

"They told me our mother died giving birth to us. That you were born first. They said that the attendant nurse who adopted you was killed in an automobile accident when you were six years old. They told me that you lived in numerous foster homes."

"You have more to learn about our special birth, David. But not now, later. Did they tell you I'm worth millions?"

"No, they didn't mention that."

"Here," Darrell said. "Turn left at the next light. Then pull in to the café parking lot on your left. Stop and turn off the engine. Keep your eyes forward."

David complied, and Darrell continued, "I'm going to blindfold you. I'm taking you to Meredith, so don't do anything dumb. Besides, you need to hear the rest of the story. It's a doozy."

Darrell tied a black sash tightly around David's eyes. "Okay, step out of the car. Do I need to cuff you, David?" David slid out of the SUV, shaking his head no to the question. As Darrell spoke he was patting David down, looking for a wire. "Give me your shoes, please."

"No, you don't need to cuff me. I want to see Meredith. I won't do anything. Why do you need my shoes?"

"Smart. Shoes are a good platform for electronics. I'll buy you another pair later. Now, get in the back seat." Darrell opened the front door and took David by the elbow, directing him to the open rear door of the SUV. Once again David heard no hint of a helicopter, only a slight breeze through the pine and live oak trees and the raucous cry of grackles arguing over a tidbit in the parking lot.

"Aren't you concerned that someone will see us?" David asked.

"Fasten your seatbelt, David." David felt that the directive had added meaning far more sinister than riding in a car.

Darrell drove for twenty-five minutes, making numerous stops and turns. Try as he may, David could not keep up with which direction they were heading. Finally they turned off the paved road onto gravel and continued along a bumpy path for another five minutes, stopping abruptly.

"All out," Darrell said. "We're here."

Darrell guided David by the arm for several yards then said, "Sit. Just sit down. Right here."

David sat.

"I'm tying you up," Darrell said. "Put your hands behind you."

David pushed back. "Why? I said I'm not going to try anything. My concern is for Meredith. You have the upper hand here."

"I may have to leave you here for a spell. Give me your hands."

David complied, feeling the cord being wrapped around his wrists. Then Darrell made several wraps around David's waist followed by a number of turns around his legs. David's anxiety was growing; his heart hammering so hard he was sure that Darrell could hear it.

Immediately the blindfold was removed. Blinking his eyes rapidly, David looked around. An empty wooden chair sat before him. He noted that he was in a stable. All doors and window openings were closed, diminishing the light. Then Darrell slowly walked into David's field of vision and sat in the chair opposite him.

David was not prepared for what he saw.

FIFTY-SIX

Present Day

Operating in the fully automated NAP, or Noise Abatement Profile mode, the RAH-66 helicopter, modified for law enforcement use, hovered quietly over the property where "Number One" and "Number Two" had just entered a horse barn. They were near the center of the stalls as indicated by their thermal images on the FLIR display. Two's hot patch was clearly defined. The subjects were within inches of one another, not moving.

Normally operated by a two-man crew, this aircraft, codenamed "Eagle Eye," carried a third man, a sniper borrowed from SWAT strapped in at the door, responsible for the safety of the kidnapped girl and Number Two. At the ready was his M24 sniper rifle fitted with a Leupold M3A scope. The crew had seen no sign of Meredith on their displays or visually. They could clearly hear the conversations of the two men below. Video, audio and FLIR images were being relayed to the command station. All operating decisions would come from command, code named "Tree Top."

"Not exactly what you had expected to see, huh?" Number One said derisively.

"I…uh…I didn't…I wasn't…" Number Two tried to respond.

"I...uh...I didn't...I wasn't..." David stammered, completely nonplussed, totally taken aback by Darrell's appearance. The man who sat before him had plainly suffered unspeakable trauma to his head and face. The left side of his face had been reconstructed—poorly—covered with some kind of grayish-yellow animal skin. There were no facial contours that looked remotely human, only lumpy areas that, combined with the bulging left eye, created a reptilian appearance to the face. The left ear was a nub. The hair on the left side had been scalped; leaving wisps of gray hair springing from wrinkled pink flesh that had the look of burn-scarred tissue. The hair on the right side was thick, dark, and naturally curled, just like David's.

"That's the typical reaction, brother. I'm accustomed to it. Have been for years. You can call me Frog Face, Snake Eyes, Ju Ju Head—wouldn't be the first time. Here, this is my photogenic side," Darrel said, turning his good right side profile toward David. It was amazing. The right side was faultless, giving Baxter the surreal feeling that he was looking at himself. The only imperfection was Darrell's bottom lip, which was swollen and covered with a white bandage and tape. A bloodstain seeped through the white gauze.

"What happened to your lip?" David asked.

"I ran into a door. No big deal." Darrell turned to face David directly. "What you see here, David," he said, touching the left side of his face with his claw-like left hand, "is what I was talking about earlier. This is a depiction of my pain, my suffering. And suffering is what matures you, elevates you, David. I have suffered. You have not. But you will. It is part of my mission to bring you along to where you need to be, little brother. So, I need you to understand your origin so that you can embrace your destiny, as I have."

"Let me be clear about this, Darrell," David said with as much authority as he could muster. "I could care less about origins and destinies right now. I demand to see Meredith. I want to see that she is okay or you get no further cooperation from me."

Darrell leapt from his chair so quickly that David almost tipped over backwards. "You colossal fool!" Darrell shrieked. Suddenly there was a pistol to David's temple. Cringing, he turned his head away.

"I can determine if you are alive or dead this very minute!" Darrell pressed the muzzle to David's head, continuing to screech, "I am in charge here! You have no say! No say!"

"Treetop, this is Eagle Eye. We have a gun."

"Roger that. Can you get a shot?"

"Negative, no visual. All doors and shutters are closed. Should we let down?"

"Wait one, Eagle Eye." There was a moment of silence on the radio while the team at Command studied the FLIR images carefully; then, "That's a negative on dropping down at this time. Stand by. All Stream Bed, stand by." Stream Bed was comprised of twenty-five agents who had moved to within a quarter mile of the site.

"Roger, Treetop. Standing by."

Darrell continued to rage, waving the pistol and pacing back and forth.

"I am first! You are second! There's a reason for that. It should be clear to you. I am first because I was chosen to lead the way. You are second. Second, because you are designed to follow. I thought you got it. I thought you were beginning to understand! What am I going to do, David? Tell me. What am I going to do with you?"

David could only shake his head. His mind raced. What could he say that would break through this craziness? *Jesus, help me.*

"You have to understand the main thing first," Darrell said, his breathing labored. He returned the pistol to his waist and sat down. "We are special, you and I. The suits didn't tell you the details because they knew that you would come over to me. Who could stop us then?" Darrell threw his head back; his laugh was from the abyss of Hell.

Yea though I walk through the valley of the shadow of death..." Didn't tell me what details?" David kept his voice as steady as he could.

"The details of our conception, David. This is straight from our mother's mouth. I read the account myself, from official police records, so surely the FBI has the same account. I read the transcript of her words, directly to them. Our mother, Jolene Waters was sixteen years old when she ran away from home in Brownsville. She was running from an abusive mother, who, no doubt had seen to it that Mom had had her quota of pain. She took a bus to Northwest Houston where she was gathered up by some helpful soul who brought her out here." Darrell paused and studied David's face for a reaction. "Get it? I said 'Out here' because right here is where it all happened. Well, not here in the stable, but up the road a ways in the house. This is where you and I were conceived, David. At the Pale Horse Ranch."

Back at Tree Top, Agent Merick slapped the palm of her hand into her forehead. "The Pale Horse Ranch, of course. That's the *Pale Horse* in the clues—why didn't I find that in the records?"

"When I discovered that, I came out here to look the place over. It was abandoned. I bought it for a steal. Anyway, it all happened on a very special day, May 20, 1966. Probably doesn't mean much to you David, but it was a high holy day for the folks out here. A Wiccan coven had been meeting here for years. Witches, David. Warlocks and witches. They had anticipated this day for months and months. There would be a total eclipse of the sun on the twentieth, and precisely at that hour the god of this world and the Queen of Heaven would possess their respective recipients; and that's exactly what happened. Satan entered Mr. Smith, the High Priest of the Coven; and, you guessed it, the Queen of Heaven entered into our mother. The offspring of their union, David, was you. And me. Afterwards, David, our mother went berserk, killing the High Priest, his wife, a young man, and another teenaged girl. She was convicted of murder and went to prison, where you and I were born." Once again, Darrell paused for effect.

David was dumbstruck; his mind seemed frozen. Hardly comprehending what he was hearing he could find no immediate response, and Darrell continued.

"You and I are sons of Satan, David. It was said by the group here at Pale Horse that we would be revealed to do his bidding in thirty-nine years. It is that time now. We must obey our true father, Satan, the one true god. We will usher in his light."

Suddenly David recalled Jesus' forty days in the dessert and His response to Satan's temptations. His every response was directly from scripture.

"You shall worship the Lord your God, and Him only shall you serve," David said.

"What?"

"It is written, you shall worship the Lord your God, and Him *only* shall you serve."

Darrell cocked his head to the side, but said nothing. David sensed that his window was narrow, that he must talk fast.

"It is also written, Darrell, that 'whoever calls upon the name of the Lord shall be saved' and that 'Jesus said, "I am the way, and the truth and the life; no one comes to the Father but by me."' David noted that there was a strange hypnotic expression on Darrell's face, as if he were almost mesmerized. "Darrell, all you have to do is believe that Jesus is the Son of God, that He died on the cross for you, call upon Him to save you, and He will."

Darrell continued to remain quiet. David continued, emboldened, "It is also written, 'But now in Christ Jesus you that once were far off are made near in the blood of Christ.'"

Eagle Eye first saw the additional image on their FLIR display as it emerged from the thick piney woods, moving fast southeastward, directly toward the stables. Next they saw it on the video monitor. The co-pilot quickly zoomed in.

"It's a young female," he said, zooming in tighter. "It is Meredith Baxter."

"Treetop, Eagle Eye. Do you have the image on your video?"

"Roger that. Standby." Treetop was obviously wrestling with what to do next. Then, "Stream bed leader, establish a 100 yard perimeter. Eagle Eye, maintain your position."

"Roger that, Tree Top—perimeter, 100 yard radius around the subjects."

"Tree Top, Eagle Eye, maintaining position."

At the mention of the blood of Jesus Christ, Darrell's head jerked to one side, then rapidly to the other, then whipped forward to glare directly at David. The acrid odor of burning sulfur filled the stall. As Darrell rose from his chair the pupil of his right eye changed from black to gray, and the pristine appearance of the right side of his face distorted into a wrinkled grotesque monster, his upper lip curling back into a repulsive grin. The voice was from some cavernous depth not of this world, filled with the dreadful resonance of all manner of evil and wickedness.

"It is also written, 'Know that thou shalt surely die, thou and all that are thine.'"

David saw the blow coming but could only turn his head. Darrell backhanded him, catching him full on the right side of the face. The strike rattled his senses, causing a shrill ringing in his right ear. He tasted blood in his mouth.

"It is also written," Darrell shrilled, waving his arms madly, weaving from side to side, "There is a way which seemeth right unto a man; but the end thereof are the ways of death!" Darrell reared to his full six foot two inch height, his right arm drawn back for another blow.

But the blow did not come. Instead, strangely, Darrell's head wrenched forward violently, and even more strangely, his left glass eyeball popped from the socket and arched slowly over David's right shoulder. Darrell gradually toppled forward like a felled tree, landing on David, sending him sprawling backwards.

Immediately David saw Meredith, standing terrified, her hands wrapped around a large oak branch. She seemed paralyzed.

"Meredith, is it . . . are you alright?" David squirmed to get Darrell off of him. "Help me, push him off. Hurry!"

The words mobilized Meredith into action. Throwing the tree branch to the side, she pushed on Darrell's large frame, grunting with the effort. Finally she managed to roll him off her father. A long groan issued from Darrell's mouth as he thudded to the ground on his back.

"Mar, hurry! Get me out of these ropes, before he wakes up."

"Stream Bed, this is Tree Top. Move in. Move in. Eagle Eye, can you put down on the south side of the stable?"

"This is Eagle Eye. Roger, we can set down."

"Roger, Eagle Eye. Put down. I say again, put down. Give us a status on Gemini One visibility."

"Roger, standby."

✳ ⸸ ✳ ⸸ ✳

Meredith fumbled with the knot, her fingers not doing what she willed them to do. "Daddy, I can't get it. It's not working. The knot's too tight!"

"Meredith, you *can* do it. You can. Keep trying."

She pushed and pulled on the rope knot, trying to get it to loosen. Darrell moaned again, stirring slightly. The knot did not budge.

"Oh, no… oh, no!" she cried. "I can't."

"Meredith, you have to. You can. Jesus, help us."

Meredith stood, her eyes filled with fear. She reached down and picked up the oak limb.

"Meredith, what are you doing?" David closed his eyes as she raised the limb over her head. With all the strength she could muster she swung the branch down on the rear chair leg, which was wrapped with the rope, front to rear around David's legs. She swung again and again, the blows jarring David. On the fourth swing the leg snapped.

Quickly, Meredith dropped to her knees, pulling at the coils of rope, unwrapping the ankles first, and then moving up to her father's waist and arms, finally lifting the last of the spirals from around his shoulders.

Darrell moaned again, loudly, moving his head, shifting his body, trying to lift himself. David kicked at the coils, standing and grabbing Meredith by the hand.

"Come on," David said. "This way." He pulled his daughter toward the west doorway. Looking back he could see Darrell rising to one knee. Reaching the closed stable doors he pushed, but it did not budge. Pushing with all his might he looked behind him. Darrell was sitting in the dirt, shaking his head, trying to clear it.

"It's barred from the outside." David looked toward the first stall's shutters. They were closed. Darrell had probably nailed them shut as well, so he did not waste the time. Instead, he turned left, pulling Meredith into the tack room and closed the door behind them.

Outside the helicopter was settling gently to the ground. Simultaneously, agents were racing on all sides toward the stable, their rifles raised to the ready, pointed toward the stable. All were garbed in black tactical gear, body armor, boots, helmets and dark goggles. All but one. John Parella was out in front of the line that swept toward the stable, incongruously dressed in his tan sports jacket and trousers. His Glock 19 drawn and pointed skyward.

David quickly surveyed the tack room. There were old saddles, bridles, halters, helmets, and shelves of supplies. Everything was covered in dust and cobwebs. A rust covered refrigerator stood against the wall. David pulled it away and tilted it; allowing it to crash in front of the door, dust exploding into the air. Unlatching the lock on the sliding glass window he tugged at it. It didn't open. Quickly grabbing a saddle he threw it through the glass. With a plastic spray bottle off the shelf he cleared away shards of glass around the window opening.

"Meredith, come on." David bent over, lacing his fingers together. "Step here, and I'll help you over." Meredith placed her left foot into her father's hands; he lifted her up so that she could get her right leg through the window. Meredith scrambled out, and David quickly followed.

A line of officers was advancing toward the stable, weapons raised. Billowing dust churned around a helicopter. An officer stood in the midst of the cloud, rifle in hand, waving father and daughter to their right toward the west stable doors. As David turned in that direction he saw Detective John Parella rounding the corner. He was motioning with his hand.

"Get down, get down," Parella shouted.

"Meredith, down," David said, pushing his daughter to the ground. He heard two rapid gunshots, one from Parella, and one from the area of the helicopter. Turning to look behind him, David could see Darrell lying on the ground just at the east corner of the stable. Scrambling to his feet, he ran toward his brother.

"Meredith, stay here."

"David, stay where you are!" Parella shouted.

"It's my brother for heaven's sake!"

Dropping to Darrell's side David rolled him over. Darrell's right eye stared skyward; his left eye socket was empty. Labored efforts to breathe created a raspy wheeze. Blood trickled from his nostrils and the corner of his mouth. A hole in his chest bubbled pink foam. A bullet had also penetrated his left shoulder.

"Darrell, can you hear me?"

Darrell nodded his head almost imperceptibly.

David bent over to speak into Darrell's right ear. "Do you remember what I said about Jesus? Believe in him, call upon His name, and you will be saved."

"Sorry," Darrell whispered hoarsely, haltingly. "I'm . . . sorry."

"I forgive you, Darrell." David squeezed his brother's hand. Darrell held on tightly.

"That's . . . what . . . she said . . . Summer."

Oh, Summer. Dear Summer. You were listening. You got it.

"Darrell, please, ask Jesus to save you."

Darrell's lips moved, but no sound came out. He struggled again to create words.

"Je . . ." was all that came out. His eye closed slowly, and he was gone, his grip on David's hand slowly loosened.

David did not know what just happened. He did know that

God was able to sort these things out. He also knew that he was filled with a profound sadness. His only brother—twin brother—was dead.

He felt a hand on his shoulder and looked up to see Parella. He was surprised to see a tear in Parella's eye. Still on his knees, Meredith nearly bowled him over.

"Oh, Daddy," she cried, "I was so scared."

"So was I, Mar," he said, hugging her tightly. "So was I."

Parella handed him a cell phone. "It's your wife."

David took the phone and stood to his feet.

"Sweetheart?" David said.

"Oh, David," Lillian said. "Thank God, you're okay. I was so worried. All I could do was pray. How is Meredith?"

"She's fine, she's right here. She saved my life." David handed the phone to his daughter, who began to weep.

"Oh, Mom," she sobbed. "I didn't know if I would see you and Dad again."

"I know, darling. Lots of people have been praying. Hurry home and give me a hug."

"Okay," Meredith sniffed. She handed the phone back to her father.

"I love you," David said.

"I love you, too," Lillian said. "Come home."

"Be right there," David said. He turned to see a flurry of activity behind him. Yellow crime scene tape was being cordoned around the stable. His brother was lying alone on the ground.

David turned to Parella and shook his hand. "Thank you," he said.

"Come on, guys," Detective Parella smiled slightly to David and Meredith. "I'll give you a ride home."

FIFTY-SEVEN

Present Day

David Baxter had elected to drive the four hours up IH45 to Plano rather than fly to Palmer Hutchins' funeral. He felt that he, Lillian, and Meredith needed the time together since the events of yesterday. Last night everyone was exhausted, and they had elected to crash. This morning it was obvious that Meredith was still operating under a high level of adrenaline. She was in the back seat of the Tahoe, leaning forward between her mom and dad.

"So he told me that the house had burned down, and that you, Mom, were in the hospital with severe burns over 90% of your body. I was so terrified, you know? It was weird. He looked just like Dad. It was horrific, you know? Except that he had the whole left side of his face bandaged; from the fire, you know? Anyhow, I start to get suspicious in the car so he sticks me with this needle and next thing I know I'm waking up in this barn. I was scared absolutely stiff."

David and Lillian glanced at one another, knowing the other's thoughts, that they were each delighting in the joy that their daughter was here in the car with them, full of life.

"So, I was all tied up to this chair and couldn't move. It cramped so-o-o bad; my arms went totally numb, you know? And my hands—I couldn't feel a thing. I was just praying and praying. There wasn't anything else I could do really. So anyway, when he comes back he didn't have the bandage on any more. It was so-o-o gross.

He looked like a snake or something. I was trying to remember the stuff I had learned in self-defense class. I was scared I would just do something wrong, and it would just make him mad, you know. At the same time I was feeling like this was my only hope, to do something. Anyway, he brought me a hamburger, which really stunk. I don't know why, but it just smelled really bad. I told him I was thirsty and had to go to the bathroom. He really didn't want to untie me, but he did. I told him I couldn't make my hands work, so he bent over to give me a drink of coke and that's when I bit his bottom lip off, and poked two fingers in his right eye at the same time. He just pushed me away real hard, screaming a bunch of stuff. He couldn't see because he didn't have a left eye, so I gave him a swing kick on the side of the right leg above the knee, you know? Where all those nerves are? It made him just bend over and puke.

"Then I ran as hard as I could. He didn't have the stall door locked so I ran and ran to these woods. There was an old house but I was afraid to go there, so, anyway I thought I had a better chance in the woods, which I did as it turns out. I was too scared to come out, you know? To try to get help. I thought he would see me. So I stayed hidden. It got sorta cold that night so I piled up a bunch of pine needles and leaves and stuff and crawled into them. It wasn't too bad really, just a little scary when I could hear animals and stuff scratching around. I didn't know if there might be wolves or what. I was really praying hard, you know?"

"We were praying hard also, sweetheart. Everybody was praying. We thank God that He answered our prayers," Lillian said, turning in her seat to stroke Meredith's cheek.

"Tell your mom what you did next, Mar," David said, then turning to his wife, "This is where she did the hero stuff. I mean big time."

Meredith laughed. "Not really. I was just scared. I don't even know if I was thinking. Anyway, I hear this car pull up, and I sneak over near the edge of the woods and see Dad, all blindfolded, getting out of the SUV with *him*, the monster man. They go into the backside of the stall, and I can't see them anymore. Then all of a sudden I see this shadow and look up and there's this helicopter, with a guy sitting in the door with a rifle. It said FBI on the side of it in big white letters."

I was afraid that if the bad guy saw the helicopter he would do something bad to my dad. I didn't know what to do exactly. I found this oak limb, that's the only thing I could find, so I picked it up and started running toward the stall. The guy in the helicopter door was waving like crazy, but I had to keep going. I went inside as quiet as I could, but it didn't make much difference because the bad guy was yelling so loud he couldn't hear me. He was hitting Dad, so I ran up behind him and hit him over the head as hard as I could. It sorta knocked him out. So we got out of there."

"Yes, we did," David said. "Meredith saved my life, and the rest is history."

"I am so grateful," Lillian said. "I am so grateful to have you both."

The Baxters arrived in Plano two hours before the funeral. David drove directly to Doris Hutchins' home on Hilltop. Her eleven-year-old son Ricky opened the front door.

"Hi," he said, flatly. "Come on in."

David offered his hand, and Ricky shook it.

Nine-year-old Tatum was on the floor in the family room watching TV. She hopped up when she saw the Baxters and ran over to give Meredith a hug. She had idolized Meredith all of her life.

"Hi, Tatum," Meredith said.

"Hi. I'm glad you came."

Doris entered the family room from the kitchen, dressed in

black. There were dark circles under her eyes. "Hi, guys," she smiled wanly. "How was the trip?"

"It was good," David said, giving her a hug. "Not much traffic. I think we made record time."

Lillian came over and hugged Doris tightly. "Doris, how are you?"

"Oh, you know," Doris said, her eyes filled with profound grief. "So, so." She paused and then she said, "Actually, I feel like I have been kicked out of the human race. All of this seems so—unreal. So unfair. You hear about it every night on TV. So and so was killed down at West End, or someone broke into somebody's house and killed them; and you think nothing of it. You forget about it almost the instant they start talking about something else. The news people can't begin to put into words the deep, heavy weight that is tossed upon you when you hear those dreadful words, 'We are sorry to have to tell you Mrs. Hutchins, but your husband has been killed— murdered.' It just kicks you in the gut. You can't breathe, you can't see, you can't think. You suddenly become non-human. How does anyone bear it? I pray to God, and it's like He's behind this massive door, and He's busy right now. He's just too busy to answer." Doris' bottom lip began to tremble, and she sagged.

David and Lillian took her by the elbows and guided her to the sofa, where she collapsed. Tatum sat beside her mother and took her hand.

"Ricky, get a glass of water, please," Lillian said, feeling guilty that she was thinking that she was so grateful that it was not her husband.

David recalled his first night in jail, how he had felt exactly the way Doris had described—as if God were behind a massive door, pretending He was not at home. He considered quoting to her the verse that had recently occurred to him, that God would not allow anything in our lives that we cannot bear through His strength, but he decided against it. Doris needed to vent her grief right now, and the best way that he and Lillian could help was simply to listen.

The attendance at Palmer Hutchins' funeral was nothing short of phenomenal. All 350 seats at Grace Fellowship Church were taken and there were at least 100 along each side wall and the back.

David was grateful to see Detective John Parella there who introduced his wife Annie, and their daughter Jenny. Parella's partner, Detective Sergeant Vincent Cramer had also come with them.

David *was* surprised to see the ADA Denise Nichols. She had come alone. David made his way over to her. "So good of you to come, Miss Nichols."

"I couldn't do otherwise, Mr. Baxter. Mr. Hutchins was a good man—an honorable man. There are so few these days." She looked away, and then back to David, catching his eyes. "I am so sorry, Mr. Baxter, for what we put you through. For what *I* put you through. It must have been sheer hell for you. And for your family." She nodded in Lillian and Meredith's direction.

David smiled. "It was undeniably difficult, Miss Nichols. Still is. But I understand. I know that you were operating on the evidence that you had. Yours is a difficult job. But, regarding your apology, Miss Nichols, I forgive you."

"Thank you, that helps." A tear glistened in her eye. "If there is ever anything that I can do . . ."

"I will take you up on that, Miss Nichols." David smiled. Returning to his family, everyone took their seats, the soft strains of "How Great Thou Art" playing in the background.

Everyone in the Baxter SUV was quiet as they headed south toward home, reflecting on the day's events.

David had delivered a heartfelt eulogy, telling how he and Palmer had met at law school at Baylor University, quickly growing to be best friends, going to a local church in Waco together, starting their families together, vacationing together, splitting ways but maintaining close contact.

"I am grateful to God for allowing me to know Palmer," David had concluded. "I have no doubt that we will meet again in heaven where we will spend eternity rejoicing before our Lord and King Jesus Christ."

Pastor Harold Jenkins had delivered a stirring message about the celebration of life, that death was not a final stop, but for Palmer it was the beginning of eternal life in Jesus Christ. He also shared with the congregation that it certainly appeared that Darrell had been saved at the last moment before his death. At this statement there were audible gasps in the audience, turning heads, whipping up an undercurrent of whisperings.

Pastor Jenkins had handled it well. "This is a day for celebrating Palmer Hutchins life, and we will do that. But it is also a day for declaring how glorious the grace of God is, and how marvelous is His faithfulness toward us. In Romans chapter five verse twenty it says, 'but where sin abounded, grace did abound more exceedingly.' That means that no matter how horrible your sin, God's grace, His ability to forgive you, is much, much greater than that.

"There is also the parable in Matthew 20 that Jesus spoke, about the owner of a vineyard. He sent out his servant early in the morning to hire laborers at a set price. He continued, it says, to hire laborers all day, right up until the end of the workday. At the end of the day the owner announced that it was time to pay everyone. He paid first the last ones hired, and he paid them at the wage he had set with the first laborers. This, of course, caused the ones hired first to think that they would be getting paid more. When the owner paid them the exact same wage as he paid the last workers, the first complained. 'We have worked all day in the hot sun. Why should they get the same wage as us?' The owner responded, 'I did you no wrong. I paid you what we agreed upon. It is my desire to pay these others the same.' The good news here, and this is something I know that Palmer would want me to share with you, is that no matter what you have done with your life—you could be the most horrible serial killer ever to exist—the grace of God is greater than that. The blood that Jesus Christ shed upon the cross for you allows God to say that you will receive the same salvation as someone who has been a Christian, serving Him, for fifty years. All you have to do is receive it, like those end of the day workers received their wages. The only difference is they worked for their wages. You don't have to work, just receive it. It reminds us of the thief on the cross next to the cross of Jesus. All the thief said was, 'Remember me when you come into your kingdom.' And Jesus told him, 'Today you will be with me in Paradise.' If anyone was a last minute entry into heaven, this man certainly was."

"Amen," David said.

"What?" Lillian asked.

"I was just thinking about the pastor's message today. I'm glad he said what he said about last-second salvation. I'm sure it made some people mad to have to think that Darrell might have made it into heaven."

"My guess is that we'll have several surprises when we get there," Lillian smiled. "Both ways. Some will be there whom we thought wouldn't make it, and we'll be wondering where others are."

"Good thing we're not God," David said.

"Reminds me of the t-shirt: 'There is only one God—and you're not it,'" Lillian laughed.

"Anybody hungry?" David asked. "There's a Dairy Queen up ahead."

"I am famished!" Meredith shouted from the back seat. "And a hamburger sounds good!"

David Baxter appreciated the sense of peace that settled over him as he headed the Tahoe onto the exit ramp.

EPILOGUE
Eternity

Darrell Baldwin Phelps knew that he was dying, although he felt no pain. He had run around the back corner of the stable, intending to yell at David, to stop him so that they could talk further. Something that his brother had said . . .

Then David was suddenly at his side. Strangely, the oddest sensation swept over him—nothing like he had ever felt before. It was love, he knew. He wanted to reach out and hold his brother, and tell him things that were beginning to seem so clear now.

"Darrell, please," his brother was saying. "Ask Jesus to save you."

Darrell could somehow see all around, 360 degrees. There was a fierce battle raging between hundreds of soldiers—opposing armies engaged in hand-to-hand combat. On one side were soldiers of light, huge and white, glowing brilliantly, extended bolts of lightening flashing from their swords, their shields radiating brilliant waves of electrical energy. On the other side were dark forces, grotesque creatures, green eyes glowing, who emanated a black light, screaming all manner of foul things, clanging swords and shields against their arch enemies.

They are battling for me, Darrell thought.

He tried to say aloud "Jesus, save me," but he could not. He wanted to say goodbye to his brother as well, but he could not. He began to say, over and over in his mind, *Jesus, save me; Jesus, save me.*

He heard a loud, thunderous voice say, "Whoever calls upon the name of the Lord will be saved!"

Instantly, the world burst into light more brilliant than ten suns. The black forces disappeared and the white army gathered around him, rejoicing and singing.

Darrell is saved, Darrell is saved. Worthy is God to receive honor and glory and blessing.

Immediately, as if the army of light had thrown him, Darrell began to hurdle toward the brightest part of light that surrounded everything, the feeling of love increasing as he went. Then, he knew he was there, and he stopped. There were people all around—thousands, millions. He could sense that they were all happy to see him; there was rapturous joy on all their faces.

Then he saw Willy Daniel Morris.

Then came Marianna Parks.

Then he saw Marie Faye Birch.

Then, Alice Dawn Marshall.

Then, Sandra Elaine Peet.

Then, Jayme Lee Parker.

Then, Misty Louise Cramer.

Then, Summer Blevins Chase.

Then he saw Palmer James Hutchins.

All of them were smiling and saying, "Welcome, Darrell. Welcome."

Then, instantly Jesus was there in all His majesty.

Darrell fell to his face, weeping and crying out, "I am not worthy, Lord. Forgive me for all of those horrible things I did."

Jesus reached down, taking Darrell by the hand, lifting him up and, smiling, said, "What things, my son? All of those things were forgotten at the cross. Your faith has saved you. You are welcome. Come, enter into my Kingdom."

Look for E.R. Webb's next exciting thriller:
The Pallium Project. **Coming Soon!**

In *The Pallium Project* nations are secretly embroiled in the pursuit for a technology so strategically important that the world balance of power is at stake. Assassination, sabotage, kidnappings and intrigue fill the pages of this new novel by E.R. Webb. In this soon-to-be-released thriller, attorney David Baxter, homicide detective John Parella, and three brilliantly intelligent teenagers known as *The Texas Trio,* who work for the NASA Johnson Space Center, find themselves joined in a race more important than the quest for the atomic bomb, or the Space Race. In the attempt to ensure that America comes out ahead in the competition for world dominance, lives and faith are stretched to the breaking point as the group finds themselves battling both physical and spiritual adversaries.

Excerpt from *The Pallium Project*
By E.R. Webb

Madirashi's routine was well known to the security guard at the entrance to the Cryogenic facility. Each month she would visit her family in New Delhi. Each month, on a Friday, she would bring her brown and tan suitcase into the lab, then in the afternoon she would leave from the lab to the Bangalore Airport to fly the 1735 kilometers home.

Today the security guard saw nothing different from the other months as he made a cursory examination of Madirashi's suitcase. Everything was routine. He did not see the thin film of perspiration on her brow, nor the ever so slight tremor in her hand as she released the latches to the luggage.

Azmat's initial proposal had horrified Madirashi. It had horrified her to the point that she said she would not do it. She knew that she held the power. Nothing could happen without her. She had access to the lab. They needed her.

"We must eliminate the professor," Azmat had said. "And the boy. They are key in preventing this program from succeeding. It is imperative."

"No," she had said, flatly. "I will not be part of such a thing. The professor and Dilawar are not my enemies, they are my friends."

"If you do not mind yourself," Azmat said, malice in his eyes, "you will make yourself dispensable. You will make yourself unnecessary, young girl."

"You frighten me this much, dog breath," she said, holding her thumb pressed against the tip of her index finger. "I won't do it. Think of another brilliant idea."

"You are becoming a Western cowgirl," he said. "Your strong head will get you under the ground."

"Whatever," she shrugged. "Think of something else."

"Okay," Azmat had conceded. "We will destroy the lab only."

"Good," she had responded with relief. "Late at night, when no one is there."

"Yes," he nodded his head. "When everyone sleeps."

Azmat had packed the explosives in a false bottom of her suitcase, over which Madirashi had carefully placed her folded clothes.

"Thank you," the guard said, looking up at her with a smile.

"You're welcome," Madirashi said, taking her suitcase, some pounds heavier than usual, and headed for the Cryogenic Lab. She sat the suitcase next to professor Kathadra's desk, as was her habit. He was rifling through a file cabinet.

"Are you okay?" he asked, concern on his face.

"I'm fine, sir," Madirashi said, averting her eyes.

"You look pale," he continued.

"No, really, I'm okay," she said, with a wan smile. "It's just that I didn't get much sleep."

"Have you eaten?" he asked.

"No, sir."

"Then go—go. You have thirty-five minutes before the cafeteria closes for breakfast. We don't have anything scheduled before this afternoon anyway. Go—you need something to eat."

Dilawar was over by the experiment, replacing the cylinder of nitrogen.

"Okay," she said, reluctantly. "I'll be right back."

"Take your time, we have plenty of time," the professor smiled.

Dilawar waved his hand. "Later."

Passing through security, she exited the Cryogenic facility and turned right. The cafeteria was only two blocks, so she would have plenty of time.

She was half a block away when the explosion ripped through the air, the concussion ramming her to her face on the sidewalk.

Immediately there were screams of horror and pain, and the blaring of automobile alarms in some sort of insane concert.

Painfully, Madirashi pushed herself off the sidewalk, stood shakily, and turned toward the madness in numb shock. The Cryogenic facility was spread across the street in a pile of burning and smoking rubble. Papers and debris floated like autumn leaves in the air. Tongues of fire licked out of the gaping hole where the lab used to be. A mangled car was on its side, burning furiously. Several bodies were on the sidewalk and street. Other people were wandering aimlessly, covered with blood, their brains refusing to accept what was around them.

"Oh, dear God!" her mind cried out. "Professor Kathadra! Dilawar!" Immediately she broke down in racking sobs. Dropping to her knees on the sidewalk, she screamed at the top of her lungs: "Azmat! You pig!"

TATE PUBLISHING & *Enterprises*

Tate Publishing is committed to excellence in the publishing industry. Our staff of highly trained professionals, including editors, graphic designers, and marketing personnel, work together to produce the very finest books available. The company reflects the philosophy established by the founders, based on Psalms 68:11,

"THE LORD GAVE THE WORD AND GREAT WAS THE COMPANY OF THOSE WHO PUBLISHED IT."

If you would like further information, please call
1.888.361.9473
or visit our website
www.tatepublishing.com

TATE PUBLISHING & *Enterprises*, LLC
127 E. Trade Center Terrace
Mustang, Oklahoma 73064 USA